ATLAS

DISCARDED HEROES: SCIONS

DISCARDED HEROES: SCIONS

ATLAS

APOLLO

ACHILLES

DISCARDED HEROES

NIGHTSHADE

DIGITALIS

WOLFSBANE

FIRETHORN

LYGOS

ATLAS

DISCARDED HEROES: SCIONS

RONIE KENDIG

Atlas
Discarded Heroes: Scions, Book 1

Published by Sunrise Media Group LLC

Print ISBN: 978-1-966463-51-1

This book is a work of fiction. Names, characters, places, and incidents are either products of the author's imagination or used fictitiously. Any similarity to actual people, organizations, and/or events is purely coincidental.

For more information about the author please access her website at roniekendig.com. Published in the United States of America.

Cover Design: Sunrise Media Group LLC

This book is lovingly dedicated to all my loyal Rapid-Fire Fiction readers who have been with me since the beginning. Those who endured the months-long wait between each of the original Discarded Heroes series. Who cheered and championed each release and reveled when Wolfsbane won a Christy Award.

To you, I dedicate the start of this new series. To see the Nightshade Scions come to life. Not gonna lie—the pressure was enormous. I did not want to let you down, but then I dived in and had so much fun revisiting these heroes and their families. It was tough, too, looking at the Discarded Heroes and asking the hard question—how has their career and subsequent choices impacted their children? That got interesting real fast.

I hope you love this story as much as I did—and embrace it as a heartfelt THANK YOU to you, my loyal readers!

With much love and prayers that God will touch your heart in these pages,

Ronie Kendig

Exodus 14:14

AUTHOR'S NOTE

Hello, Rapid-Fire Readers! First—I want to thank you for taking the journey with Dante and McKenna. While it was fabulous and oh-so-fun to write the story of Colton "Cowboy" Neeley's eldest daughter and Griffin "Legend" Riddell's son, I always look for ways to bring a heaping dose of reality into story. For this series, I asked my husband to pick three diverse countries whose settings are not as common in thrillers and went from there.

For ATLAS, I started researching the beautiful country of Armenia and stumbled across the Armenian Genocide, and wow, my heart just ached. The United States Holocaust Memorial Museum states:

> **Sometimes called the first genocide of the twentieth century, the Armenian Genocide refers to the physical annihilation of Armenian Christian people living in the Ottoman Empire from spring 1915 through autumn 1916. There were approximately 1.5 million Armenians living in the multiethnic Ottoman Empire in 1915. At least 664,000 and possibly as many as 1.2 million died during the genocide, either in massacres and individual killings, or from systematic ill treatment, exposure, and starvation.**

"At least 664,000" Armenians died. Nearly half their population! Many suggest the number is closer to a *million*. Unable to imagine losing half the population of a people group, I wondered why I hadn't really heard about this genocide. Compound that with the fact there is still an active campaign against Armenian Christians, and I knew that's where ATLAS needed to take place, if only to highlight and remember—*honor*—those who died.

In 1967, the Tsitsernakaberd Memorial in Yerevan was erected on a hill and dedicated to the memory of the millions who perished in the first genocide of the twentieth century. The Tsitsernakaberd Museum & Institute was opened in 1995 in commemoration of the 80th anniversary of the Armenian Genocide.

Over the last couple of decades, numerous peace talks have failed to produce the much-needed accord to bring relief to Armenia. Many times talks would happen but nothing would be solidified. Thus, the reason for the peace talks idea…So imagine my surprise when in August 2025, President Trump managed to bring both countries to the proverbial table. I feared my story might become irrelevant, but since there is—a month later—no formal agreement even still, I have chosen to leave the story as is. I ask you to pray for these people groups, for peace to prevail.

Here are a few links to more information about the Armenian Genocide:

The Armenian Genocide Museum

http://www.genocide-museum.am/eng/Description_and_history.php

The Armenian Genocide Testimony Collection

https://sfi.usc.edu/collections/armenian

The Holocaust Encyclopedia

https://encyclopedia.ushmm.org/content/en/article/the-armenian-genocide-1915-16-overview

Truly I tell you, whatever you did for one of the least of these brothers and sisters of mine, you did for me.

Matthew 25:40 NIV

ONE

Yerevan, Armenia

GOLD GLITTERED ACROSS THE OLD DOMES of Saint Cross Church in the bright, wintry sunlight, the scenery blurring past. Trees bare of branches and dead grass gave proof that winter had finally asserted its icy grip on Yerevan. A red-and-white sign hulking on the side of the road had both Armenian and English, strident evidence that McKenna Neeley was far from home.

An ache constricted her chest, especially sharp after having spent Christmas and New Year's away from her family. Mercy, she missed Daddy and—well, everyone. They were the best of blended families after Daddy married Piper, then gifted McKenna with the three siblings she'd always wanted. As Nana had told her before she passed, "the only steps are on the front porch." Thus, she'd never used stepmother or stepbrother. They were family, and soon, she'd be able to hug their necks. Take a long, relaxing ride on her mare. Maybe Daddy would join her for the ride—or Sophia. Gosh, she just could not wait!

Guiding her Hyundai import around a slow-going truck, McKenna reminded herself Daddy was only a call away. The ten-hour time difference, however, had worked against their ability to actually connect. Not to mention he had his hands full with her siblings—Ben had joined the Marines last summer, following in Daddy's footsteps, but senior year was in full swing with the twins, keeping their parents distracted, running in a dozen directions since Sophia and Spencer had very different interests and college goals.

Nobody had meant to miss calling on Christmas. But a last-minute emergency with an American citizen in-country forced McKenna into the office and then a hospital follow-up, instead of lounging on her cozy couch for a video chat via her tablet. Add particularly tense relations between Azerbaijan and Armenia, and she had been going ninety to nothin' from sun-up until sundown for the last ten days. Altogether, it meant she hadn't heard from Daddy in three weeks!

Tears pricking her eyes, McKenna took the circle to the right, then made a U-turn when traffic allowed. She felt alone and forgotten by her family but knew that wasn't true. She zipped around other cars, rethreaded the circle, then parked at the curb in front of the shops to get pastries for the office.

It'd sure be nice to have Sophia and Mom come over and visit, do some shopping with her. She'd once done that with Serena Beck, one of the junior consular officers, but it wasn't the same.

Shaking off the sadness, McKenna stepped into the chilly morning air. Hurrying across the sidewalk with hexagonal pavers, she pressed the fob to lock her car and aimed for the local favorite, Crumbs Bread Factory & Café. It was a decidedly American name for an Armenian bakery, but the pastries were next-level delicious.

Inside, the thick smell of yeast and sugar somehow made her feel as if all would be well with the world. She purchased pastries for her coworkers, added baklava for her boss, a cream-filled pastry for herself, and paid for the treats.

"*Shnorhakalut'yun*," McKenna thanked the cashier, but her phone ringing drowned her words. Grimacing an apology for the grating ringtone, which sounded like a rotary phone, she whirled toward the door with the box of goodies and fished the device from her purse. She shouldered into the door and left the café. Cold air smacking her, she hunched against the bitter wind to answer the call. "Hello?"

"Where are you?" rasped Serena's hushed voice.

Her coworker's urgent tone told McKenna two things—it must be an emergency, and it required McKenna's expertise of language, compassion. "About ten minutes out." She negotiated around a small crowd of chatty women. "Why? What's up?"

Dawg, she did not want to start the week again by visiting someone in the hospital. Of course, she was glad to help—that's why she did this job, after all—but some cases just broke her heart.

"We have VIPs incoming," Serena said.

Nothing new. The embassy and consular offices regularly had VIPs. McKenna unlocked her car and opened the driver-side door.

"The Tartan is losing her mind."

Also not unusual. The Tartan—her immediate supervisor, Cicely Robertson—served as the Ambassador to Armenia. A bit uptight but with good reason, since political tensions were high. Too, the embassy and consular officers were responsible for ensuring the safety of American citizens, which often got tricky when said tensions were high. It sure didn't help that Deputy Chief of Mission Harel Olafssen was gunning for the Tartan's job. What little slack there'd been in the office before his arrival at Christmas had pulled taut.

VIPs though . . . "Any idea who?" she asked, tucking herself into her Elantra. Setting pastries on the passenger seat, she pulled the door closed. "There weren't any on the schedule."

"No idea. Just get back here. You're the only one the Tartan trusts with all this."

Even though McKenna was a junior officer. "On my way." When she set the fob on the console and hit the Start Engine button, she saw a strange reflection glide across the GPS screen. Her heart leapt into her throat—someone was in the backseat!

She snagged the keys. Gripping the apartment one between her fingers as a weapon, she wasn't fast enough. A muscular arm encircled her throat and cut off her breath.

"Don't move," a deep voice ground out against her ear, "or it's over."

Pulse jamming, she stifled her panic, catching his arm—and her gaze shifted upward. Through the rearview mirror, she caught sight of her attacker. Dark eyes. Dark intent.

Wait . . . It took a second for her mind to register and process what she was seeing. *Are you kidding me?* She let out a strangled cry. Dropped the key and reached back, slapping her would-be attacker with a growl.

"Hey!" He recoiled and fell away.

McKenna twisted in her seat and unleashed a flurry of strikes, heart thudding—in anger this time, not fear. "Dillon Jacobs, you beast!"

He pitched backward, shielding his face and side. "Hey, hey, hey!" There was nowhere to go in her small import, so he was powerless against her very strategic smacks on his sorry self.

"You menace," she snarled and swatted his leg. Easing back, she let out a ragged breath, shoving her bangs from her face as she released a tremulous huff. "You scared me half to death!"

His laughter rumbled through the chilly car as he straightened. "You really should have better situational awareness, Mickey. Your dad would be ashamed."

"My dad would tan your hide for breaking into my car—"

"Didn't break in," he said, jabbing a finger in the air, then running a hand over his shorn black hair. "When you got out, you took too long to lock it, giving me ample time to slip in."

Slumping in her seat as her pulse returned to normal, McKenna faltered. Could not believe she'd been so careless and left that opening. That he was here.

He caught the headrest and pulled himself forward. "What if some thug—"

"*You* are a thug!"

"—got in?" He cocked his head. "A beautiful American woman walking around without security . . ." He sniffed. "Good thing I was here to protect you."

"I need protection *from* you, Dill-pickle!"

He glowered. "You promised to stop calling me that."

"And you promised to stop hitting on me." She arched an eyebrow at him.

Dillon had always flirted with her—he flirted with every girl that met his gaze. But it was never the kind that had him coming to a foreign country to see her. So his unexpected arrival wasn't about *her*. Besides, as Scions—the children of the infamous Nightshade team—they were more like siblings than love interests. Long ago, an unwritten rule had developed that Scions looked out for each other but never dated. While Dillon had never met a rule he didn't try to break, she had made it clear years back that nothing would happen between them. And yes, maybe it did have to do with a much older member of the Scions, but that ship sailed long ago.

"Don't tell me you're still carrying a torch for Dant—"

"Look." Amid a riot of frustration, she flashed her palms at him. "No torch."

But . . . wait, hold on . . . She frowned, noticing the knot between his brows, and shifted to face him better. "Dillon, what are you doing here?" Her honed instinct that he and the other Scions had always called "motherly" rose through her, hot and virulent. "What's going on? You okay? Does your mom—"

"Leave her out of this."

"She's worried about you. We all are."

Another glower. "I don't have time for this, Mickey."

"But you have time to sneak into my car and scare the life out of me?"

He peered out the windows and glanced around. "We're too open here. Is there somewhere we can go to talk privately?"

McKenna's phone buzzed, reminding her of the situation at the consul's office. She let Serena's call go to voicemail. "Sadly, no. Something's going on at work. I need to get there and help sort it out."

He hooked his muscular arms around the front passenger seat and looked through the windshield. Stretched his stubbled jaw. The rowdy, hotheaded boy she'd grown up with had definitely become a man. Those eyes and his rugged, devil-may-care resolve had brought down many a pretty girl. There was also his bad temper and thrill-seeking hunger that drew the vultures. But this smelled different, like . . . more. Like trouble.

"Okay, listen." She tucked her long blonde hair behind her ear, snagged her keys, and began working one off the ring. "Meet me back at my place at five. I'll try to get off early, but with VIPs arriving, it's unlikely. Just wait for me there."

"No way," Dillon said, refusing the key. "Your condo building full of embassy workers is too heavily monitored. I don't want my face on security cameras."

She paused. Frowned. "*What* is going on?"

His brow furrowed as he held her gaze for a long second, debating whether or not to tell her. "I got a lead on my dad."

An anchor plunked in her stomach. She grieved that he hadn't accepted his father's death. "Oh, Dill—"

"Don't, Mick." Dark eyes flashed, lips thinning beneath raw intensity. "He's alive. I know he is, and what I found proves it."

Something jostled in her chest as she studied him. "You have a lead?"

He had a killer instinct for all things military and tactical situations. But . . . the DIA and General Lambert both said his father, Max Jacobs, died on assignment fifteen months ago. "How have you unearthed a lead that neither the government nor Nightshade have managed to find?"

His expression tightened. He again looked out the window, working that jaw muscle. "Because they aren't looking." A ragged breath rose through his chest. "I am."

It was tempting to argue with him, to remind him he was only twenty-four, but the guy filling up the backseat had a tenacity and propensity to "deal with things" that often got him into trouble. A lot of trouble. But, she had to concede, it also got him answers. And ticked off those in authority. "You—"

"Don't argue with me, Mickey," he said. "I'm fed up with people telling me I'm wrong. I refuse to give up on my dad. I don't—"

"I wasn't going to," she said softly.

His gaze snapped back to her, dark eyes darting around her face. "You believe me." His eyebrows lifted, then relaxed as a smirk tweaked his lips. "I knew you would." He caught the door handle and pushed toward it. "Meet back here at five. In the café. Deal?"

Mind scrambling to keep up with his swift subject change, she could only watch him exit the compact car. "Y-yes. Deal," she called before the door closed. Running a hand over her face, she exhaled heavily. He'd found a lead . . .

When she looked in his direction again, he was gone. She scanned the street. How had he vanished so quickly? And what had he found? But the bigger question nearly choked her: Was Max Jacobs really still alive?

Xinaliq, Azerbaijan

Darkness descended on the remote village that sat at the foot of the Caucasus but was also strategically located atop a rocky formation. With night's surrender to day, warmth should be pushing the mercury, but a chill pervaded the air due to the almost eight-thousand-foot elevation. In the distance, lazy, thick clouds caressed the tallest peak of Bazardüzü with its over 14,500-foot elevation.

A cold breeze rushed him and thrust its icy fingers around his collar, trying to dig beneath his armor plates. Hunching his shoulders to stay this side of frozen, Dante Riddell adjusted the strap of his M4A1 and freed the bite valve to his Camelbak. After a big swig, he secured the valve and resumed patrol. He hoped the veeps managed to find that common ground needed so he could get back to a warmer climate.

Omen Tactical Group had been tapped to run additional security for Secretary of State Henry Derriscort, who was here on a clandestine meeting with representatives from Armenia and Azerbaijan. For years the two countries danced around a peace treaty but never found enough common ground to seal the deal. But a call from one side signaled that the treaty might now have a legitimate chance.

Ops like this were typically handled by routine security details—Derriscort's never strayed far from the SecState, so they were already on-site—but this rendezvous had been set up last minute. When Derriscort learned local spec ops were tasked elsewhere, he insisted on an added layer of security and secrecy, believing himself on the precipice of effecting unprecedented peace between Azerbaijan and Armenia.

"OTG, what's your sitrep?" came the deep voice of Pike Auberon, founder and boss of Omen. One of the best men Dante had ever met, outside Pop and the Nightshade team, the former master chief had a solid reputation for decisive, effective, and reliable ops.

"Red Two quiet and secure," reported Brick Archer from the far north corner of the small village where he monitored the road leading up the hillside.

"Good copy, Red Two."

"Same at Red One," comm'd Tariq Wadi, the team medic who had northeastern oversight.

From an outcropping on the southeastern edge, Dante slid his gaze over the rolling hills. All quiet. "Blue Two clear," he reported.

Another all-clear from Dade Tycho. Then Pike and Luther Landry holed up in a two-story structure.

"Vehicles inbound," comm'd Crow Rawlins from his higher vantage, where he was likely stretched prone with his sniper rifle trained on the incoming caravan. "I can confirm positive ID on Vidadi Asgarov in the second SUV. Plus one bodyguard."

"Good copy," Pike replied. "Keep eyes on him. Omen, stay alert. If word has gotten out about this meet-up . . ."

"We'd be hot and heavy with some unfriendlies," Dade said in his country twang.

Movement to Dante's three o'clock position snagged his attention. He adjusted to that direction and scanned, but found nothing. Probably shadows from clouds drifting across the sky.

If it'd been him, Dante would've held the meet in a location with more exfil options. Out here, it was them, the elements, and clear lines of sight for klicks with only one way in and one way out—that road. Didn't help that the village was more spread out than anticipated, forcing Omen to expand the distance between each operator to establish an effective perimeter detail. But this was his chance to prove to Pike that he could act on instinct as much as ROE. That he'd listen to that instinct and not the rules.

Rules had been Dante's bread and butter his whole life, guiding him through tough obstacles and hard life. Now, it was getting up in his business. Messing with him and his career.

The brown landscape shifted again, pulling his gaze back to the hills.

Alright, twice wasn't a coincidence . . . M4 at the high ready, he used his scope to scan the base of the hill, hunting whatever distracted him. But he still found nothing. What was going on?

Shoulder against the rocky edifice and eyes on that spot where shadows had morphed, Dante listened to the comms chatter of the team reporting the convoy veering into the village and navigating the hard-packed roads.

A *clack* reached his ears. The pervasive quiet of the remote village amplified sounds. While he could hear crunching as the vehicles moved deeper toward the designated meet location, this sounded smaller. Closer.

Something was out there . . .

Quietly, he took a knee and traced his reticle over the area. His eye twitched as something again shifted. Dust? Too small to be a vehicle. Could be a motorbike. "Possible movement in Blue Two," he reported.

The clatter of rocks stilled him. More trickled off to the near-distant left. How had someone gotten this close? That was right there. Nearby.

Withdrawing into the soft shadows of the cleft overhang, Dante waited a few seconds. Then swung out for a quick look-see. Drew his gaze along the path, up the slope. A shape loomed there.

"Holy—" He flinched at the nearly thirty-six-inch goat, hooves clacking along a path, plucking tufts of grass from the rocky façade. All while it made its way steadily toward Dante.

And this wasn't no cute pet goat like Aunt Phee had back home on her farm that was as tall as his knees and loved people. This thing was big. Like I'm-gonna-eat-your-momma big. And it had some serious scimitar-shaped horns that spiraled out and back over his shoulders. Bulging eyes locked on him.

Oh, huh-uh. Dante pulled away again, annoyed he hadn't seen the thing before now. Worried it'd put a horn through his gut. He peered back and found the goat fully trained on him now.

Baaaahhhhaaahhaaahh.

The loud, obnoxious bleating sounded like a staccato laugh.

Now the goat was mocking him.

"Blue Two, report," Pike ordered, concern in his tone. "You need support?"

Remembering he'd signaled possible movement, Dante shook his head. Refocused on patrolling. "Negative," he gruffed. "All clear. Just a stupid goat."

"Shoot the goat," Brick comm'd, his tone way too light, mocking. Like the goat.

"You are sick." Dante visually swept the area, then eyed the goat. Why only one? Did a local own it for milk? Or should he be on alert for a herder? More goats?

"VIPs are exiting vehicles and entering the structure," comm'd Dade.

That meant Pike and Luther would go inside with the SecState and VIPs. Time ticked by as the talks began, things apparently going smoothly.

Dante maintained watch, confirming no new goats, no herder, and no unfriendlies. Just Big Horn chomping his way closer and closer. It was irritating—right along with the scalding memory after their last mission when Pike rebuked him for his "unwillingness to learn to assess and adapt to mission needs, rather than rigidly clinging to the rules of engagement."

Each word had seared into Dante's heart. Now he was trying to figure out what that meant exactly. Rules worked. They were there for a reason. He could still hear Pike's deadly accurate words: *"You'd be an amazing operator if you could get your head out of your b—"*

"How's your buddy, Atlas?" Brick comm'd.

Dante blinked, glad to be yanked from that stinging memory. "Chews as loud as you do."

"I'll show you ch—"

"Stay focused," Pike ordered, silencing them.

Another rebuke. Great. Putting distance between him and

Big Horn, Dante stretched his jaw and monitored the fields. He groaned at the sight of two more goats headed in his direction.

Unbelievable. *What, do I have goat scent on me or something?*

A *clack-scritch* came from behind.

He pivoted just in time to see Big Horn take an impossible vertical leap onto the overhang under which Dante had taken cover. "You have *got* to be kidding me," he hissed, swiveling out with his M4 trained on the goat.

Ears angled to the sides, eyes bulging, Big Horn cocked his head at Dante.

"Atlas, problem?" Pike asked in a low voice, likely trying to avoid alarming those with him.

"Guessing the goat called for backup," he muttered. Was he imagining it or did this one seem . . . ticked? He checked the black-and-white one, now chomping grass near one of the smaller homes. Okay, he—she?—looked happy. Going about his business. But Big Horn . . .

Still on the rock. Still staring. Was staring a challenge of power with goats like it was with dogs?

He was not going to disrupt a historic meeting of two countries finally willing to try to make peace happen because of goats! "All clear," he forced himself to say.

But in that second, something made his gut clinch. A change. With the goat. Couldn't figure out how, but he had this sense that his standoff with Big Horn was about to go from mocking to lethal.

He pointed at the big guy. "Bro. Stay there, out of my business, and I'll stay right here. Out of yours." He touched his chest. "That way, we're both happy. Cool?"

Hold up. Why was it lowering its head . . . flattening its ears?

"No-no," Dante warned, shifting away. "No, we are not doing this." Maybe he shouldn't have pointed. And he might not be up on goat behavior—who thought they'd need that intel on an op?—but this reeked of aggression. He backed up again.

God, I asked You to help a guy out, not hurt a guy with a goat.

Might sound the same, but they were different. When the goat angled his neck closer, Dante yielded another step. "Way different."

Hooves clacking against the rocks, the goat gave a thrust of its neck and stabbed its horns at Dante.

Yeah, not good. "Dude. I got the message. But I can't leave."

Big Horn bleated again—but this wasn't laughter. Or mocking. This was a scream. A primal scream.

Dante keyed his mic. "Chief, might have a problem . . ."

"Go ahead," Pike said, dead serious.

No way was he outing himself in a standoff with a goat. Dante shifted aside, then realized he was stupidly trying to angle so he could present his smallest side to Big Horn. Like that would make him less a threat.

"Atlas, *report.*"

He clenched his teeth. "There's another goat. He's throwing aggression at me."

"Deal with it," Pike bit out.

Right. Man, he felt stupid. Scared stupid.

"Shoot the goat," Brick repeated.

Weapon up, Dante took aim. He'd apologize to Aunt Phee for killing her goat's cousin, because he was not being taken out by a freaking goat.

Big Horn bleated, tucked its chin, and charged him.

"Son of a—" In that split-second, he knew shooting wouldn't stop that thing from impaling him. He leapt aside, narrowly avoiding being skewered in the thigh. When the psycho skidded around, Dante released the M4 on its sling and drew his Ruger.

"*Don't* shoot the goat," Pike hissed in warning. "We don't need to draw attention to our VIPs."

Tightening his lips, Dante holstered the gun. Now what was he supposed to do? Do HammerTime with a ticked-off goat? He needed options so he could save what little respect he had left in Pike's eyes.

As the thing once again pulled down its chin and flashed the horns, ready to charge, Dante readied himself. Eyed the small cleft above.

Hooves clattered toward him, the small thunder of aggression echoing loudly.

Dante launched at the overhang. Caught it and swung to hike himself up—but a loud crack sounded. Immediately, he felt the infinitesimal shift of the rock. "Oh cr—"

Crack!

The shelf gave way, slamming him back to the ground.

Bleating seared the night, the goat—which had careened past him when he'd jumped—screamed as it nearly slid off the incline.

"Atlas." There was something about Pike's question, the way he said Dante's callsign, warning that "little" respect had now evaporated.

Big Horn swung around again.

"Oh, come on!" But then an idea struck. Dante hopped to his feet. Positioned himself at the sharp drop-off of the path. It was whack that a three-foot-high goat was wiping out his self-respect. Time to return the favor.

Just don't miscalculate. Because Omen would never let him live it down if a goat took him out. As the thing neared, he waited . . . waited . . . Leapt as the air stirred. Dove up and hard right. Heard the clatter of hooves and sliding dirt. Scraping . . . a shriek of panic as the menace slid off the edge and down the incline.

"He's doing the mamba with the goat," Crow reported for him. "He's safe. Goat is out of range now. Blue Two clear."

Flat on his back and heaving breaths, Dante died a little right there, humiliated. Humiliated the team knew he'd nearly lost against a goat. Humiliated that he'd been too busy avoiding impalement by goats, that Crow had to give his sitrep. Staring up at the defiant clouds that forbade the moon from shining clear, he huffed. Plates and gear dug into his spine as he made himself answer too. "All clear."

"Atlas," Brick called with a snicker, "OTG is OTG. You coming down or spending the night with the herd?"

I see, God. You got jokes.

TWO

Yerevan, Armenia

WHERE HAVE YOU BEEN?" HISSED SERENA as she fell in step and paced McKenna down the long hall. "It's crazy here."

"What's happening?"

"The Tartan is tied up in a meeting off-site, but that dinner you've been working on?"

Tugging off her jacket as she balanced the box of pastries, McKenna gave her coworker a look, daring her to threaten all that hard work. "Literally for months . . ."

"Mm-hmm." Dalita Apkarian joined them with a firm press of her lips. "The same one you and I stayed late every night last week preparing for."

McKenna reached her desk. "Don't," she groaned.

"Yeah, add fifteen heads to that and find accommodations for them."

"What? How—who?" She tossed her jacket at her chair, then set down the box. "What happened? Who on earth—"

"This is our chance, Harel."

At the strident tone of Ambassador Cicely Robertson, McKenna fell silent and peered over her shoulder.

Her boss stalked toward her office with the embassy's chief of mission hot on her heels. It was a minor miracle she wasn't railing at him. The two agreed on little, and the chief rarely had a kind word for the woman he saw as incapable and pandering to the locals.

"Amazing that this happens just two months after I get here," Olafssen said.

Ambassador Robertson stopped short of her office. "Don't you dare, Harel. I have been working night and day with my team and Congressman Derriscort to drive a wedge into the objections." After unlocking her door, she looked at McKenna. "I've just sent you an email with some names to add to the dinner. I'll explain later. For now, get on that."

Not sure it was possible to find more space at the dinner, McKenna also knew it was her job to get it done regardless. "Yes, ma'am." She eyed the pastries, suddenly remembering the one for the ambassador. "Oh—" The bang of the office door silenced her.

"What do you think is going on?" asked Asher Bøhn, another junior consular officer who stood next to her.

"Something important, clearly." Jacket draped on her chair, McKenna sat down and rolled closer to the desk.

"Might explain why Olaf was so grumpy," Serena suggested, using the nickname they'd given the deputy chief. "You know, more than normal."

"I heard a rumor," came Dalita's quieter, plaintive voice, "there was some big, secret meeting in Azerbaijan."

McKenna furrowed her brow as she considered the local employee, curious how the Armenian woman could know about the meeting . . . Obviously it wasn't a secret if a local worker knew. But she had to hand it to Dalita, who'd often heard rumors that turned out to be accurate.

A big, secret meeting, huh? Could it possibly mean what she thought it might?

Yeah—a lot more work. That meant there was a very real chance she wouldn't get to go home for a vacation. That longing in her chest sharpened. At this rate, she wouldn't even get to see Sophia and Spencer graduate. Completely unacceptable!

"Peace talks, I'm guessing," offered Asher.

"Peace talks," scoffed Vugar Gharibian, one of the LEs, as he moved past them. "It is too late! A million of our people have died, and now they want to sweep that tragedy away."

McKenna pushed her gaze out to the window to the hill in the distance, where the Tsitsernakaberd Memorial complex stood with its eternal flame, dedicated in memory of those who perished. During the spring of 1915 and the fall of 1916, the Young Turk government conducted a campaign of deportation and mass killings against Armenian Christians of the Ottoman Empire. They also conducted a secret meeting with Azerbaijan in which the end goal was the annihilation of the Armenian people. The Armenian Genocide was closely linked to World War I and Ottoman fear that Armenians living in the Empire would be convinced to join the effort, so deportations were the beginning of the ruthless campaign against Armenians, killing over a million through starvation, exposure, massacres, and individual killings.

In that respect, Vugar was right—it was too late. And it hung over Yerevan like an oppressive storm cloud.

Talk of peace between the two countries stirred the embers of hope that the terrible fighting, which had persisted for decades, might at long last find resolution, peace.

When she looked back, she saw the others heading back to work, the weight of Vugar's venom quelling desire for office chatter. With a sigh, McKenna shifted her thoughts toward today's distress—how to add fifteen more seats to an already maxed-out dinner gala. But first, she checked the email from Cicely. It had instructions to secure a dozen rooms for security contractors and temporary documents for the attached list of incoming VIPs.

Aloud, McKenna continued reading. "'Request an urgent video meeting with . . .'" She gaped at the names spelled out in the email. This . . . this was the whole Foreign Relations committee that handled foreign policy, including the chairman himself! And—

She drew in a quick, quiet breath at the mention of the secretary of state. Sweet wings of mercy! Could it really be true that a historic peace treaty was about to happen? It'd be a good thing, assuming the details were carefully negotiated, but she knew that some on both sides would decry such a measure. The peacemaker in her had to believe that peace would be good.

Knowing time was not on her side to get the list done, McKenna got to work for the ambassador. Set up a secure chat room for this afternoon's meeting, issued invitations to the names listed. Then she recorded all her actions and turned her attention to accommodations. Since the embassy's rooms were already maxed out because of the dinner, she'd have to book the newcomers at a hotel. Which meant a visit down the street due to sensitive cybersecurity protocols. That and face-to-face always helped relations between businesses and the embassy. It also might enable her to be back at the café to catch up with Dillon.

Woof, this was going to be a long day.

The ambassador's door opened, expunging Mr. Olafssen from its domain.

A riot of emotions surged through McKenna at the sight of the stern-faced deputy chief of mission—he was here, serving Armenia and America, so she would grant him that respect, but he was not easy to work with, to put it mildly. Then there was the fact he searched for mistakes to blame on Cicely to get her removed.

"McKenna, come on in," the ambassador called from her office. "Bring Serena and Asher—and those pastries!"

Verifying the other officers had heard the summons, McKenna

grabbed the box. She carried it into the office, retrieved a plate and napkin from a credenza, then placed them on the ambassador's desk just as Asher closed the door.

Lifting a piece of baklava to the plate, Cicely glanced at her phone that had lit up. "I see you've already started on the list." Her gaze bounced to McKenna.

"Yes, ma'am. I've sent the invitations and logged everything in the system."

"Good." The ambassador took a bite, then licked her thumb. "Last night in a small village in Azerbaijan, Armenian and Azerbaijani representatives met to decide if there was any possibility of a preliminary peace talk. Miraculously, they both agreed to move forward."

"Brilliant!" McKenna heard the others make similar exclamations.

"So," Ambassador Robertson continued, "that dinner we already had in play will now include the secret delegation. I know that was a lot to throw at you this morning, but with Secretary of State Derriscort en route, the timing couldn't have been better."

At that name, McKenna started. "I saw his name on the meeting list but did not think he'd be coming."

"He was, in fact, at the covert meeting in Azerbaijan."

"Wow. I can't believe this might actually, finally be happening. That'd be amazing"—her mind rattled beneath Vugar's earlier objection—"and contentious."

"Indeed." Cicely took a bite and chewed slowly, pausing to read another message that woke her phone. "The peace delegation is traveling under anonymity and with haste to avoid any potential word leaking out. Nobody is to mention the names beyond my door."

McKenna and the other consular officers nodded their understanding and agreement. This meant the additional accommodations should be placed under a general embassy reservation, not individual names. Good thing she'd make the reservations in person.

"I know you'll have things well in hand, Miss Neeley, but the timetable is rushed."

So, no sleep tonight. Touching her temple, McKenna fought a wave of overwhelm. "Not a problem." This was par for the course here, yet she grieved the strengthening chance that her vacation Stateside wouldn't happen.

After finishing off her baklava, Cicely gave her an assured look. "I can't imagine any of this interfering with your PTO request."

Relief swarmed McKenna. It amazed her that, with all Cicely had going on, she remembered and ensured the time off would be honored. "Thank you, ma'am." With a nod, she brought up her data pad. "The lodgings here were all booked due to the dinner."

"Put them in the Holiday Inn on Republic Square."

"My thoughts exactly," McKenna said with a smile. "Since it's so last notice, I'll go over there personally to make the reservations." The embassy/consul had worked with the hotel often, so it made things smoother and more trustworthy. Too, it gave her a chance to develop a stronger rapport with the local community.

"Do what you need to."

"And I'll alert Chef to ensure no shellfish or pork for two of our arrivals." She knew for a fact that many of the Azerbaijani presidential detail were devout to Islam and considered both of those foods haram.

McKenna's phone buzzed. Surprise leapt through her at the name of the caller—"Catalina Derriscort." She looked at the ambassador, frowning. "Does she know her father's here?"

"Due to the delicate nature of this meeting, I cannot imagine he would have told her."

"So don't answer her call." McKenna pocketed her phone and returned to jotting on her iPad.

"This is a very precarious situation. If anyone outside this office learns who will be here, we—and they—could be targeted." The ambassador shook her head. "The last thing we need is for word to get out and an extremist try to kill someone."

"Are you saying Prime Ministers Abbasov and Harutyunyan will be here?" Asher asked, his eyes wide.

"Not this time," Cicely stated. "If this dinner with their representatives and the secretary of state goes well, then Abbasov and Harutyunyan will meet later at an undisclosed location." The ambassador exhaled heavily and rubbed a spot between her eyes. "Okay, I won't keep you. There's a lot of work to do. McKenna, get over to the hotel and secure those rooms. I don't want any hiccups. You know private contractors when things don't go smoothly."

"On it," McKenna said as she exited, closing the door behind her. She grabbed her jacket and purse, bundled up, and headed out of the embassy building.

Chilly air scraped her cheeks as she rushed to her car. And the encounter with—

Oh shoot. Dillon! She hoped she could get to the café to meet with him later. The thought of standing him up killed her—she wanted to know what he'd found that made him believe his dad was alive. Okay, she'd need to be careful with her time to make that happen.

In her car, she locked the doors and pulled onto Admiral Isakov Avenue. As a consular officer, she'd learned fast to make the most of every available second to get things done. First, she called and updated Chef Aillet about the additional plates they'd need. Chef was always pleasant and accommodating. Unlike her homeperson contact, Emin, who acted as if he had to move heaven and earth to make changes to the seating plans to prepare the banquet hall.

McKenna dreaded him answering and prayed it'd go to voicemail.

He answered.

Shoot. "Uh, Emin—" *Be cheerful!* "Hiiii, this is McKenna Neeley from Ambassador Robertson's office."

"Ah . . . oh . . . yes, ye?" He sounded distracted.

"I hate to tell you this," she said, continuing in Armenian, "but we must add fifteen people to the dinner tomorrow night."

"*Voch', sa anhnar e,*" he spat, no longer distracted or nice.

"I know," she replied in Armenian, hoping her effort at his language would help, "but we must add a table. I will—"

"It is not possible," he repeated.

She drew in a calming breath and let it out. "I understand the dining hall is not large, but we must figure this out. It's very important." She eyed the time—not even noon. Should be fine. "I'll come and help you sort it later. What time do you leave, Emin?"

Silence.

McKenna frowned. "Emin? Did you hear me?"

Nothing.

She eyed her phone and found a blank screen. "He hung up." She tossed her hands in the air. "He acts like I enjoy making his life difficult, and here I'm even willing to do the work for him." Which she would, because she would not let Cicely or this incredible opportunity down.

Miraculously, she found a spot along the curb in front of the Holiday Inn. She wrinkled her nose—to have such an American name in this exotic locale seemed . . . wrong. The lesson with Dillon fresh in her mind, she locked her car as soon as she exited it, hurried inside, and strode through the lobby to the front desk.

"Ah, good morning, Miss Neeley," greeted the assistant manager. "How can we help you today?"

"Hello, Mrs. Petrosian. I need to block fifteen rooms under the embassy." She drew out the credit card and passed it over. "Arrival within the next twenty-four hours and a week-long stay." It was a guess—she couldn't imagine them staying longer, but if they did, she could work it out later.

"Sure, sure." Mrs. Petrosian went to work reserving the rooms in the computer.

After setting up a per diem for each room and ensuring all details were correct, McKenna scanned the printout one final time for accuracy.

"My brother asks at least once a week if you are still single," Mrs. Petrosian said around a wry smile.

McKenna laughed. "Still single, but sadly, too busy for a relationship." At least, that's what she told herself and anyone who asked for a date—or proposed, as Mrs. Petrosian's brother had done, by proxy of his sister. "Thank you for your help."

"We—"

A raucous laugh reverberated across the lobby. "You are the goat!" The comment earned chortles.

McKenna turned and spied a half dozen men stalking toward the front desk. "Speak of the devils . . ."

Private security contractors had a very distinct bearing and presence that she was intimately acquainted with, considering her own father had been in that line of work for most of her life. But did they have to be so—

"Bro, do not—"

One guy made a sound like a sheep—no, a goat.

"What did I tell you, bro?"

That voice! McKenna's breath jammed in her throat. Her thundering heart yanked her forward—and right into the burly wall of ebony flesh she knew very well. "Dante!" She threw her arms around his neck and hugged him tight, elation coating every thought. He was here. All the way from Virginia. And her heart was about to jump clean out of her chest.

She released him and stepped back, laughing. "Mercy, how are you doing? What are you . . . ?" Why was he staring at her like that? Didn't he recognize her? "It's me—McKenna. Surely it hasn't been so long that you've forgotten—"

"Mick." He swallowed, stealing a glance to the side—his buddies. Then stretched his jaw. "Haven't forgotten."

Frowning in confusion and no little amount of hurt, she felt her smile slip away. Only then did her mind catch up with the last few seconds and register the jeers and hoots thrown at Dante as she'd hugged him. Oh, mercy. "Sorry." She retreated another step and tucked her hair behind her ear. "I was just so surprised. Why are you . . . ?"

"Work." Dante hoisted his ruck into a better hold.

"Right. Of course." Withdrawing her enthusiasm—what had she been thinking, hugging him?—she was suddenly aware that the Dante Riddell of her teen-crush years was not the same Dante standing in front of her. This was a whole lotta man—an operator who'd seen and done things she could not fathom. He had an edge to him now that hadn't been there before. A wave of embarrassment tumbled through her at how familiar she'd been with him.

His rich brown eyes wouldn't meet hers. Why was he being so weird?

No, not weird. He was Dante. Distant, disciplined Dante. He'd always kept to himself around the other Scions. Said it was the age difference, though she'd never bought that. But he'd always been friendly. Yet, nothing more. Never more.

Time to leave. She swallowed and nodded to the men. "I, uh, guess I should—"

"Hey." An operator with a ginger beard shouldered into Dante and smiled at her. "Want to introduce us to this beauty?"

"Step off," Dante bit out, his expression tightening.

Ignoring the bad mood, the brawny, barrel-chested guy stuck his large hand toward her. "Brick Archer, ma'am."

Had to appreciate the twang and Southern charm of the big

man. Skating a glance at Dante, she wasn't sure if his coldness was about more than embarrassment. Maybe anger? At what though? Regardless—unlike him—she would not be rude. "McKenna Neeley."

"Pardon my intrusion, but I'm wondering how you know this goat," Brick asked, thumbing toward Dante.

"Oh, um . . . our dads worked together." The Scions had long been instructed on how to answer that question, considering their dads handled very sensitive missions. It also made explaining the Scion connections to each other simpler, easier. "However, I'm also with the consular offices, and I assume you are"—*careful with details in public*—"our unexpected additions to security—"

"Yes." A tall, handsome man edged in, his dark hair threaded through with silver at the temples, which glinted beneath the lobby lights. His steely eyes moved to her like a storm. "Pike Auberon, CEO of Omen."

"Oh." Sweet mercies. *The* Pike Auberon? Holy what—Dante was on Pike Auberon's team? Why hadn't he ever said so? Everyone with any connection to military operations knew this guy, and she understood immediately his reputation was well-earned. "I . . . I'm McKenna Neeley, junior consular officer working with Ambassador Robertson." She indicated to the front desk. "Mrs. Petrosian there can help you with the arrangements I've made for y'all. There's a per diem as well."

"Thank you," Pike said. "We need to get checked in and cleaned up. If you'll excuse us."

The way he shouldered in her direction, effectively driving her back a step, told McKenna her work here was done. And apparently, so was her friendship with Dante.

Swallowing the wad of grief lodged in her throat, she backstepped and eyed her onetime friend, but his gaze was on the men. The twenty steps to the double doors were made in humiliating silence. She'd hoped he would stop her. Talk to her.

But she understood—he wasn't interested in her. Not like that. Never had been. Probably never would be. But weren't they friends? She couldn't even explain why it hurt so much.

Do not cry. Do not cry. You are an intelligent, competent officer.

And he was a skilled operator, lodging that icy dagger of rejection into her heart. Again.

Spine vibrating with a tremor of rage at himself for turning his back on the only person in his entire life—outside family—to treat him with respect and kindness, Dante knew he should catch up with her. Make nice. The shock of seeing her was one thing, but having her jump in his arms had short-circuited his brain.

A thump to his shoulder snapped him around, ready to take Brick and his flirting self on. But he drew up sharp at finding Pike standing over him. Dante retracted that coiled viper in his gut, steeling himself and his expression. "Chief."

Pike cocked an eyebrow to the left, in Mick's direction. "That's a mistake."

Nope. No way would he let the chief think he was distracted. "It's not a problem. She knows we're just friends."

The former Navy SEAL master chief stared at him. Hard. "You're not hearing me—*that* is a mistake."

All Dante could do was nod because he had no idea what Pike meant. Was McKenna a mistake? Was being her friend a mistake? How else could she be a mistake?

"You disappoint me, Atlas."

Boom. Right into the thick emplacements around his heart. His honor. Pulse ricocheting around his ribs, he stilled. He wanted this man's respect so bad but always fell short. "Aware of that, boss."

Pike gave a slow shake of his head, then pointed to the front desk. "Check in and shower up. We're back down here at fifteen-hundred for a prelim walk-thru of the embassy."

Escaping to his room was the best course of action. Dante tossed his ruck in the corner and placed his hands on his shaved head. Paced, working through letting down Pike. Hated that he'd hurt McKenna. She didn't deserve that.

Man, he had to get his head on straight. "'I serve with honor on and off the battlefield,'" he quoted the Navy SEAL creed, moving to the window and pivoting as he continued. "'The ability to control my emotions and my actions . . .'" A breath rattled through him, a cool swarm of calm worming into his chaos. "'. . . regardless'"—he nodded in affirmation that it shouldn't matter what was happening, he needed to maintain control—"'of circumstance, sets me apart from others.'" Yeah. Set apart . . .

Because he was a loser.

He clenched his eyes. Tilted his head back and stretched his jaw. Made himself finish. "'Uncompromising integrity is my standard. My character and honor are steadfast—'" He bit out the words that were painful . . . maybe not accurate . . . He had failed. So many times. Let down Omen. The Navy. Pop. Now Mick. "'My word is my bond.'"

Hunched forward, he palmed the ledge of the window. Pressed his jaw to his shoulder. Inhaled deep . . . exhaled. If he lost this contract . . .

Man, what *is wrong with me?*

With a growl, he straightened and turned. Threw a fist in the air and huffed. That's when he noticed the clock—had to be downstairs in twenty. Needed a shower. He grabbed his shave kit and cleaned up. Appreciated the heat and steam of the shower that seemed to clear his head. After a quick shave, he considered his reflection. "You got this, man."

He hoofed it down to the lobby with two minutes to spare. Twenty-eight minutes later, he and Omen cleared security at the embassy. They reconnected with the secretary of state and his security detail on the second level. Then Pike and the SecState entered a conference room where five embassy personnel waited.

A petite, fifty-something woman with short, brown hair stood and extended her hand. "Secretary Derriscort, welcome."

The politician nodded as he accepted her greeting. "Good to see you again, Ambassador Robertson. How are we doing on the dinner?"

She pointed to the side. "My right hand, junior consular officer McKenna Neeley, is handling tomorrow night's dinner details for me."

And like that, McKenna was in Dante's line of sight and jacking up his thoughts again. In the hall, he eased back, adjusting to the side for a clear shot into the conference room. Lot of bodies in that room. Someone had to watch their six.

He eyed Brick, who grinned like a hyena. How did the dude always know . . . ? Looking away, Dante checked the hall. Empty. Three doors. All closed. Exit sign indicated to the right. He eventually brought his attention back to the room—on Pike. Who had taken a seat and swiveled to the left as the soft voice of McKenna drifted from somewhere out of sight.

Dante planted himself there, arms crossed and feet shoulder-width apart, listening.

"The agenda for the dinner will be simple," she said. "Three courses—appetizer, main course, and dessert—so plenty of time remains for a cocktail hour afterward, designed to encourage casual, open conversation."

"Music? Dancing?" Hamer, Derriscort's lead security officer, asked. Head on a swivel, he clearly wanted to plan for all contingencies. Dancing made securing a room more challenging.

"Uh, no," came McKenna's voice from somewhere inside. Somewhere Dante could not see. "It's not deemed appropriate, considering the purpose of this gathering and the existing tensions between the two countries."

"How many in attendance?" Pike asked.

"With the addition of your team, sixty-five." After quiet settled over the room, McKenna spoke again. "If there are no more questions, I can go over the planned arrival and departure schedule."

On the glass inset in the door, McKenna's reflection slid into view. Hair down, she looked sharp. She'd added a business-suit jacket to her blouse and slacks. A class act. It'd been a hot minute since he'd last seen her . . . it'd been . . .

Hold up. When *had* he last seen her?

For the last few years, the Scions had chatted on Discord, and they usually had their cameras on. But he'd been in locations he couldn't reveal, so he'd stuck to audio only. No, that hadn't been the last few years. That'd been at least six or eight. Man, it had been . . . ages. Ops had taken up his time. So . . . when had he seen her in person? He recalled her laughing, screaming—the tandem-jump gift Dillon had given her. For her sixteenth birthday.

Bro. Had it seriously been a decade? All he knew was that Mick had not looked like that. Or felt like that.

His brain buzzed with the memory of her in his arms. The soft curves . . . she hadn't had those before. She'd been a stick in her teen years—tall and thin. He was ashamed to admit he hadn't even recognized her at the hotel. Oh, he'd seen her a'right. A fine woman like that did not go unnoticed. So maybe he'd been staring and that's why he'd been so shocked when she'd jumped in his arms. It wasn't until she'd said his name in her sweet voice that the hammer struck. Her squeaky little voice—the other Scions called her Mickey Mouse because of it—used to grate on his last nerve when they were younger. But here she spoke with authority and intelligence to a room full of key political figures. Kinda felt proud.

She'd always been smart—more a mother to the other Scions than a cadre member.

A throat cleared and he met Crow's gaze.

Rawlins arched an eyebrow. "Need me to get out of the way?"

Only then did Dante realize he'd shifted right up against the team sniper to maintain a line of sight on Mick. "Just wanted to be sure there wasn't visual intel I was missing."

"Like what she's wearing or if she has the hots for you?"

"Shut up, man."

Suits stood and crowded the door, forcing Omen aside as the conference room emptied.

Pike signaled the team over. "Embassy security is going to give us a walk-thru of the grounds."

Embarrassed at his own distractibility, Dante fell in behind the others, his gaze snagging on McKenna, who shot him a furtive look, then glanced away. The two security teams were meticulous in surveying the embassy and its grounds. Making notes of potential problem locations and blind spots. An hour later, they headed out. And he couldn't help but scan the embassy for her. Not gonna lie—he hated when they made their exit and headed back to the hotel, where the guys worked out and did some laps in the pool.

"Group up," Pike said, as he dragged a hand over his face dripping with chlorinated water. "Hamer asked us to walk the banquet hall and first level prior to the dinner tomorrow. We'll head over at 1640 hours."

"We going all monkey suit?" Brick asked, flinging water from his red beard. "Those suits choke me."

"Why don't you keep that," Luther said, indicating the shirtless burly Irishman, "concealed in tac. But this"—he slapped his chest—"is what tuxedos were made for, baby."

The team snickered.

"Sorry to disappoint," Pike said. "We'll be in kit. SecState wants an obvious security presence as backup to the standard suit-and-tie detail."

"In other words, bullet bait," Dade complained.

Anyone looking to take out security would first see those in full kit. The suit-and-ties were harder to spot in a crowd of similarly clad bodies.

"I say bring it," Luther countered. "I mean, there's a reason we're called Omen—good omen for those who need our help, bad for those getting up in the face of justice."

Pike nodded, glancing around the team. "We don't need distractions." Funny how his gaze landed on Dante just then. "Be ready. For anything."

"Like goats."

THREE

Yerevan, Armenia

WOULD HE STILL BE WAITING?

McKenna raced back to the café's little bricked courtyard, hoping and praying Dillon would be there. Paying attention to the speed limit and negotiating the gnarled traffic, she stole a glance at the dashboard clock. Eight p.m. Yikes.

She groaned that the route and layout of the streets demanded she actually pass the café and circle back. Straining for sign of him, she glided by, searching the people and shadows. Was that—

A honk from behind warned her that she'd slowed too much.

With another groan, she focused on taking the circle and zipping back. Prayed there was a spot along the front curb again. Annnnd of course, there wasn't.

So, she had to park a block away. Keys in hand, she grabbed her purse, locked the door, and hurried to the café. Scanning as she reached it, she knew he wasn't here. It was just like Dillon. Hotheaded and impulsive. He'd probably written her off at 5:01. But she'd really wanted to know about that lead. Auntie Sydney would be . . .

Mercy, there just would not be words for how distraught she

must feel with her husband dead—gone?—and her son now missing.

Brushing her blonde hair from her face, McKenna did a complete one-eighty, again probing the shadows and alcoves. *Please, Dillon . . .*

She ducked into the café and checked the tables to no avail. Back outside, she walked the perimeter slowly.

Shoot. Dillon wasn't here; she had to accept that. Only she, with her uncanny knack for messing things up, could see two Scions on the same day and have both encounters go wrong.

Woof. She was setting a record.

While she was here, she might as well get dinner from the café before heading home, where a lot of work waited. Once armed with a gourmet salad, she gave the courtyard one more perusal and returned to her car. Inside, she double-checked that he wasn't hiding out in the backseat. By the time she pulled up in front of her flat and parked, she felt the thick blanket of sadness weighting her. She missed her friends and family.

McKenna climbed out, shut the door, and locked it. Shifting the keys to find the one for the door, she rounded the corner.

A dark shape careened at her.

"Augh!" She braced but the impact of the man's shoulder knocked the salad from her hand. "Hey—be careful!" Furious, she spun after him. Noticed that tall, athletic frame, and her heart climbed into her throat. "Dillon?" She started forward even as the shadows and darkness of the alley swallowed him. "Dillon!"

Was that him? The broad shoulders, shorn hair—

Another man erupted from the shrubs a block down and gave pursuit.

What? Awareness tremored through her—Dillon was in trouble! She was not a fast runner, but she had a car. Back in her Hyundai, she whipped the car around the block and drove in the direction Dillon had gone. "C'mon, c'mon. Where'd you go?" she whispered as she slunk along, eyeing side streets and courtyards that were simply fenced driveways.

The twenty-minute search turned up nothing, and she wasn't sure whether to be concerned—had he been attacked, hurt?—or irritated. Had his mile-wide noble streak forced him to stay hidden so he didn't endanger her too?

She had to choose to believe the latter or panic would overwhelm her. Calling the authorities was out of the question because she had a big feeling Dillon wasn't in-country legally, since he was searching for his dad. It was very unlikely he was flashing his passport when he entered countries, because that would log his location with the government.

Back at her place after the search, she hurried up the sidewalk, retrieved the still-closed salad box—unbelievable!—and rushed into her condo. She abandoned her purse and salad, then grabbed her phone. Daddy would know what to do.

As it rang, she chided herself for calling in the parents but felt this was an emergency. She eyed the clock and winced. Wow, it was late th—

"Mick?"

The concern in her dad's voice sent a warm squall through McKenna. "Daddy." Tears stung just hearing his sleepy voice.

"What's wrong, darlin'?"

"I . . ." She dropped onto her oversized comfy chair, tucked her legs beneath her, and bent forward. "It's so good to hear your voice."

"Likewise. What's going on?"

"I didn't know what to do." She had to be careful not to sound the alarms. "You're not going to believe this—Dillon was here."

His silence proved heavy and telling. "Dillon Jacobs was in Yerevan?"

"He said he'd found a lead about Uncle Max. Said he's not dead."

Quiet rankled the line.

Not wanting to hear him decry Dillon, who'd earned a bad-boy reputation for very good reasons, she rushed on. "I couldn't talk to him much—things are happening at work, and I had to get to the office." The Nightshade parents may have written Dillon off, but as a Scion, she could not. Would not. "We agreed to meet at a café after work, but I was late. When I finally made it, he was nowhere to be found. So, I came home to get some work done—and he was here! Nearly bowled me over, racing past me. Then I realized someone was chasing him, Daddy! I tried to follow in my car, but they were either long gone or . . ." She squeezed her eyes shut.

"Don't go there, Mickey." Daddy always had sage advice tucked in that deep voice of his. "He's Max's son—God, help him—so I'm sure he's fine. But how'd he know where you live?"

McKenna blinked, frowning as she lifted her head. "I . . . have no idea. He hasn't participated in the Scion group chat in a year. And come to think of it, I'm not sure how he knew I was even here." She straightened, pressing her back into the thick cushion of the couch and held her hair out of her face. "I'm worried about him, Daddy. I couldn't find him."

"That boy's tough," Daddy said in his Southern drawl. "He may be many things, but I'll hand it to him—capable is one of them. Dillon can take care of himself."

"True." Her daddy's words did not really quench the worry. Likely, he'd make some calls later. She had to believe that. Trust that. "It's been such a long day. I was—Oh! I saw Dante."

"Riddell?" His voice pitched, the shock obvious. "You saw both Dante and Dillon today?"

She laughed. "Strange, right? Yeah, Dante is here for—"

"Stop talking, Mickey. This line ain't secure."

She clenched her eyes, cursing her carelessness. "Right. Sorry. So easy to forget when it comes to family." And that's what the Scions and Nightshade team were.

"I know. Just be smart. You don't want to put either of them—or yourself—at risk."

"Well, I'm pretty sure that isn't going to happen since Dillon is off to wherever and Dante didn't want anything to do with me."

"Come again." That edge to Daddy's voice stilled her.

She knew that stiffness. It was the same one she'd heard the day she unwittingly admitted that Mitch Daniels had stolen a kiss during lunch at co-op. "Oh, Daddy, please don't. I . . ." *Humiliated myself!* "I was so surprised to see him that I hugged him. In front of the whole team."

"Ah, that'd do it," Daddy said. "But if I need to read his dad in on this . . ."

"You would positively mortify me."

"Might be worth it, if it meant you didn't hug him again."

She couldn't help the smile. "Honestly, Daddy. I told you we Scions agreed long ago not to date. We're like siblings, so it'd be gross." Except it wouldn't be. Wasn't. Not with Dante's tall, broad frame and corded muscles. Definitely not gross.

"If Legend knew his boy was rude to you, he'd beat him into next year."

"He didn't mean to be. I caught him off guard."

"Still. He was rude to my darlin', and that ain't acceptable."

Yeah. He was. There was a small—very small—part of her that wouldn't be mad if Dante got chastised for being so cold to her. He'd made her feel like a dog put in its place with how he'd sidestepped her. "It's okay."

"Not on this planet. You got your Beretta?"

She chuckled. "You know I wasn't allowed to bring it over." Like she would ever target Dante—well, with anything other than her heart. "Besides, while the Beretta air rifle helped me medal in the Olympics, it doesn't have half the range of my Remington 700." A birthday present from Daddy. Even their banter couldn't erase all of the frustration from today or the concern she felt about both Scions. She let out a hostage breath.

"I hear that sigh and can tell you're still carrying a torch for him."

That Dillon had said the same made McKenna wrinkle her nose. "Hard not to, but I'm a grown woman. I see the writing on the wall." She huffed and changed topics. "Anyway, how's everyone?"

"Doing good. Heard from Ben, and he's doing well at training. Sophie got accepted to Carnegie Mellon, and Spencer is talking Navy. Don't worry—I'll get him straightened out. Boy's head is in the wrong place, wanting to be a frogman like Uncle Max."

Inter-service rivalry never died, even with Nightshade. "He practically hero-worshipped Dante for a long time too, so that doesn't surprise me," she said with a sigh. "And Mama?"

"Here. I'll let you chew her ear. Love ya, darlin'."

"Love you too, Daddy. See you in a couple of weeks." *God willing and the creek don't rise . . .*

"Hey, Mickey," came Mama's sweet voice. "How are you?"

"Doing okay. Things are a bit crazy, but I'm alive, happy, and healthy, so . . . I can't complain."

"Just as long as you haven't accepted a marriage proposal from some handsome Armenian and plan to stay there."

McKenna laughed. "I promise. Even if that man existed, I miss home too much to stay here."

"That's the answer we want to hear."

"Darn right," Daddy called through the line, making her ache all the more for them. To feel his arms around her, reassuring and protective. To see him laugh.

"Still coming at the end of the month?"

"Absolutely!" Tears running, she couldn't wait to be home.

"How's work going?"

"Good," McKenna sniffled, wiping her nose. "I'm doing good. Helping people who can't help themselves and coordinating dinners for the ambassador."

After a fifteen-minute chat, they said goodbyes. McKenna grabbed her laptop and went to work. Lot to get sorted as she ate her now-tossed salad. She checked her mail and found a request for confirmation on the seating from Emin. He had been so difficult when she'd met him before heading out to connect with Dillon. But things were sorted. She forwarded the email to the ambassador for approval. Then did final sign-offs on the guest list additions.

"Haven't forgotten."

McKenna drew in a breath, recalling how Dante had said that. What had it meant? And the way he'd told Brick to "step off." That . . . sounded like jealousy. Or possessiveness.

Nah, just a big brother looking out for his little sister. Because wasn't that how he'd always referenced the other Scions? *Little.*

Although she had just stared him in the face a few hours ago, she had this irrepressible urge to look up photos of him. It wasn't social media she went to but the photo from nearly ten years ago. There was a better one on her desk at work, but here . . .

She browsed her phone and found the photo that always made her heart pitter-patter. When her sixteen-year-old self had the worst crush on the brand-new Navy SEAL. It was a photo from Daddy's phone that she'd sent to herself, then deleted the sent notification. Uncle Legend had gone out to his son's BUD/S graduation and sent Daddy the picture of father and son, smug as all get-out and handsome to boot.

She zoomed in on Dante. Handsome then. His rich, dark skin had always been beautiful and tempted her fingers to trace the sharp planes of his face. He'd often shaved his head—probably to emulate his dad. This photo was almost ten years old, and now he had a decade of military experience to harden his features and toughen up the edge that made his jaw that much more . . . rugged.

The ridiculousness of her thoughts made her cringe. She tossed her phone aside and dug her fingers into her hair and groaned. Then she hugged her knees to her chest. "What are you doing,

McKenna Margaret?" She slumped to the side and curled into a ball. "Being pathetic!" She grabbed the couch pillow and stuffed it over her face and head. "God, why did You make him so gorgeous?"

Stomping to her feet, the pillow sliding to the area rug, she fisted her hands. "I am better and stronger than this. I'm not here to catch a man's eyes but to help the people of Armenia and American citizens abroad." Tugging her sweater down, she straightened her shoulders. Drew in and exhaled. "I am strong, confident, and capable, but I am weak. God, give me strength so everything I do glorifies You . . . which would mean"—she slouched onto the couch—"not pining after Dante Riddell." Grabbing her laptop with one hand, she thrust the other into the air. "Back to work!"

* * *

Not even the fading light of the day could hide the majestic and ominous presence of Mount Ararat looming over Yerevan in the distance. Its spine cast a reflection on the Yerevanyan river basin and lake squatting on the southern edge of the embassy. Man, there was something impressive, humbling, about formidable mountains, and this one ranked high.

M4A1 on a sling, Dante palmed the stock as he patrolled the rooftop. Nodded to an embassy guard as he approached.

The guard inclined his head.

"What's the three-story structure there?" Dante pointed across the river basin, knowing what it was. He wouldn't be stupid enough to work security for a VIP without doing his homework: studying street maps, structures where snipers could get vantage, and all possible exfils in case of an attack. But it was good to talk up the locals and as a single unit, rather than an us/them situation.

"Swimming school. Closes at eight." The guard smirked as, if on cue, the interior lights at the school winked out, but exterior lights still threw their weight around, chasing off night. "Water's about twenty-six degrees this time of year, so unlikely anyone would be in it."

Dante gritted his teeth at the thought of the freezing lake. As a SEAL, he'd learned fast the dominating, powerful force of water. Like a fool, he'd done the polar plunge on a dare from his buddies during a training rotation in the Hindu Kush. Wouldn't make that mistake again.

He scanned the road that curved around and out of sight on the north side of the building. "How do things feel?"

In the time it took the guard to eye him and figure out what he meant, Pike's voice thrummed in the comms. "First guests arriving. Omen to positions."

The guard bobbed his head. "Quiet, normal."

"Let's hope it remains so." Dante patted his shoulder. "Stay frosty." With that, he ducked inside and hustled down the stairs, answering the command to return. "Atlas en route. Roof is clear and quiet. Guard on each corner. Basin clear."

"Good copy," Pike replied.

Adjusting his weapon to the low-ready, Dante pushed through the door onto the second level and spotted Luther at a juncture with Crow.

"Chief wants you in the hall," Luther said, thumbing toward a double set of doors.

Dante faltered. "Inside?" Where McKenna would be. Not that he was thinking about her. Or had spent all night with her on his mind. Or remembering how she jumped into his arms.

Luther's lips quirked. "Scared you'll see She'sJustaFriend again?" He backhanded Crow's chest rig. "Maybe you should introduce yourself."

"If you're sure about that friend thing," Crow said with an unrepentant grin, "I'll give her my number. Unlike you, I'm not afraid to slide past 'friend' to 'more than friend' with someone like that."

Bros were just messing with him. But it got up under his plates and burned. "Get off, man." That had too much bite to it. Should bring it down. "You're too"—he eyed his buddy with feigned contempt—"small."

Crow's brown eyes widened. "Did you—"

"I think he just challenged you, bro," Luther said.

Dante shook his head. "I ain't going to be goaded."

"Yo. Hold up. Don't you mean"—Luther smirked—"goated?"

Laughter bellowed through the hall, and Dante knew he'd never live down Big Horn.

"Game on. Watch this." Crow started for the dining hall where staff awaited the arrival of guests and VIPs.

Dante put a hand to the guy's chest and stopped him. "Stay."

"I don't report to y—"

"Atlas." Pike's sharp voice cut through the hall.

Backing up, Dante pointed a warning at Crow, then pivoted and hustled to the main doors. In the small huddle with Pike were the ambassador and the chief of mission, along with Renzo Rossi, second in charge of the SecState's security detail. "Chief?"

The early-forties Omen founder eyed Dante. His presence felt more like a land-based hurricane than a breeze. When he swung his gaze into someone, the person felt it. Sometimes by the warm trickle running down their leg.

Which wasn't Dante. This time. However, he did fight the urge to step back.

Pike's hand landed on his shoulder as he eyed the huddle. "This is Atlas. He's the man for the job."

I am? What job?

"In mythology, Atlas carried the weight of the world on his shoulders." Renzo eyed him, as did the ambassador.

No doubt the guy said that for a reason, a power play. "Technically, he held up the sky and heavens." Though Dante felt their intense scrutiny, he steeled his expression. Same as Pike. He greeted the others with a nod, as if this happened every day. Which it didn't. The chief had never singled him out for an op like this.

"Auberon says you're skilled in jiu-jitsu," Renzo stated.

Feeling the intent shift, Dante nodded. "I am."

"We want you inside the event hall during the dinner," Rossi said, his words gritted out. Like bro was ticked. "Picked up some chatter that has us concerned. A possible attack on one of our VIPs, and if something goes down, we'd prefer the hostile be secured, not killed."

Only one reason for that—to pull intel out of the attacker.

If they wanted Dante inside, then they were doubting someone they already knew. Or one of the guests. And if they were wanting a guy in full kit in plain view, they also wanted the threat of force clear to this individual—and likely non-lethal. CQB—close quarters battle—at its finest. "Understood."

"He'll do," Ambassador Robertson said, "but he needs a suit."

At that, Dante flinched, then relaxed that he could refuse. "Afraid I do not have one."

Robertson signaled a security member forward but spoke to Dante. "If you'll follow this officer, you can get changed."

"Changed?"

The ambassador nodded. "I'll see you back in the hall once you're in proper attire."

Monkey suit and dinner with politicos. Was that laughter coming from heaven again? Hey. As long as he got to put someone in a spine twister, the price of a strangling suit might be worth it. Maybe.

Pike held out his hand. "M4."

Some operators might object, but a master at BJJ, Dante preferred the Gentle Art. He handed over the M4 and unholstered his Glock.

"Keep that," Pike instructed.

The guard led him through a coat closet to the back, where a rack of jackets hung on the wall. It took him ten minutes to don a black shirt over his plates, conceal his Glock along his spine, then shrug into the best-fitting jacket.

"Seating is assigned," the guard said. "So you'll need to find the officer to know where you'll be sitting."

Dante worked the tie. "They know I can't speak Armenian, right?"

"Won't need to," the guard said, leading them through a series of rear passages until they entered the banquet hall via a side door. "Let's find . . ." He stretched his neck, looking around the room.

Chatter and the clink of ice in glasses greeted Dante as he got the lay of the land. First thing he noticed was the U-shaped setup of tables with eight seats at the head. Behind the middle chairs stood three tall, proud flags—the Armenian and Azerbaijani with the American flag at the center. It was the US Embassy after all. Tables were dressed in black cloth, floral arrangements, and fine china. Wait staff mingled, serving wine and possibly champagne. Others offered hors d'oeuvres to the guests streaming into the hall.

"Over here." The guard negotiated his way past all the glittering attire. "Ma'am."

A curvy woman in a navy dress turned to look over her shoulder—

Shoot. Me.

McKenna came around, her eyes alighting on Dante. "Oh."

Now, *that* had to be mocking laughter coming from God.

She'd tied her hair up—that's why he hadn't realized it was her at first. The crisp, professional lines of that dress contradicted the teardrop cutout just below her throat that was tauntingly left bare. Gathered fabric along her waist made sure every perfect curve got noticed, yet it wasn't tacky or sleazy. Modest came to mind. She wore black heels, smart and minimal jewelry. It was like she owned casual sexible—he meant sexy. Son of a goat—*sensible!*

"Thank you, Randy," Mick said as she eyed the tablet in her

hand. "Mr. Homer, your seat is over here." Voice tight and low, she strode toward the front of the tables and set a hand on a chair. "Here."

Homer. She had to go that route.

"Hesiod," he corrected as he checked the seat and name placard that clearly read: Homer.

She hesitated, throwing that frown at him across the three inches separating them. "What?" The navy dress somehow brightened her face and accented her shape that haunted his dreams. Why'd she have to wear that? Wasn't there a nun habit available?

Hauling his thoughts back to the Atlas debate, Dante clasped one hand over the other, business casual as it were, angling toward the rest of the hall. "In Homer's *Odyssey*, Atlas was a marine creature."

McKenna shifted closer, stirring the air—and something in him—that strained his focus. "Mm-hmm," she said, her voice a near whisper, "and were you not a SEAL?"

He snapped his gaze to her.

"Marine creature," she said, her delicate brows lifting as she shrugged, making her point.

"True." He liked how she teased him. "But Hesiod's Atlas was a Titan who took part in the war against Zeus."

Tilting her head to the side, she was right there—a breath away. Unfazed by his challenge or him. "So, you fancy yourself a god?"

"Ti-tan," he corrected, emphasizing the syllables with his hands and voice.

A near-smile ghosting her lips, she tapped the second chair. "Your seat, Mr. *Ho-mer.*"

He did not miss how she broke up those syllables or the message she sent downrange with her insistence on calling him Homer. And man, if he didn't find himself smiling as she strode toward the gathering crowd. Girl had it going on in all the right ways.

Mick met a short, balding man. They chatted, laughed, then she led him across the room and introduced him to some politico. She looked so casual and comfortable among the locals, and nobody seemed to feel awkward around her. Hold up, was she speaking Armenian?

Rather than plant his backside in the chair as she'd instructed, he chose to walk the room. He might not speak the local language, but he was more than adept at reading body language. If they had concerns about someone, it'd be good to get a feel for relations. Any way you counted it, half the people in this room had been at war with the other half for the last several decades. Which meant some let hate into that mindset. And that led to operators like him interdicting.

In the middle of the room, the ambassador and chief of mission talked with the Armenian Minister of Foreign Affairs, an ever-growing crowd around them.

Didn't like that cluster—too tight, too hard to reach the VIPs and interdict if necessary. He shifted through the crowd, taking in faces, expressions, tensions . . .

"Heads up," Pike comm'd. "SecState's on-site with AzerB MFA."

With both MFAs present, Dante looked for Mick to ensure she was aware, but by her close proximity to the ambassador and Armenian MFA, who were making their way to a side door, she was a step ahead of him.

She paused and glanced back, searching for—

He felt those blue eyes connect with his. Straight to his core. She cocked her head to the side, indicating he should follow. Quick strides carried him across the room, and he stepped up behind her.

Aside, she whispered, "Ambassador wants you to stay close to us and the MFAs."

"Staying close," he confirmed quietly to her, but also to ensure Omen had his twenty and understood the situation.

The SecState entered the private antechamber with the MFA from AzerB and their security detail, along with Pike and Luther.

Dante visually checked those already in the room, reading posture, proximity, and protocols. Seemed chill. He looked at McKenna again, liked that she was watching him. Checking him out? Wait . . . what was with the small crease between her eyes? Was something wrong?

Three more times, her gaze wandered to his as the delegation asked after families and well-being—customary among the West Asian countries. That undercurrent of concern about her made him work his way closer to Mick and the VIPs. He tried to angle in to find out what was wrong, but someone had her engaged in a conversation, so he again took in the crowd. From the queue of embassy officials, a pair of dark eyes met his—a woman. Late twenties. She quickly averted her gaze. Turned away from him.

As in she did not want him paying attention to her.

But then he sensed Mick's distress again as the politicos lined up to make a formal entrance into the dining hall. He veered toward her once more. Relieved when he reached, he shouldered in. "All good?"

She warily met his gaze and wet her lips. Hesitated.

He stayed with her, advancing toward the door. "Tell me."

"An LE is . . . late. Missing." She bounced her shoulders and shook her head. "I don't know."

"LE?"

"A local employee," she clarified, brushing aside one of the locks of hair she hadn't tied back and used the motion to hide her words. "He left at lunch and hasn't returned. He's supposed to be here, helping."

Dante merged with the delegation as they moved through the door, then eased behind McKenna. "That normal?"

"No," she whispered, catching his arm and drawing him to the right-flanking table, where she found her seat.

Right next to his.

"He's usually quite reliable," she said as they both sat down.

"But earlier today, he was very upset about this meeting. Vugar is a really nice man—grew up in one of the outlying villages near the border. His grandparents were killed by some Azerbaijanis trying to wipe out Christians and that village."

As guests settled into their seats, Dante once again assessed the crowded room and thought about the peace treaty decades in the making and the damage one rogue LE could inflict. "If he has security access, cut it. Now."

"You can't—" Her eyes widened as she considered him, then she focused on her tablet and went to work. "I am doing this strictly out of extreme caution. Vugar would never do anything. It's not like him."

"Desperation makes people do crazy things," he muttered. "We need to protect what's happening here. It's too important."

Mick straightened, brushing hair from her face as a breath staggered out of her, and her gaze landed on her boss. She seemed rattled. Worried. Afraid.

And it undid something in him. "I got you."

Those blue eyes swirled back to him and latched on, lingered. "I know."

Why was his heart drumming out of his chest?

She shuddered a breath, then refocused on the delegation.

Why'd he go and say he had her? He had this mission. It wasn't personal, not like that. But he knew if something went down and he didn't protect her, there were a half dozen operators past their prime but still very lethal who would come after him. Forget that— he'd hate himself.

On the table, McKenna's phone lit with an incoming call. She looked at the screen but silenced it and focused on her work.

Right. Back to work. Studying those present, he noted hand placements. Posture—whether one person was rigidly faced forward or angling toward another on their right or left. Expressions. Smiles—there were a lot of smiles, each with a different meaning.

A man leaned forward, enabling Dante to lock gazes with a woman. The same one with dark eyes who had been tracking him earlier.

She started. Went rigid. Jerked her gaze away and hunched over her phone.

Hiding from him. Why? "Tycho," Dante subvocalized, swiping a hand over his mouth to cover it. "Female, black hair, blue blouse. Stay close."

Low-key, Dade Tycho casually adjusted position toward the woman.

A hand stuffed into his periphery, startling Dante. He flinched, narrowly avoiding catching the man's wrist and doing something impolite, like breaking it.

"Hello." The man's smile made his eyes disappear as he bounced his hand in the air, urging Dante to shake it. "I do not know you."

Same, bro. Same.

"Mr. Papian," McKenna said, inserting herself into the awkward situation, "this is Mr. Homer, a colleague of mine."

She had to go there again . . .

"Ah, you are from embassy?" Papian asked, eyes vanishing behind thick eyelids.

With a nod, Dante shook the man's hand. Which was nasty— sweaty. But he buried his reaction because he was not that man who embarrassed another.

Papian stared at him for a long second, and Dante could swear there was some sort of . . . question there. But it never got verbalized before the man returned to his own space.

Hands in her lap as servers delivered the first course, McKenna leaned in front of Dante and said something in Armenian to the man, who glanced at Dante, then laughed.

Dante gave her a questioning look, which she deftly ignored, leaning farther across him to whisper conspiratorially to the older man. Who laughed—a lot.

Peering over them to the room beyond, Dante shook his head. "Not cool, man," he muttered, convinced he was being mocked. "Not cool."

Laughing, McKenna set her hand on his arm and continued her conversation with the older man, not caring that she invaded his personal space. That her perfume was tangling up his mind. That her face was inches from his—and her small smattering of freckles was distracting. That the guys were going to torment him over this. More importantly, that she was impeding his line of sight on the room.

Papian shifted aside so a server could set a plate in front of Dante, who was glad for the space, but that food looked like something Big Horn had left behind. "Aw, nah man." He caught the server's eye and made a sawing motion at his neck, indicating to take it away.

McKenna was already eating hers and furrowed her brow. "It's *vospov kofte.*"

"Tss, my coffee ain't never looked like that."

"*Kofte*, a lentil patty." Her blue eyes were vibrant beneath the chandeliers and her amusement.

Teasing her, he held a fist to his mouth as if he might vomit, but he was smart enough not to mock the food too much.

"You are uncouth," she sniffed.

"I think you mispronounced *wise.*"

She chuckled and shook her head. "It's a traditional dish here. You should eat something."

"You saying I'm looking light?" he balked.

"I'm saying," she said, her smile fading, "you will insult the people who are here to make a peace treaty if you keep shunning their food."

"Fair," he had to concede as the server removed the *kofte* and set a bowl of some yellow soup-thing. An improvement.

"That," McKenna said, "is Dushbara—dumplings with mutton."

He wiped that out in no time and seconds before a third plate landed in front of him. This looked like a small loaf of bread with a wedge cut out and the center spilling rice, meat, and vegetables. "Now *this* is what I'm talking about. A man could grow on this."

"That's Shah pilaf. Chef made small versions for each plate, but it's a traditional dish," she said, then wrinkled her nose—something he recalled from her much younger years. "You realize you prefer all the dishes from Azerbaijan?"

He hesitated, mouth watering over the pilaf. "That a problem?"

"No, just . . . interesting."

Conversations dulled as the guests dug into the main course. He ate, keeping his eyes and ears open. Noting Papian finished off his food, excused himself, and went farther down the table to talk with someone. As staff removed the dirty plates, Dante felt himself relaxing, knowing one more course, then they'd mingle for cocktails. He'd be out from this table and back in tac gear.

Mick cut a piece of bread from her pilaf. "Why is your man there watching Dalita?"

My man? He didn't have to look to know she meant Dade. "She hit my radar. Seems nervous."

She tucked her chin and touched her lips, hiding a smile, as she finished a bite. "That would be because she's attracted to you."

He faltered but shook his head. "It's more than that."

"More than her being attracted to you?"

He wasn't here to banter and flirt. Though, he thought he heard a tinge of jealousy in her voice. Kinda dug it.

"Dalita is a very good worker and friend," McKenna said, her tone carrying only a modicum of defensiveness. "I trust her."

"And the LE who didn't come back from lunch," he said, checking the guests who were finishing up as staff worked fast to clear the tables for dessert, "also a good worker you trusted?"

Hesitating, McKenna looked toward the girl for a long moment. "I see your point."

"Stop staring at her."

She pulled her gaze back. Sat quietly as the tables were cleared. Something changed in her, brought down her spirits. It wasn't much different than when the clouds slid in front of the sun, dropping everything into shadow.

"What's wrong?" he asked quietly as dessert carts rattled into the hall.

Spine flush against the seat, she laid her hands in her lap and watched the goings-on. She drew in a ragged breath and let it out. "I . . . I'm sorry for yesterday."

Dante eyed her, confused.

This time, she wouldn't meet his gaze. "The hug—uh, it was . . . instinctual, seeing you after all these years. I was . . ." She pressed her full lips together and swallowed. Lifted her chin. "I didn't see my family for Christmas or New Year's. Missed Daddy's birthday. Spent mine alone." She twisted her lips, as if fighting tears. "It's been hard, lonely."

Then why had she chosen this life? Gone across the globe to work in a foreign country? Still, he knew the pain and price paid for a career away from family.

"Seeing you in the lobby was like . . . having family here. Someone I knew. I was so happy when I saw you." She glanced down, swallowing. "I didn't mean to embarrass you." She nodded, finally meeting his gaze. "When I hugged you . . . it didn't mean anything."

Except she yanked her gaze away with those words and looked down again. Which meant she didn't believe the words she spoke. He and every other Scion knew Mick had a crush on him. Even now with her retracting gaze . . .

"Hey, we are family," he said, but quickly did his own retraction. "Scions. Eternal friends."

She breathed a grunt, as if he'd said the wrong thing. Then she chewed her lower lip.

To his right, the Armenian politician returned and gave them a side-eye.

Dante knew he'd messed up—again—with McKenna. "Hey, lis—"

The server stretched between them, delivering a layered cake to the table, effectively cutting off their convo.

Though frustration coiled tight in his gut, Dante acknowledged the waiter. But when the waiter moved on, apparently so had McKenna, who'd gotten up. He watched her cross the room and cursed himself, the viper in his gut squirming.

Dante fisted a hand as he stared at the dessert before him. He liked Mick—she was sweet and attentive. But . . . they'd never be together. Their careers dictated it. Being "family" demanded it. He felt an obligation to look out for her. To not hurt her.

"*That's a mistake.*" Pike's chastisement from earlier echoed in his head.

The guy next to him shifted, bumping elbows with Dante, which drew his gaze. In that split-second, two things were very clear. One, the man next to him was not Papian. Two, the man had a weapon.

"GUN!" Dante surged to interdict.

FOUR

A CRASH ERUPTED BEHIND HER.

Even as McKenna whirled toward the noise, she registered fast-moving operators pouring from the shadows and bolting toward the commotion. She flinched as shouts of "gun!" peppered the air. Her gaze skidded to where she'd been sitting two minutes ago.

And froze. It took a second for her brain to comprehend what she saw—Dante thrusting backward, his chair and Papian, whom he had in a chokehold, plummeting to the industrial-grade carpet. Lips tight, nostrils flared, he worked with a fierce, lethal determination to subdue the man. His raw power and intent screamed that he was not to be messed with. Strong, focused, and decisive, he locked his legs around the local, forcing his face into the floor.

That wasn't Mr. Papian. So who was he, and how had he gotten a gun past security? Why was this happening, especially when they'd finally gotten the two countries to talk? The loss crushed her.

Operators bolted past her, moving with lethality. From the head table, the SecState's detail rushed him, the ambassador, and MFAs from the room.

An operator collided with her, urging her to leave. "Clear out!"

Startled into motion, McKenna was flooded with the warning clanging through her to get to safety. To hurry before someone got hurt. The frenetic moment thrust her back to the night so long ago when Poppa died. The chaos . . . the panic. Nana's sobbing.

A woman nearby shouted for someone.

Only then did McKenna realize what she was doing—fleeing. But it was her job to make sure the guests were safe, and how could she even think to leave Dante in the middle of that nightmare?

"Quickly and calmly," she heard herself saying even as she slowed, motioning to the doors. She returned to the banquet hall door, the crush of bodies swarming the exit forcing her aside. Spine to the wall, she slipped in and looked to where they'd been sitting.

On the floor, chairs upended around him, Dante stretched his upper body over a man's torso, threading around the arm of the man, who howled at the move, face contorted in agony.

With one knee bent and propped for traction, Dante used his straight leg to kick at something. The gun!

Had the man fired a shot? She didn't recall hearing one.

Omen swooped in to assist Dante, two crashing on the gunman to help immobilize him. The most bizarre thing of all was the contradiction of perfect calm on Dante's face to the chaos around him.

"You got him?" Pike asked as he went to a knee.

"I got him," Dante bit out, his attention wholly trained on maintaining control of the man while Brick fastened cuffs on the gunman.

In what felt like seconds, Omen had the man secured. Four men grabbed a limb each and hauled him out like a dead body.

Dante got to his feet and stretched his neck, as if this—taking down a gunman—was an everyday occurrence. And maybe it was—for him. But to her, this . . . was shocking, frightening. Especially with Dante embroiled in the threat.

He trailed Omen through the doors, and his gaze briefly hit her.

"You okay?" McKenna asked, hands shaking as she struggled not to reach for him and embarrass him again.

"I'm good," he said with a quiet nod, then stopped. "You need to get somewhere safe till this is sorted."

"Right," she said, glancing about, feeling breathless. Disoriented. "Mick."

Lost in her confusion about where to go, she swung back to him. "Yeah?"

He cocked his head, indicating the passage. "C'mon." He cupped her elbow, tugging her along with him.

Adrenaline dumping now that the attempted shooting was over, that Dante was safe, she shuddered a breath and hurried with him.

"Do you know who the man was?" he asked.

McKenna faltered as they rushed down the corridor. "I . . . no." She frowned, remembering the moment she'd realized it wasn't Mr. Papian . . . "I know everyone on the list, except him."

Pike circled back and tapped his earpiece. "Atlas, get Ms. Neeley to the ambassador."

Her phone buzzed in her hands, and she stared down at it, blankly. Her brain refused to translate the letters into words. She blinked. *Get a grip!*

"Upstairs," Pike said, his voice stiff and harsh. "MFAs are in a saferoom."

Of course. "I-I know where that is. You don't have to take me," McKenna mumbled, feeling a semblance of coherency taking hold. "Just around the corner."

Pike's gaze hardened. "Don't leave her till she's with them. Two rights and a left. Get her there and hold tight."

"Understood, Chief."

Pike glanced at her, then Dante. "Once we get this guy below and transferred to local authorities, we'll be topside."

"Got it." Dante inclined his head to her, encouraging her to move.

McKenna took the lead, heading up to the saferoom. She reached for the access pad, her fingers shaking. She clenched them into a fist.

"Mick." Dante leaned in. "You good?"

Peering into his rich, brown eyes, she felt her heart stutter. Adrenaline, right? "Yeah . . ." Last thing she wanted or needed was for him to think she was too rattled—that'd get back to Daddy, who'd pressure her to leave her job. "Sure." Head on straight, she entered the code, which unlocked the first door. In the forechamber, she glanced back, waiting for the exterior one to lock. Once it did, they waited for the inner one to release.

When she heard the shink of the mechanism, McKenna reached for the handle—but so did Dante. His large hand swallowed hers. The surprise of the contact made her yank back and give an awkward laugh. Right. "Thanks," she whispered and hurried through into the windowless, nondescript room with seats, tables, but not much else.

The petite frame of Cicely engulfed her in a hug. "I am so glad you were not in your chair when it happened," the ambassador said.

"Me too," McKenna admitted, though she wouldn't share why she hadn't been in her seat.

"You," the Azerbaijani Minister of Foreign Affairs pointed to Dante. "You are the reason we are all safe. How did you—"

"Doing my job, sir."

The secretary of state's security officer moved between Dante and the VIPs. "Lay it out for me, start to finish."

Dante nodded, folding his hands in front of him. "I was sitting there. The man in the seat to my three was a Mr. Papian"—he looked at her, as if unsure he had the name right—"and he'd vacated his seat after dinner. During dessert service, my right line of sight was partially obstructed, but I thought he'd returned to his seat. But then the guy bumped my elbow—and I noticed this guy was bigger. And when I shifted my gaze to him, I saw the K-2 in his hand. I interdicted. Brought him to the ground to immobilize him using a submission posture."

The Azerbaijani Minister of Foreign Affairs stepped in and extended his hand. "I am very thankful."

Dante accepted it, but looked uncomfortable with the attention. "Just my job, sir."

"Yes, yes," the Armenian MFA added, giving Dante a vigorous two-handed shake. "You are a hero! We are all glad you were there. Very quick action, young man!"

With a cockeyed nod, Dante stepped back—a deliberate move, it seemed, to distance himself from the attention.

Secretary of State Derriscort shifted forward and clapped him on the back. "I knew Omen was the right team for this. Well done, son."

Dante's cheek twitched, and even McKenna did—for some reason, he'd always disliked men calling him "son." Except his Nightshade uncles.

McKenna's phone rang again, and she glanced at the screen. This time she comprehended the name—Catalina! She glanced at the secretary of state—Cat's father!—who had moved aside again with the Azerbaijani contingent. This was Cat's third call since the dinner started. Should she mention to the SecState that his daughter was calling? What was going on?

A light touch came at her shoulder—Dante. His close position splashed nervous jellies through her belly.

"You good?" he asked.

Nodding, she stared at her screen, debating whether or not to answer. Definitely didn't want anyone hearing if she did—Cat and her dad were not on the best of terms. "This is the secretary of state's daughter."

Dante's brow dug deep as he drew aside. "Why—"

"Catalina and I were college roommates," she whispered, putting her back to the others. "It's unlikely she knows her father is here, but . . . she keeps calling."

"That normal?"

She shook her head. "I rarely hear from her, but she had to get her papers cleared for this visit in-country, and I handled it. That's the only reason I even know she's here." The phone lit with another call, and she groaned. "She's not giving up."

Dante touched her arm, guiding her to a corner as he checked over her shoulder, then lowered his head to hers. "Answer it. Quietly."

McKenna cast a furtive look at the VIPs, and Dante slid between her and them, shielding her. She accepted the call and put the phone to her ear as she hunched. "Hello?"

"McKenna! What on earth—I've called you three times!"

"Things are pretty crazy right now." To say the least—she wouldn't risk security by saying there had been an attack here. "I've been working like mad trying to coordinate a big dinner tonight—"

"I know."

She did? How? This dinner was off the books and below the radar.

"Listen, Mickey," Catalina said, "I haven't been able to reach my dad, and I know he's there."

McKenna's heart thumped as her gaze bounced to the secretary of state, then Dante. How could Cat know if she hadn't been able to talk to her dad? "You know I can't divulge any information—"

"Don't need you to. But what I do need is a favor—after you hang up, tell my father to come out to this village and see me." *Pling.* "I just dropped you a pin to my location," Cat stated, clearly used to getting her way. "It's imperative he visits. Tell him, if he thinks Abbasov is serious about peace, he needs to see what's really happening out here."

Shielding her phone, McKenna faltered at those ominous words and eyed the huddle of men in hushed conversation. "I don't think—"

"Just do it, McKenna. And I don't mean this as a threat, but ... if I die, then this will be on your head. You're a sweetheart, but you think people are good."

Assaulted by that accusation, at the use of inflaming scenarios to force her hand, she hugged herself and shifted into the corner formed by Dante, the wall, and herself. "You used to think the same."

"Yeah," Cat said with a caustic laugh. "Being out here cured me. We're sorority sisters. We go the extra mile for each other. Right?"

That was a low-blow tactic. "Cat ..." She felt Dante hover closer, and man, he smelled good, straining her focus.

"Make him come out here, Mickey. There are Azerbaijani soldiers sweeping toward us. Three villages used to sit between this one and NK. Now, we're all that's left," Catalina said. "It's a Christian community. They just want to live in peace with their faith. I know you believe in God, McKenna. Maybe that's why you're there—to help stop this."

McKenna swallowed hard. No, she'd come out here ... *To help those who can't help themselves.* Her self-defined purpose condemned her unwillingness.

Dante jutted his jaw at her, asking what her friend was saying.

"McKenna, is everything okay?" the ambassador asked.

"Tell him!" Cat shouted.

She turned away and hunched more. "I'll do what I can. Gotta go." She hung up and let her forehead rest against the wall. *God ... what are you doing?*

Cicely touched her shoulder. "McKenna? Everything okay?"

McKenna straightened and exhaled heavily. "I ... I need to talk to you and Secretary Derriscort. Alone."

— • —

"This isn't a wise course of action," Pike said to the SecState. "We have no proof your daughter wasn't being coerced or forced to say those things to lure you out there."

This was good. Dante knew if the team loaded up to take the SecState to some remote village, a fair chance existed that Mick would tag along, since her friend was the one who'd called in the request. He knew she was a strong, capable woman now, but that was a whole lot of ugly she did not need to be tangled up in.

"I agree with Auberon," Hamer stated. "Risks and unknowns are high. With what happened tonight, going out there is too dangerous."

"What it is," Secretary Derriscort growled, "is my daughter. Out there." He stabbed a hand at the windows. "And you think suggesting that she's being forced and coerced will convince me to not go?" He shook his head as he paced.

"How did she know you were even here?" McKenna asked aloud, then shrank when eyes swiveled in her direction. "Your presence here wasn't readily available knowledge."

When Dante nodded, she looked at him with a small smile of appreciation for confirming her words.

"The big blue-and-white jet marked *United States of America* on the nearby airstrip ..." Brick Archer shrugged. "Dead giveaway, if you ask me."

Dante elbowed the guy and frowned at the sarcasm. If they needed assurance of the threat level to avoid visiting this village ... "And you're one man short, right? Someone didn't show up to work today?" He studied the ambassador. "Any word on him?"

"Vugar Gharibian," Ms. Robertson said with more than a little frustration. "Security located him at a nearby bar, plastered out of his skull. I don't think he's a threat—just . . . disgruntled."

"Still," the SecState groused, "we don't need employees like that."

The ambassador's lips thinned.

"He's grieved," McKenna said, then cringed.

Secretary Derriscort locked onto her. "Wait." He straightened to his full height and moved toward her, eyes narrowing. "McKenna Neeley . . ."

Something primal rose through Dante at the way the guy stared her down.

"Yes?" McKenna held her ground.

"You're Cat's college friend, right?"

She paled, eyes widening. "Junior and Senior year roommates at Carnegie." By that expression and the stiffness sliding into her demeanor, she seemed to understand why the SecState asked.

So did Dante.

"And you speak the language here."

McKenna hesitated. "I do . . ."

Hold up. Wait. No, this was not good. "Sir, I think—"

"Both Armenian and Azerbaijani," the ambassador added, clearly proud of her officer, yet not understanding what this would mean for Mick. "Russian too. She's brilliant!"

Mick's cheeks flushed beneath the praise, but she also looked . . . concerned.

Like Dante. "She—"

"Good." The SecState stabbed a finger at Mick as he looked to Hamer. "We're going out there, taking her, these men"—he motioned widely to the operators—"and an armored vehicle or two. Leave at first light. See what's happening. Drag my daughter back to the States with me." He grunted and folded his arms. "Kicking and screaming if I have to. I am not letting her stay in-country with what she's suggesting is happening out there."

Dante's heart spasmed at the thought of Mick in the field. "Sir—" he said at the same time as Mick.

She faltered but plunged ahead. "While I appreciate your confidence in me, Mr. Secretary, I am not field-rated nor cleared. I'm trained for—"

"Cat called *you*, young lady." He gave a grim-but-fierce nod. "You're her friend. Don't you want to help?"

She drew up, face paling. "Of course I do. That's not—"

"All those shopping trips my wife took you and Cat on, the ski trips. And this is how you repay her?"

Looking mortified, McKenna's mouth froze open. Then she recovered and swallowed.

Dante wasn't letting this politician call McKenna's character into question. He held his hands in the time-out position. "Hold up. I call foul."

"What's foul—"

"Miss Neeley just went through a traumatic experience," Dante argued.

"We all did!"

No way he'd let anyone, even the SecState of the United States, bully Mick into endangering her life. "There's a difference between being 'friends' and 'field qualified.' Taking a junior consular officer on an op into a potentially hostile situation—which is what your daughter has suggested is the case—is not logical. It puts her life at risk, why? Because she's got language skills?"

"Oh, so now you think my daughter is in danger?" the SecState argued. "Besides, this young woman is an Olympic sharpshooter, so"—his jowls rattled as he shook his head—"she can handle herself well enough. I can't believe you want my daughter to die!"

Gaslighting at its best. Politicians were masters of this witchcraft. "No, sir." With all the power Derriscort had, Dante knew not to provoke the guy. "That'd be you. Panic and concern for your daughter is clouding your judgment."

So much for not provoking him.

The politician's gaze darkened. "Clouding my—"

"Harry, you cannot be serious," Ambassador Robertson said, quietly and firmly as she set a hand on his arm. "You've given them no time to recon or put security measures in place. You're one of our country's most powerful men, and if you'll think about it, even you know going out there without a plan and time to prepare is not wise."

"Fine!" Jaw tight, the SecState glanced at his watch. "It's now twenty till midnight." He eyed Pike, then lingered on Dante. "You have eight hours to get prepared."

"Harry," the ambassador complained. "Be sensible."

"My daughter is out there!"

"If we don't do it, he'll go alone," Hamer said, looking to Pike. "And then we'll have more Brass and heat breathing down our necks than if we just go do a look-see and get back here before anyone's the wiser."

Pike shook his head and smoothed a hand over his beard, clearly not liking this.

"I'd appreciate your help."

The chief stretched his jaw. "Adapt and overcome." He shrugged. "We are here on your dime . . ."

"Seriously?" Dante balked.

Ignoring him, Hamer motioned to a map on the wall and moved toward it. "The pin dropped by the SecState's daughter was just outside Hermon in the Yeghegis Municipality of the Vayots Dzor Province. That's 146 kilometers—one-point-five-hour drive. Forty mikes by bird."

"Helos are loud and draw attention and they're also prone to RPGs, which these terrorists favor," Pike countered. "Long drive, but that's my vote."

"There's a couple armored vehicles here that could be used," the ambassador suggested.

"You have four," the SecState snarled.

"Yes, and I need one for my meeting with the parliamentary members in the morning, and another should be left for the deputy chief of mission's use," the ambassador said.

"Wait, so you wouldn't be going?" McKenna asked, concern tugging at her features.

"I cannot," the ambassador said, looking aggrieved. "I would argue against you going but . . . things being what they are, it does make sense to have someone with a brain on that trip."

Lady got some teeth on her. No wonder Mick liked working here.

"Besides," the ambassador said, her gaze shifting to Dante, "I think you'll be in good hands."

"Considering she's already been in his arms . . ." Dade muttered, earning snickers from the team.

"And the goat," Brick reminded.

"Bro, not nice."

Pike's glare silenced the jokes—and all opposition. "Let's get to work." Then he eyed McKenna. "Meet back here at zero-five-hundred."

Startled, Mick was nodding even as her gaze moved around Dante, but he caught her arm. "Hey." He hated this. Hated that she was going. Hate the fear playing havoc on her face. "I got you. Get some rest. See you back here in the A.M."

Though she tried to smile, it never made it past her lips, then she furrowed her brow and trailed the ambassador out of the safe room.

Annoyed with the turn this had all taken, Dante left with Omen. They set up in the basement, going over maps of the local area, contingencies, resources available, and prepping gear. By 0500, they were loaded and waiting out front with the three armored vehicles when Mick returned in her blue import.

She strode across the parking lot wearing green cargo pants and a brown wool jacket with buttoned epaulets. A plaid scarf coiled around her neck and fluttered behind, likely waving bye to civilian life. Man, it ate his gut up that she was roped into this. He saw the weight of it all over her downturned expression and wanted to lighten the mood. "What's in the pack? Book and makeup?"

Fire lit her eyes. "I'm the daughter of a MARSOC Marine. My daddy taught me how to pack for survival."

Alright now. That was some fighting spirit. Wasn't surprised, especially with Cowboy being her pop. "Leather personnel carriers were smart."

She wrinkled her nose. "Huh?"

He smirked and pointed to her feet. "Boots."

Groaning, she shook her head. "It is too early in the morning to be using five words when one is clearer."

"Know how to handle a weapon?" Crow Rawlins asked as he sauntered over.

"Bro." Dante shook his head, pivoting to deal with the punks. "Mick's an Olympic sharpshooter."

"No joke?"

McKenna shrugged. "My dad was a sniper and taught me everything he knows."

Crow asked, thick brows lifting to his ball cap as he gave her an appreciative once-over. "Sweet."

The team considered her, and Dante did not like the way they looked at her. Nothing hotter to a bunch of grunts than a woman who knew how to handle a weapon and hold her own. Last thing he wanted was to spend hours with them trying to hit on her.

"Mick." He indicated toward the second black armored SUV. "With me."

"Hold up," Brick said, trailing them. "Why's she with you?"

"Cuz I know where to keep my hands and eyes."

"Do you?" Brick taunted. "Didn't last night—almost didn't see that shooter until he nearly shaved a couple inches off that big head of yours."

Ignoring the jibe, Dante opened the door but then saw the concern on her face as she climbed in. "They're just messing with me."

Seated, she tucked her hands in her jacket pockets again and hunched.

He eyed her. "Cold?" Or feeling the need to protect herself?

"Couldn't find my gloves."

He tugged out his Mechanix insulated pair. "Here."

She frowned. "I can't—"

"I do not need Cowboy all up in my face because you got frostbite while I was with you."

She sniffed a laugh. "Yeah, he'd do that." Gloves tugged on, she held out her now-protected hands. "They're huge, but warm. Thanks."

"Only the second part matters." Dante hiked up next to her.

McKenna gave him a long look, something weird in her expression, then shifted her gaze front.

"You sleep okay?" he asked.

She nodded but did not look at him or say anything.

Was she mad? "Something wrong?"

Mick gave him a side-eye, then took in the team. "I do not need you defending me to them. I can handle myself."

"Never said you couldn't," he said, understanding he'd stepped in where he wasn't wanted or needed. "Just went crossways in me, them doubting you."

She shifted to him with a tangled brow. "You haven't seen me in over ten years. How do you know what I can do?"

"Group chat, remember?"

"You never comment."

Where was this coming from? "Maybe," he said, noting Brick headed their way, "but I read them."

She huffed. "It's rude not to reply, ya know. Still think you're too good for us?"

"Check your anger, Mick. It ain't like that."

Another frown. He just couldn't win, could he?

"Hooah!" Brick yanked open the front passenger door and stuffed himself into the seat. He reached back and patted Dante's leg. "Watch out, lover-boy. Brick is here!" When that earned him a scowl, the big guy belted out a laugh. "Guess I hit a nerve."

"He seems to have a lot to hit," McKenna threw his way.

"Uh-oh, Goat. She's got your number."

Dante stared straight ahead. This was going to be a very long op.

FIVE

Yeghegis Municipality, Vayots Dzor Province, Armenia

WINDING WITH SWITCHBACKS, THE ROADS into the mountain village threatened car and altitude sickness. The operators weathered the ride with ease. Unlike McKenna and her roiling stomach. But after her comment to Dante about not needing to be defended, she could not vomit and humiliate herself. So, she did her best to focus on the view. The village lay at the joint of a V-like crevasse gouged between two lush mountains. It also made it very difficult to locate, but after conversations with some villagers, the team had it in sight.

Utterly relieved when they finally pulled to a stop on the plateau where the homes and buildings were tightly clustered, McKenna grabbed the handle to thrust open the door.

Dante reached across her and caught her hand. "Wait."

Desperate for clean air, she speared him a look, only to find him indicating through the front windshield. Just beyond the vehicle hood, Pike and Hamer exited the lead vehicle and walked into the open. When Dante looked over his shoulder, she did the same. Four more operators were out, weapons held low—but make no mistake, they were ready for any confrontation.

"Security first," he said quietly.

A petite brunette emerged from one of the white buildings and greeted them.

"There's Catalina," McKenna noted.

"Clear," Brick called and bailed from the SUV.

Seeing the Derriscorts reunite, McKenna broke out of the SUV and inhaled greedily of the icy cold air. Imbued with courage and balance, she straightened. Ignored the very powerful presence of Dante as he stepped close, scanning for trouble but obviously waiting for her. *With* her? She wasn't sure which, but with how he so clearly slammed her into the Friend category with his "eternal friends" thing, she would respect his wish—no matter how much it smarted—and that meant being around him less.

McKenna headed toward the front of their convoy.

"No, I absolutely do not have to leave," Catalina hissed at her father and yanked away. "Not until you come in and talk."

Uncomfortable with the clear tension, McKenna took a moment to take in the breathtaking view now that she didn't feel ready to vomit. Below them in steppes were three rows—streets?— of homes that they'd navigated past in their journey to the plateau. Verdant greens and yellows blurred into a stunning watercolor tapestry. The mountains descended into a beautiful valley that, in the far distance, spawned a city. Mist lazily curled around nearby peaks and drifted toward them, as if looking to baptize them in its magnificence. It would be impossible to stand here and not appreciate the incredible beauty and handiwork of God.

"You good?"

She flinched at Dante's proximity—how had he gotten so close without her noticing? "Peachy." When he winged up an eyebrow, she just shook her head, turning back to the cluster of operators, security, and locals.

Cat's eyes landed on her and bulged. "What on earth are *you* doing here?" Her tone reeked of concern and a dash of anger. "I didn't expect you to come with them."

McKenna wondered at the near-rebuke. "Neither did I, but I"—she couldn't help but look at Cat's father—"was told to come."

"It's a good thing she did," Secretary Derriscort asserted. "We got lost twice, and she asked locals for help with the language skills the rest of us were lacking."

"So, this is your fault," Catalina purred at her father as she again considered McKenna. "You always were the smartest of our sorority sisters."

"If by smartest you mean not drunk and battling a hangover during finals," she said with a sniff, "then, yes, I was the smartest."

Catalina's laugh echoed across the open road and valley.

Pike angled closer, pulling gazes to himself. "You told Olympian here that the AzerB military were in the area?"

"I did," Cat said, her expression sharp and resigned. "If you'll come inside, I'll tell you what I know. No need to stand out in the freezing cold."

"Cat," Secretary Derriscort said with pleading. "Just come back with us. Come on. You've had your fun out here. And we don't want to give your mother a coronary, so let's get you back to the States. Besides, your mother wants to take you out for your birthday."

"My *birthday*?" Catalina decried, her eyes widening. "I live *here* now, Dad. I'm not abandoning them because things get a little difficult. I asked you to come out to the village to see what's happening here. The politicos you are cozying up to in order to bolster your name and reputation with a record-breaking peace treaty are not allies. They are in bed with Russia and Turkey. Buying time with sweet words until they get weapons and troops in place. You continue on and you'll all but hand over Armenia and her people to them."

"Cat, there are things happening you don't understand—"

"Clearly, the same should be said of you!"

"Okay, let's take this inside," Pike said, herding the father and daughter into the two-story structure.

McKenna trailed them inside and took in the immediate room that served as a kitchen and a living room, both rudimentary at best. A table and chairs were the only real furniture that anchored a counter and sink, but there was not much else besides a couple of local men who stood with their arms folded.

"Go ahead and tell us what you know," Hamer said, his attention fastened on Catalina as the security detail crowded into the small setting.

Pike planted his feet and rested a hand on his tactical belt, gaze ticking to Dante walking the perimeter, peeking into rooms whose doors were open.

Catalina nodded to a man who was at least a foot taller than her and thin. "I'd prefer you heard from Areg. This is his home, village, and people."

Hands on the small wooden table that shifted beneath him, Areg considered the soldiers.

It had to be awkward having them intrude here, but McKenna could guess he was relieved to finally have someone listen to his concerns. In her job as a consular officer, she'd seen that over and over—a thread of hope sluicing through the darkness that had overtaken their lives.

When the man did not speak, Catalina moved to his side and whispered to him. The two shared a long look, then he finally bobbed his head in acquiescence.

"If you take a walk up the hill near the monastery, maybe ten minutes away," Areg said around a thick accent, "you will see them with binoculars. They are at our door, and this treaty, the more talks of peace—it is all designed to distract. Make you and other politicians look the other way, while they wipe out village after village."

"How many Azerbaijani troops?" Pike asked.

Curly brown hair touched Areg's shoulders as he shrugged. "First time, maybe five trucks. Then fifteen. Now...?" He pursed his lips. "Too many. They keep the military vehicles hidden in buildings and behind shops where they are beneath camouflaged canopies. But in town after town, they kill and raze."

"I don't understand." Secretary Derriscort crossed his arms over his chest. "They took Nagorno-Karabakh, and there are still skirmishes near there, but this is farther west. Why—"

"They want all of it. One day," Areg said with a grave shake of his head, "Armenia will be"—he fisted one hand over the other and then flicked them apart, like an explosion—"gone."

Catalina touched his back, her expression wrought with grief. "Azerbaijan, backed by Turkey and Russia, has been playing the long game. They're shrewd with their tactics. If they gain control of the corridor between countries, they will militarize it and then it'll be too late. They will devour Armenia. Add to that the active targeting of Christians in the region..." She let out a thick breath and shuddered. "Befriending Azerbaijan is like taking small doses of poison over a long time. It might take a while, but you will die because it is poison."

Mr. Secretary nodded. "I hear your concerns—and I agree with you."

McKenna fought the urge to roll her eyes—that was a classic Potomac Two-Step phrase. And he'd said it way too fast to have any amount of thought or true consideration behind it.

"But I am in an untenable position, Catalina," Secretary Derriscort said. "I *must* entertain talks if they say they are open to them. Do you realize how long we've been trying to make this happen?"

"Of course I do," Catalina railed, knitting her brow. "But you've seen the pictures of the two presidents, shaking hands and expressions grim? All a facade. Peace will not happen because

Azerbaijan is waiting for its allies to send more money and back them in militarizing the corridor."

The whole situation was so sad and made McKenna's heart hurt. Cat's words were haunting echoes of what Vugar had asserted many times. A whisper of concern lingered about how Catalina had known her father was in-country. She should not have known, so who had told her? That question and its likely answer tugged at McKenna's focus.

"While politicians stall," Catalina snapped, pointing east, "the military troops encroach on Armenian lives and villages—and nobody does a thing! Do you know what the Armenians are doing? They're burning their homes and relocating graves before the troops can desecrate them! And you want me to worry about birthday shopping? Worry about placating—"

"I want you to be able to worry about shopping," Mr. Secretary said, digging a hand through his still-thick hair. "Or whatever you want to worry about, but I want you alive."

"I *am* alive! And this—these people—are what I worry about. I want them to survive, especially since country after country has failed or abandoned them!" She moved to her dad with a pleading look. "You're here, Dad," she said, placing her hands on his folded arms.

The symbolism of that—his folded arms and her open hands—was not lost on McKenna.

"*Look*," Catalina urged, impassioned and ardent. "Look at the proof of what's happening. They need our help. Armed, military help."

"It's more complicated than just seeing a skirmish and—"

"Skirmish?" she scoffed. "Hundreds of thousands were forced to leave their homes! Recall the Armenian Genocide?"

"Oh, come—that was decades ago!"

"And this political dance around a peace treaty is over a decade old, Dad. When will they have paid enough?"

"Cat. Please."

As the two continued arguing, McKenna noticed the team start shifting. Hands touching comms pieces. Her gaze hit Dante as he moved toward her. It was startling and impressive to note the subtle change in his posture that had gone from casual to anticipatory. Readiness.

Which unsettled her. "What's wrong?" she asked Dante quietly, glancing back at Omen's leader, who was fully attentive to the Secretary and Cat, even though he touched the piece in his ear, indicating he was aware of whatever was happening with the security details.

Hooking his head toward the door, Dante pushed it open and hovered on the threshold.

Closing the gap between them, she felt the cold wind snake past him and tug at her cargo pants. "What is it?" she asked, frustrated he hadn't answered her first question. That's when, beyond his shoulder, she noticed the operators outside watching the sky, sending darts of dread through her. "Dante."

"Oh," he said quietly, gaze still roving the area, "you talkin' to me now?"

Irritation rolled into a concoction of anger as she shifted closer, both to see better and that irrefutable sense of safety she found near him. "If there's danger—"

"What'd you think we'd find up here, The Sound of Music? Just stay—" He locked onto something and squared his stance, eyes narrowing and weapon raising. He peered through the scope.

What had he spotted? Gloved hands in her jacket pockets, she braced against the bite of winter slithering in through the crack as he checked the situation. The glaring brightness of daylight pushed against her cornea as she tried to figure out what he was seeing.

Dante pressed his comms. "Movement on the southeastern plateau."

And like that, operators were in motion. A chill that had nothing to do with the winter wind swept down her spine.

"Mr. Secretary, we need to leave or get out of sight," came the terse voice of Hamer.

McKenna glanced over her shoulder to her friend, who suddenly seemed aware of the alerting operators.

Catalina rushed to the window and peered out. "Oh no—that's them," she murmured, watching, squinting. "They're coming. We have maybe an hour before they reach the plateau."

McKenna's heart thudded a little faster at the thought of enemy vehicles descending on this village.

"Probably saw the shiny new SUVs," Brick muttered as they headed outside, "and figured out someone important was inbound. Want to up the hostage ante."

"Dad, you have to get out of here," Cat insisted, her expression a mask of worry.

"I'm not leaving you," Secretary Derriscort countered as he caught her hand and drew her out of the house with him.

"Need to call an aerial extraction for you, sir," Hamer said, hurrying his charge toward the vehicles.

McKenna noticed the Omen team grouping up on Pike.

"We staying to help the locals?" Brick asked, concern embedded in his gaze.

"Negative," Pike said. "We don't have the armaments to support a response. And the best thing we can do is draw the enemy away from the village."

"We sure got more than the locals do," Brick groused.

Fire flashed through Pike's gaze at the challenge to his order. "Exfil the SecState and—"

"I'm not leaving without my daughter!" The wind whipped at the Secretary's salt-and-pepper hair.

"You are—you must!" Catalina proved just as defiant. "I came to help the Armenians, and I am not leaving them when they need me most."

A low hum carried on the windy plateau, making McKenna still, then look around. Only then did she realize the men were doing the same, except they were staring down the barrels of their weapons. She moved to Dante. "What is it?"

His answer was two shots into the air. The loud pop of the rifle firing jarred her. A second later there was a loud crack, and something dark plummeted from the sky. "Drone!"

* * *

"Another one," barked Luther as he sent the second crashing to the ground.

Brick hustled to where the first had impacted just over the slope of the hill. Another shot rang out, then he hoisted the drone and hiked back up the incline. The unmanned aerial vehicle was about six feet long—nearly as tall as Brick—with a light-gray body and cone-shaped nose. It reminded Dante of a miniature Globemaster.

The tac teams tightened up, the situation shifting from casual to concerned as they inspected the UAVs that had come to spy.

Dante felt a strange thrumming at the back of his mind, warning him to maintain visual on McKenna at all times. Overprotective much?

"Russian," Pike gruffed as he studied the damaged UAV. "They used these in Ukraine."

Brick tapped the thing. "Open that puppy up, and I bet we find American chips and tech."

"What . . . what does this mean?" McKenna inched closer, hugging herself. Fear had taken up residence in her expression, which twisted Dante's gut.

"That Catalina is right," the SecState conceded, turning to his dark-haired daughter, who seemed unusually pale. "I won't let anything happen to you."

"I'm not worried about myself," Catalina balked. "It's the people. They're farmers, not soldiers."

"Delta Five-Five-Four requesting emergency evac for Eagle Four," Luther called in to Command. "Say again, Delta Five-Five-Four needs immediate evac." He followed it up with coordinates, then nodded to Pike. "Running 'em up now."

Pike shifted his attention to Areg and Catalina. "A hike up to the monastery would give us a better vantage, show us their base where they are holed up?"

"We don't have time for that!" Cat objected, looking between the men. "It'll take twenty minutes just for you to get back to the main road!"

"We have forty to work with before the bird is here." Pike nodded to Areg. "Show us."

Already in motion, Areg hooked an arm in the air, indicating for them to follow him, and started jogging.

"For Pete's sake," the SecState grumbled as he fell into a lope. "It's not easy running in a three-piece suit."

"Try a dozen-piece suit," Brick countered as he pounded past them in battle rattle.

Dante hung back. Had nothing to do with McKenna. He just had to ensure the SecState didn't end up in cardiac.

"Stop . . . babysitting me, Dante," she hissed. "I'm in shape and able to take care of myself." With that, she trotted ahead and fell in step with Brick.

Couldn't win for losing. Mick was an odd duck. Intelligent, sharp as a tack—even with her tongue. Razor-sharp wit. While she laughed with the team, she'd only doled out smack to him. Not to anyone else.

Guess I'm just lucky like that.

By the time they reached the monastery, Omen was already

hyperfocused on a spot down the southwestern slope. Others were calling out intel and recording locations, vehicle, and body counts. Dante dug the all-weather notebook from his pocket and jotted down range-finding numbers. Counted the structures. Followed the roads in the village until his gaze finally settled on the landscape itself.

There was something ethereal about being up high, getting this kind of vantage. The slopes and rises made him think of kings kicking back over their vast domain. Smoke from distant fires mingled with the mist crawling through the valley. Challenged visibility. The serenity of this location warred with what was happening—possible full-on engagement with AzerB troops.

The SecState, Hamer, and Pike chatted about ramifications, bounced around whether it'd be an armed conflict or if the bad guys were just coming for a cup of Joe and a chat. Unlikely.

Dante spotted McKenna off by herself again. But told himself to stay put—didn't need another earful. He should just do his job.

"Check it out," Brick said, shouldering over and pointing. "Gas station. Ten o'clock."

Grateful for the distraction, Dante peered downrange with his binos. Found the gas station. Standard stucco buildings set into the sloping face of a hill in the far distance. That town was easily ten times the size of this one and had gas stations, shops, people moving about.

Wait. A familiar twang vibrated down his nerves—that wasn't a truck or van. It was an armored military vehicle! "Heads up! They got Sandcats, Humvees, Cobras." His gaze raked over a stark camo pattern of a troop transport. "Is that a Marauder?"

"Two of them," Luther affirmed. "That's a lot of incoming armor."

Brick let out a low whistle. "And troop transports. Dudes are not messing around."

"With them this far west, they're not here for peace talks," Dante said.

"Roger that," Brick agreed.

Dante glanced at McKenna, who stood at the edge of the steep slope, hands stuffed in her pockets, trying to see what everyone else was studying. What did she think of this, considering all her work to put that dinner on and foster a positive environment for talks? Her gaze went to her boots, likely out of frustration. Defeat.

Somehow, Dante found himself behind her. *What're you doing?* He tapped her bicep with the binos. "Hey."

She flinched and those blue eyes snapped to him in question as he slid the binos around in front of her.

"Take a look," he said, keeping his voice quiet and hoping to disrupt that "don't talk to me" look marring her face. "Eleven o'clock." Did she catch that he wasn't babying her? That not explaining the clock positions meant he knew she had this?

Hesitantly, she took the binoculars and followed the line of sight. She scanned, then tensed. "Sweet mercies . . ."

"Yeah."

She slowed her inspection. "The uniforms—distinctive dark green and brown camouflage."

"Azerbaijani."

"So many . . ."

"*Too* many," Dante corrected. "But the real problem is at your two." That's where he'd seen a caravan of six military vehicles barreling down the road from that village.

She trailed the binos along the road . . . to the highway . . . "Oh no."

"Yeah. Good thing chopper's inbound."

"No, look!" She thrust the binos back at him, stabbing a finger toward the trouble. "There—three o'clock."

Dante eyed her speculatively but did as instructed. There, smaller but more nimble armored vehicles tore down the road.

They'd hit the road faster than the twenty minutes it'd take them to exfil. "Chief! Three o'clock, close to the valley floor."

Curses peppered the air as the teams kicked it into high gear.

"Out of time, people," Pike barked. "Where's that chopper? Back to the vehicles. Let's move! We'll meet them if we have to."

The telltale thwump of rotors told them the chopper was closing in long before they could see it.

"Delta, on the SecState," Hamer barked.

And two of the four security detail flanked the Secretary, practically lifting him by the arms as they negotiated the rocky terrain back down to the vehicles.

Keeping pace with Mick, Dante eyed the bird in the distance, growing more prominent with each whomp that signaled its approach. When she slipped and hissed, he caught her. "You good?" He hauled her up and eyed her left leg—she was limping now.

She nodded, barely faltering despite the pain pinching her expression.

"Broken?"

Still moving, she shook her head, grimacing. "Bad sprain."

"Your dad would be proud."

"He usually is." She huffed a laugh, hobbling the last couple of yards.

"Head to the vehicles down the road," Pike ordered. "Bird's landing here."

Dante urged her aside while the three armored SUVs were relocated to face the road down, which the team would take as soon as the VIPs were gone.

"Derriscort, SecState, and Olympian over here. Be ready. When the bird touches down, get inside," Hamer said, indicating to the father and daughter.

"I'm not going," Catalina objected. "I can't—"

"Ma'am." Pike stepped in, shouting to be heard over the

increasing *whomp* of the approaching helo. "It'll help to have you back at the embassy. Tell them what you've seen. What you know."

Wary, concerned—likely wondering if he was pulling wool over her eyes—the daughter glanced between Pike and her father, then relented.

McKenna swung in front of Dante, hair whipping and snapping in her face from the rotor wash. "It feels wrong to leave you—"

"This is my job," he shouted back. "Not yours."

"I can handle myself."

He nodded, the chopper making it difficult to hear, then leaned closer. "You need to go. I don't want anything to happen to you."

She started, stilling, her gaze on him. Expectation there.

Oh, not good. *Fool, watch that mouth.* "Your dad would put his sniper skills to use and take me out."

A smile wavered on her pink lips. "No, he'd make sure you saw his eyes first."

"My point," he shouted with a grin.

The dolphin nose tipped up, the rear of the Mi-8MTV-5 lowering into view behind her, rotors whipping the air and turning lightweight rocks into ballistic projectiles. The twin-turbine helicopter seemed relatively new and was a capable military transport. Gunners manned a 7.62mm machine gun, which let Dante breathe a little easier knowing she'd be on that and away from the unfolding nightmare.

"Olympian, now!" bellowed Pike.

Dante palmed her head, hooking an arm around her shoulders, and ushered her toward the open door as the wheels touched down. The SecState and his daughter climbed in ahead of Mick. She put her foot on the deck, then pivoted back to Dante. Hugged him.

He felt the breath of words that were too quiet to hear over the wind and rotor noise. Then she was inside, slipping past the VIPs to one of the tandem seats.

Forcing himself to leave her there was not unlike trying to defy gravity. Still. He hustled toward the SUVs with the others and watched from behind his GATORZ eyewear as the chopper lifted off. It swung around, skimmed the lower village, then pulled up and veered west. Back toward Yerevan.

The Russian-made bird was designed for rapid airlifts, and he was glad for it. Glad Mick was on her way back to safety. She'd be okay.

Tat-tat-tat.

The distant sound of gunshots whipped Dante around. He crouched, instinctively drawing his weapon to high ready as he took cover.

"RPG!" Roared Luther through the comms as he unloaded his M4 on a target downhill.

A second later, the unmistakable shriek-hiss of a rocket-propelled grenade launching was lost to the din of the rotors that were still too close.

Dante choked on the breath lodged in his throat as a blur streaked toward the helo.

No!

The rocket impacted the tail of the chopper. Exploded. The bird whirled and spun away from them, taking his heart with it.

"Noooo!"

SIX

Yeghegis Municipality, Vayots Dzor Province, Armenia

BRACE! BRACE! BRACE!"

At the pilot's shout, McKenna crossed her arms over the harness of the bench seat as the helicopter began spinning. The centrifugal force pinned her to the hull. "God, help me," she cried, terrified this would be her last—

A body crashed into her, an arm or hand nailing her nose. She felt blood spew and saw it in the air as they spun. Equipment hung suspended. Others seem to race past them. An enormous groan shuddered through the hull.

"Dad!" Catalina's scream pierced the air, but the chaos made it too hard to discern location or . . . anything.

Closing her eyes, McKenna swallowed the raging panic. Felt bile climbing her throat.

Crack! Boom!

The chopper flipped, thrashing them like some violent amusement park ride. Thank goodness she had buckled in. In her periphery, she noticed Mr. Secretary was crushed against what was left of the burning hulk that was the tail. Another tumble and the section vanished altogether, taking him with it.

"Daddddy!" Cat shrieked.

Heart crashing into her ribs, McKenna fought the tears at the seemingly never-ending violence. They were slowing, but the groaning through what was left of the helicopter shuddered as they slid.

She recalled the steep incline she'd been standing on. Panic lit down her spine. Please, God! She did not want to die here, away from Daddy and the family. This . . . this was too much like . . .

No. No. Do not think about it.

Feeling something sliding along her cheek, she thought to check it, but no way would she let go of the harness, the only thing keeping her safe. Wind whipped and tore at them through the chunks of the chopper that had been ripped away.

Groaaaan.

"God, please!!"

The chopper canted sharply to the left. Flipped once more. Slid . . . slid . . .

How were they not dead yet?

Any second, she expected a fireball to roar through the fuselage and rush McKenna into the arms of her Savior. A serene peace—which felt utterly foolish considering the chunks of the helo tearing away—engulfed her.

"Unbuckle!" commanded a voice—a soldier who gripped the lip of the door, then jammed his boots into the hull as he worked the latch. "We need to jump as soon as we can."

Unbuckling felt counterintuitive with the wreckage still in motion, but she knew to trust him. Freeing her five-point harness with shaking hands was a chore. Add to that the violence of the careening helicopter and it was next to impossible. She whimpered, fighting the buckle.

"Go! Let's go!" he shouted from where he'd wedged himself into the opening.

With a strangled shout, Catalina leapt at him and he caught her.

McKenna pried at the buckle, frantic. Felt her fingernail break, but the buckle refused to yield. Panic choked her, made her movements clumsy.

Perfect love casts out all fear.

But I'm in a helicopter that's about to kill me, in case You missed the latest update. Still, she told herself to calm down. Think it through. Just like the second before she fired her Remington. Inhale. Exhale and—

The buckle broke free.

With an exultant laugh, she wrested to get free of the straps.

The helo pitched to the side—McKenna felt herself being yanked away, but by a miracle, her arm tangled in a strap. Granted a painful miracle since it jerked her to a hard stop, but it prevented her from being flung out the tail. Agonizing fire tore through her shoulder and ripped out a scream. She flopped to the deck, crying, only then realizing they weren't moving anymore.

"Fuel!" the soldier shouted. "Get out!"

McKenna pushed up—and that terrible pain in her shoulder seared and face-planted her again. With a strangled cry, she knew that staying down meant death. She had to get up. Get out. Arm tucked to herself, she struggled onto her knees, hunched.

But then . . . she felt something . . . a vibration . . . Like gears shifting, a jolt rang beneath her.

Horrified, she splayed a hand out to steady herself and looked back. What she saw stabbed cold shards into her gut—nothing! There was *nothing* behind her. No tail. No grass. No hill. Just . . . nothing—a gaping void.

She twitched back to the front, shaking. Whimpering. Gulped adrenaline. Shot her gaze to the opening. "Help!"

"Stay still!" Pike appeared at the front, the windows gone from the flight deck. "We're coming to get you, but the bird's on the edge of a cliff."

Tears blurring her vision, she could feel the desperate claws of the void scraping at her back. As if it were a black hole, its invisible force exerting itself against her. Palming the deck, she tried to steady herself. Her rational-but-desperate mind wanted to strike a deal with God in exchange for her survival. *Kinda guess I'd do anything, God.*

"Hold tight," Pike said, his voice unnaturally calm. "No wild parties, okay?"

"You just take all the fun out of things, don't you?" McKenna stared up the length of the helicopter, realizing how it canted. How hard it was to maintain traction and her grip. If something jarred it . . .

"Focus on what you control, and that's you." Daddy's words echoed through time.

Okay, right . . .

Her gaze hit the strap around her forearm—the only thing that had saved her. She firmed her grip on the nylon and slowly slid her other hand toward it.

Creeak.

She stilled. Swallowed. Tasted blood again, but that was a secondary issue. She tried again for the strap with her left, and the chopper again objected.

"Don't move!" Pike bellowed, then angled in. "McKenna." The firm, direct way he said that pulled her gaze to the Omen chief, and behind him stood Dante, hands on his head as he considered her situation. "He likes you—a lot more than he realizes. Let's keep you safe so he can figure it out. Yeah?"

She choked back a sob. The chief was confused. He'd say anything to make her focus on survival.

"Mick."

Her heart careened as his voice coiled around her. "Dante," she whimpered.

"We're securing the helo to the SUVs. We'll get you out. Just hang tight."

McKenna eyed the strap by which she literally hung, the pain excruciating. She wanted to laugh, but tears squeezed out instead. "Okay." She adjusted her left hand to the steel brace of the bench seats, then tucked her boot into a support and felt the chopper slip a fraction. "Oh, sweet Jesus, help!"

"Easy, easy!" came shouts from outside.

But they didn't understand—her arm felt like it was literally being severed from its socket. Desperate to counterbalance her body weight and alleviate the agony, she struggled to think about anything else. Finally, she shifted. Found a position that did not offend the dying helo and provided a modicum of relief.

"Incoming."

Cheek pressed to the deck, arms splayed to the side as she braced, McKenna heard something clink and clunk. Ever . . . so . . . slowly . . . she slid her gaze toward the nose of the helicopter. Through the broken windshield came Dante, who was harnessed to a vehicle at a higher elevation. Muscles straining as he lowered himself into the belly of the beast, he was a study in focused determination, power, and strength.

Never had he looked more beautiful.

"Okay, Mick," he said as shots peppered the afternoon, "as you can likely hear, we have company. So we need a quick egress from this deathtrap."

"Agreed," she growled around the fiery pain. "My arm is caught."

"Yep. A'right," he said quietly as he neared. "I'm going to slide over your body. Hook a harness around your waist and tether you to me. Then we'll sever the strap that has your arm caught. As soon as the bird starts moving, and you feel yourself free, use your hands to shield your face and hold on."

That was the plan—*hold on*? Was he kidding?

"Clear?"

Trust . . .

Well, she knew—even if to him they would only be "Eternal

Friends"—that he would do everything to protect her. The possibility existed that something in his plan would fail and she'd be sucked into the afterlife. She swallowed.

"Mick."

"Y-yeah—clear." She blinked, feeling him negotiate the harness along her waist, slipping under her belly, around her left hip, and up between her legs.

Dante tugged, tightening the nylon. "Okay," he said, his face next to hers, words whispering against her cheek, "on three . . . One . . ."

Gut clinching, she watched his KA-BAR move toward the nylon strap. "Dante," she gasped, fear threading her veins like a toxin.

His cheek touched hers. "I got you, Mick." Hand sliding beneath her belly, he said, "Two . . ." He tugged her to him, her spine to his chest.

"I hope your Eternal Friends thing didn't literally mean eternity." He huffed a laugh. "Three." His knife chewed the nylon.

Like her nerves, it frayed beneath the pressure of his blade.

Hand over her face, she tensed.

The helicopter resented the applied tension and groannned.

She whimpered.

With a determined grunt, Dante severed the last thread. His arms cocooned her, his strength reassuring despite the terror of the moment.

Wailing and groaning, the chopper threw itself toward the void.

Dante tightened his grip on her.

Metal moaned. For a second, silence clapped her ears. Then she felt a gust of wind as the deck tore out from under her. "Augh!" She jolted, but the tether held. Dante held. Metal scraped her arms and shoulders. Fire sliced her biceps. Yanked her sideways. Though she cried out, she felt Dante's firm grip. He had her, as promised, even as silence reigned and they were airborne.

A second later, they hit the ground. A double impact—first the ground, then Dante's weight colliding with her back.

"Yeah! Hooah!" rang out from around them.

McKenna dug her fingers into the grass, trembling. Crying. Drinking in the relief as if from a fire hydrant.

"Mick, it's safe."

No. No, it would never be safe. Danger lurked around every corner. Stole those she loved.

Gentle hands cupped her shoulders—and she cried out at the pain. Braced even as she allowed him to help her up. She kept her gaze down. Couldn't look at him. Wouldn't look into those soulful eyes and see his disappointment over her weakness. Tremors wracked her body and she strangled the tears.

Dante tugged her close and held her tight.

A sob broke from her throat. Whether from the cold, the adrenaline, or the pain in her shoulder, she did not know. She cradled her arm to herself, grateful for him. For his warmth. His protection. For his strength that had literally hauled her to safety.

"Mick, we—"

She looked up and those eyes were there—no disappointment. Just raw concern and his own mirrored relief drenched her. A trembling hot mess from the shock, she cupped the back of his head, tiptoed up, and kissed his cheek. "Thank you," she said. But the crashing adrenaline buzzed, telling her that kiss on his cheek? It *hadn't* been on his cheek. It'd been on the lips.

She'd *kissed him* kissed him.

His eyes rounded like saucers even as she sucked in a breath.

"Yeah! Get it!" Brick shouted near them.

Mortified and hating herself for causing him more mockery, she cringed. "I'm sorry. I just—I didn't—I wanted to thank—" She lifted her arm but cried out as pain ricocheted through her.

"Let's move!" Pike said, jogging up behind them and urging them onward. "Hostiles incoming!"

Dante couldn't think. His brain felt sluggish.

Brick slapped his shoulder. "Way to go after what you want, Goat!"

Ignoring him, Dante caught up with Pike and Mick as they moved toward the SUVs. If it hadn't been for the large tree and the supplies they'd brought with them, McKenna would've died today. And that kiss wouldn't have happened.

Which . . . it shouldn't have.

Pops would string him up if he found out.

But he wouldn't. No way. No how. Dante was not a fool. He knew how this game was played. Besides, Mick hadn't meant to kiss him—she'd been in shock, and she'd been shocked at her mistake. Like he'd been.

Best course of action—play dumb. Never happened. Nothing to talk about.

"Atlas," Pike called as he pointed to the third black SUV. "Rear support. You, Olympian, and Archer."

Grateful for the clarity to smack him into action, Dante lifted a hand in confirmation. "On it, Chief." He stopped short, catching McKenna's elbow and backtracking toward the third SUV. Even as he did, he spotted Crow hunched in the back of the secondary vehicle, where the rear seat and two-thirds of the middle row were laid down so SecState could lie flat as the combat medic ran an IV. In the jumpseat, the daughter sat, sniffling and holding her dad's hand.

Armed with a couple M4s, ammo, and an AT-4 rocket launcher, Luther strode past them to the rear SUV to load up the back. As Dante pivoted to McKenna, Brick lowered the back seat and the 2/3 seat, just like the first vehicle.

McKenna hesitated, watching them reconfigure things. "Guess they're expecting a firefight."

"Better to prepare and not need than to not prepare and need." Dante gestured her into the right, rear passenger seat. "If shots open up, lay down and stay down."

She glanced at him, fear twisting her features, and man, it cinched up his gut. But she mustered that Scion strength and swiveled around. Gripped the roll bar with her left and hauled herself up into the SUV. When she reached up over her left shoulder to grab the seat belt, she grimaced, her expression tight.

"Pain?" Eyeing the scratch up her bicep, he stepped on the running boards. "You hurt?"

Weariness and red rimmed her eyes. She nodded. "My right shoulder . . ." Again, she tried to buckle in, and a strangled yelp died in her throat.

"Lemme see." Braced in the well of the door, he reached toward her shoulder. Didn't want to catch her off guard and hurt her further, so he waited for her permission. It came in a tight nod as she stilled, leaning against the headrest. Gently, he probed her shoulder joint. Pressing—

"Augh!"

Her yelp thrust a dagger into his gut. He ceased assessing. "Dislocated. I can pop it back in, but it'll hurt like the devil."

She winced but nodded and went for the buckle again. "Do it."

"You sure?" He eased in, CQB putting his face irresponsibly close to hers.

Mouth tight, she whimpered her agreement. Then her eyes were on his. "I'm sorry," she said quickly.

He hovered over her in the almost nonexistent space between her knees and the front driver's seat, peering down into those blue eyes that mesmerized him.

"I didn't mean . . ." She shook her head, bobbing the blonde strands from her face as her gaze trekked over his. "I didn't mean to, uh . . . y'know."

He appreciated the way she hesitated, her cheeks going pink. A nice pink. Especially on her. Not gonna lie—McKenna Neeley had become one fine woman. Even with scrapes and bruises forming on her cheek, she had come into her own. He couldn't help but notice the changes he'd missed. Straight nose, lips that were not full but also not thin—soft, he knew from that kiss—and a delicate spatter of freckles. All framed by wavy blonde hair. She didn't need all the goop and Botox. Beauty seemed to have borrowed her as a model for its handbook.

As for that kiss . . . he wasn't mad.

But that was the wrong direction for his thoughts. What had he been saying?

"It hurt when it happened, but then . . ."

Right—her pain, the shoulder. She'd apologized for the kiss. "Adrenaline does strange things to the body." Which was probably why his neck was feeling all weak, sagging toward her mouth.

Step off, fool.

"It was an accident—the kiss," she said, cringing as she held her shoulder. "I . . . I was just so relieved that you saved me. And I wanted to thank you—a kiss on the cheek."

"Missed by a couple inches," he teased, smirking at her, positioning himself to get a solid hold on her arm and shoulder.

"I know. I'm sorry. I didn't mean—"

"Mick. Slow your roll." He set his hand on her knee. "I know it was an accident. Happens. Okay, ready?" He lifted her elbow out perpendicular to her body. Locating the socket, he pulled and rotated the arm. Felt it in his gut when she cried out. "Simply socket and ball issue," he said, distracting her. "On three. One—" He wrenched them in opposite directions, detecting the ball slip into the socket.

McKenna howled, but just as fast, her eyes widened. "It's better." Then she slapped him. "You missed 'two' and 'three.'"

"Always was bad at math."

The passenger door thudded shut as the vehicle shifted beneath Brick's weight. Engines revved around him.

"Anticipation is more painful and drawn out," he said and stepped back down, patting her knee. "Now, hold tight. It's going to get rough."

Grim determination dug into her expression, and she nodded.

Dante closed her door, then hiked behind the steering wheel. Eyeing Brick, he put the SUV in Drive but saw something in the big guy's expression he couldn't read. "What?"

"Want to pat my knee too?"

"I'll pat you alright—right upside your head," Dante warned as he brought up the rear of the caravan, heading for the main road.

Brick sniggered as he adjusted in his seat and checked the sideview mirror. "Might want to pick it up. They're gaining on us."

"Can't go faster than the chief," Dante muttered, riding the tail of the secondary vehicle, whose bumper he rushed up on when Primary slowed to take a curve. He nailed the brake.

"I said faster, not slower, Goat!"

"No, you said pick it up," Dante bit out, swerving to avoid yet another sudden stop of the forward vehicle.

"Then this is about to get fun fast." Brick unbuckled and threw himself over the back of the seat, past McKenna, and into the rear of the SUV. "Might want to stay down," he warned her as he swung his body around and aimed his boots toward the lift gate. Sat there, arranging weapons. He donned his brain bowl and dragged one of the rucks closer. Set it in front of himself. As a barrier.

Dante tugged his focus to the front. "C'mon . . . c'mon . . ." The switchbacks were complicating the situation—the need to slow so they could take the curve put their lives in perilous danger.

Crack!

Thwat-thwat-thwat!

"Contact!" Brick barked through the comms, then shouted over his shoulder to Mick. "Stay down!"

Alarm shot through Dante. He stretched his spine to peer into the rearview mirror and check McKenna, who'd ducked. Had she taken a bullet? "Mick. You good?"

"Yeah," she huffed.

Thud!

His focus shot forward, realizing he'd tapped bumpers with Secondary. He muttered an oath and pulled the steering wheel left to avoid another collision. Secondary rounded the bend and accelerated, and he negotiated the tight turn.

Crack! Ping!

Instinctively, he ducked, grateful each switchback put them lower than the terrorists breathing down their neck. Even as he thought it, Dante felt a violent fire tear across his cheek. He winced and started to look back to understand the trajectory of that bullet. It hadn't come from behind. It'd come from—

He darted a look at the roof and spotted a hole bleeding daylight. Not good. "Contact! They're shooting through the roof," he said, so McKenna and Brick would know, but also to alert the other vehicles to protect the VIP. Again, he gunned it, rushing up on Secondary. He would not be the guy who let any of the VIPs—SecState, the daughter, and especially Mick—die on his watch. The thought of Uncle Colton coming after him . . .

Nope. Not happening.

He whipped to the left and did his best to gun it, knowing there was that fraction of a second after the switchback that left him wide open to the terrorist's sights. He might as well have a painted target on this chest.

Sunlight splintered through the windshield and left him blinded. He stole a glance at Primary and saw it fishtail after the last turn. The back end swerved, and a tire slipped over the edge.

"No . . . no . . ." Dante willed Primary to find traction and get out of the way. "C'mon!"

Dust plumed. The din of chaos from Brick laying down suppressive fire, the danger of Secondary slowing to a crawl as Primary fought for grip all roiled with his own jacking adrenaline.

Primary finally found ground. Jerked and tore off. Secondary took a beating from the terrorists. The roof looked like a pegboard.

Crack! Pop!

Fire lit down his arm. Dante hissed even as the windshield spiderwebbed beneath the concussive force of the barrage. The punishing impact of a bullet hit his chest plate, punching the air from his lungs. He bent forward and strained for oxygen as pain exploded across his chest. Struggled to breathe. Focused on grabbing his M4 and using the stock to break out the window so he could see. He swung once—no good. Twice—the shatter-proofing held the thousand tiny chunks together like glue. He hammered it again and the entire thing surrendered.

Dante pitched the M4 on the passenger seat and fought to make the next turn without sending them careening down the hillside. If the drops hadn't been so big, they would've just endured the battering and rushed straight down it.

"Son of a french-fried toad!" Brick railed from the back. "You piece of—"

Through the rearview, Dante saw the big guy hoist an RPG onto his shoulder. He took aim, and behind them, vehicles veered right and left. But he nailed the third one. It went up in a flaming, bucking ball.

"Hooah! Take that!" Brick returned to his M4 and resumed defending them.

"What took you so long?" Dante hollered to the rear as they hit the final switchback.

"I was waiting on you to save the day, Goat! But you're so lazy, making me do all the hero work."

Once around the turn, he hit the gas. They revved forward, the engine roaring as they took a slight curve, then straightened out and accelerated. Dante checked the sideview mirror. Saw the terrorists swinging back into action around the burning hulk of the Humvee that had taken the RPG. They were racing to catch up.

Ahead stretched a long, straight road. To the left, villages took shelter beneath a mountain. Right—a sheer drop-off. Behind, terrorists gaining.

So help him, if there was a goat around the next corner . . .

SEVEN

Yeghegis Municipality, Vayots Dzor Province, Armenia

CHEEK PRESSED TO THE INDUSTRIAL-GRADE carpet that lined the rear seat they'd laid down, McKenna adjusted forward. She'd made the mistake of looking back, but the spent casings from Brick's weapon hit her face. As things leveled off, she fought the fear and the pain rolling over her in alternating—and sometimes simultaneous—waves.

Bracing against the back of her seat both helped and aggravated her still-tender shoulder. During the firefight, parts of the SUV had broken—or gotten shot—then struck her head. Glass littered the floor and seat.

McKenna peeked forward at Dante. Reached with her left hand and touched his seat. *God, please . . . keep us safe.* She let her fingers trek to his tactical vest. In all the years she'd imagined being with him—it had never been like this.

That's when she noticed things had quieted. Were the terrorists gone?

She lifted her head, and when nobody objected, she used her left hand to brace against Dante's seat and pulled herself straight.

The handheld walkie crackled to life.

"OTG be advised," Pike comm'd, "Primary has engine trouble. Eagle is critical. Tertiary, what's your sitrep?"

Eagle is critical. That was Cat's dad—the secretary of state. How far were they from Yerevan or somewhere he could get medical attention?

"Light two windows," Dante said into the walkie, glancing down at something, then he shook his head. "Engine light is on but we're still operational." Even as he said it, steam hissed from the front end.

"Took a bullet. Got it plugged for now," Brick said from behind her.

Realizing that was likely when he'd done the fake cursing and then shot an RPG in retaliation, McKenna settled in her seat.

"GOAT . . ." Brick called in low warning.

"I know." Dante gripped the steering wheel tight, his bicep bulging beneath the effort of controlling the vehicle even with wind thrashing them through the missing windshield.

The ominous note made her tense. When Brick started shooting again, she ducked, only to realize . . . nobody was shooting back.

She glanced over her shoulder. Her breath whooshed out at what she saw—the terrorists closing in. But now, instead of one vehicle behind them, another warbled into view. Coming straight on. A man's head and torso rose from the center of the Humvee. He hoisted up a long tube.

"RPG!" Brick bellowed.

The warning rang in McKenna's ears. Froze her in shock.

Being hit by an RPG would most likely be life ending. Daddy had taught her a lot about weapons. She knew rocket-propelled grenades did not move the way movies depicted them—slow and steady. They were as fast and deadly as a round fired from a rifle. Only much bigger and more devastating.

We're going to die!

Yet the erratic rhythm of her heart seemed to slow down time.

Instinct warned her to dive even as Brick's bulky mass pitched into the gap she vacated.

In that split-second, the rocket blurred through the missing back window. Streaked over Brick's prone form. Barrel past her, its red-hot wake searing her face and shoulder.

Clenching her eyes and mouth, she pressed her face into the back of Dante's seat. Knowing this was it—they were going to blow up.

The SUV rocked. The air warbled violently around them. She waited for the devastation. For the fire. And wait . . .

Shouldn't they be dead? Or burning alive?

The thought pried her gaze up.

"YEAH!!" Brick shouted, then laughed.

She flinched and looked at him, only then understanding what happened. There'd been no impact! The streamlined weapon, known for piercing armor and vehicles alike without complication, had—thanks to the missing windows—sailed through the back and straight out through the front. Then it had impacted in a tree, sending up shards of bark and wood, even as the vehicles ahead swerved to avoid it.

Brick bellowed a laugh, clapping as he lay staring up at the roof.

Dante whipped around to them, keeping the SUV moving. "Did you see that?"

McKenna did not know whether to laugh or cry. "Unbelievable!" Hands trembling, slumped back, she cradled her arm. *Thank You, God.* Nerves vibrating from that near-death experience, she closed her eyes. Steadied her breath. They were safe. It was going to be okay.

"Thank You," she whispered aloud this time.

Brick pulled himself up.

She rolled her head to the side and shared a smile with him.

"That right there was the hand of God. Put that in a book and nobody would believe it," Brick chortled, shifting and lifting his weapon. "We're going to be good. Your boy there has this handled. Right, GOAT?"

They really thought a lot of Dante, didn't they, to keep calling him the Greatest of All Time? It warmed her heart that others saw in him what she'd always seen.

Brick looked in the rearview and jerked. "Incoming!"

McKenna glanced behind them. And tensed.

The entire back window was filled with the front end of a Humvee.

"Hold on!" Brick shouted.

Pop!

The impact pitched them forward.

Dante steadied it out, but a second rear impact knocked them sideways.

"Why aren't they shooting?" Brick shouted, firing at the terrorists.

The violent impacts and thrusts felt like getting pummeled with a ball-peen hammer. Nervously, she eyed the steep slope of the mountain on the right side. It wasn't like the full drop the helicopter had taken, but it wasn't much better.

"They're forcing us off the road!" Dante struggled, the SUV jerking and rocking. Airborne for a second, they were freed of the jarring and contact.

But McKenna gulped at the sight of the sloping hillside. Remembered the gaping void and chopper. She'd gotten one miracle. The RPG had been a second. Would they get a third? When things again went quiet, McKenna knew it was too much to hope for. Her stomach squeezed as she peeked over her shoulder again.

The Humvee had eased off . . . only to ramp back up. She expected them to ram the SUV, but instead, they angled to the side. Caught the rear bumper. The SUV whipped around. And at the moment it lined up with the Humvee, the terrorists broadsided them.

Up became down. Cracks and pops ricocheted through the SUV. She felt them falling. Something struck her temple. Life blurred into emptiness.

EIGHT

Yeghegis Municipality, Vayots Dzor Province, Armenia

YOU'RE BETTER THAN THIS. STRONGER."

"No, I'm not, Uncle G." *Dangling from the monkey bars, Dante knew if he let go, he wouldn't get that new football gear he'd been promised. His arms trembled and ached.*

"Find what you got inside. It's there. Dig deep."

Then . . . Gray teased the edges of his dad's face as they sat at the bar in his jazz club. Wrinkles betrayed the fact Legend had finally owned the years of that reputation.

"I like her, Pop."

"Course you do. She's Cowboy's baby girl—good people. You'd be a fool if you didn't." Dad stabbed a finger at his shoulder. "But get this straight—if you hurt her, you answer to not just me, but Cowboy, Midas. Azzan. And a host of other well-seasoned operators." He dipped his hand in the glass of water and flicked it at him.

Dante flinched.

"And we will baptize you in fire for that mistake."

Groaning, he felt something strange tug at him.

"So get up off your backside, boy, and save her!"

Another groan.

"Move!"

Sunlight speared his eyes as he strained them open. Dante lifted his head and winced at the pain spiking his neck. With a groan, he pulled himself up, blinking at the ground. Wet. He lifted his palm and realized he wasn't sitting at a bar. Or in an SUV. He was on the ground, in the open. Exposed. Vulnerable.

And it was raining.

Everything snapped into focus—the village, the helicopter, the chase. Getting rammed off the road. *Mick!*

Dante whipped around and came to his knees, realizing he was halfway down the steep slope. Must've been thrown when the vehicle flipped and went over the side of the road. Mentally, he checked his body for injuries—clear.

Where was the SUV? "McKenna?" He scanned as he pushed to his feet but saw nothing. How long had he been out? Where was Brick?

Pivoting, he spotted the wreckage of the SUV near a house at the base of the hill, a good thirty yards farther down, spewing a column of smoke as flames licked through the hull. On its side and roof crumpled, the SUV looked like it'd been through a compactor. The left passenger door hung askew, thudding in the whipping wind.

Thunder boomed, startling him just before the sky unleashed its bounty, the rain going from a drizzle to a violent downpour. Steam hissed from the engine.

Amid the roiling smoke and crackling fire, McKenna's blonde hair rifled in the wind. In the SUV! "McKenna!" He threw himself forward. Slipped and slid down the unforgiving hill, rocks clawing his calves. Grass slickened by the rain, he fought for traction. Kept moving. "Mick!"

Earth and rocks spat at him. Shots!

He dove for cover behind a large rock, panting hard. Couldn't have been out long if the terrorists were still around. The hard surface digging into his shoulder, he peered around the opposite side.

There, at the top of the ridge, a man stood backlit by headlamps in the driving rain. He looked to the side, shrugged, then hustled out of sight.

Relief rushed through Dante, but it was short-lived when his gaze hit the mangled SUV. Heart in his throat, he wondered if Mick was still in there. He'd seen her hair—had she jumped out? A quick scan of the hillside was still clear. So . . . she was still in there? At least the rain was putting out the small engine fire.

Before launching down there, he checked his six—and his breath jammed in his throat.

The guy returned, this time with an RPG on his shoulder! Aiming at the SUV.

No! Terror striking a violent chord in his chest, Dante vaulted forward, not caring if he got shot. He had to save her. Even as he slipped and skidded, the RPG shrieked past him. The distant yet all-too-near detonation seared his eyes. Punched backward by the concussion, he howled at the thought of Mick still in the SUV when the rocket-propelled grenade detonated. He hit the ground hard. Groaning, he dragged himself onto all fours. Stared in mute horror at the now-burning hulk.

Gotta get her out of there.

Staggering, he scrambled to the SUV. Heat stung his face as flames roared and leapt. He stumbled to the side, trying to peer through the right passenger door to where she'd been when they went over the side. Amid the blinding, searing flames, a solid mass shifted. "Noo!" He surged forward, but a burst of flames drove him backward, scalding his forearms. "Augh!!" he howled, hands going to his head. Tears burned his gritty eyes. "Noooo!"

Agony forced him to fight his way forward. Though he squinted to see her, he could not. That tall shape was gone, the blaze too powerful. "McKenna!" He stepped back, fury rising like the flames.

"No! You can't do this! No. No." He shook his head and thought to throw himself into the greedy maw of the inferno for failing her.

Vomit rose in his throat at the thought of her dead, how she'd died. That it'd been his fault. His knees buckled. He went to the ground and pounded his fists against the earth.

Wind and rain tore at him, but nothing more than knowing he'd so terribly failed the sweetest, smartest woman he'd ever known. That kiss she'd given him . . . it'd be the only one he'd ever get. He railed into the storm.

The wind howled back at him. And the high-pitched frequency warbling in his ears made it sound like someone calling to him.

This . . . No, this had to be fixed. *God, You . . . You* got *to roll back time or something.* Vision blurred, he shook his head as he stared at the burning hulk. "We need some burning-bush action here—afire but not consumed." Please. He pressed the heels of his hands to his eyes. Sobbed.

A hollow voice barked at him. Drew his attention to the small house. There, through the wavering smoke and rain, a figure wavered in the doorway. Moving like a specter in the chaos.

No . . . This wasn't . . . couldn't . . .

Blonde hair haloed a bruised and ash-streaked face.

His pulse jacked. "Mc . . . Kenna?" Had to be a trick. He was concussed.

But she waved him over frantically.

Dante didn't have to be told twice. He pushed to his feet and tore across the three meters that separated them. Plowed into her. Caught her in a hug and held her tight. His chest heaved a sob as he crushed her to himself. He set her down and framed her smudged and scraped face, staring into those sparkling blue eyes. "How . . ."

She gave him a shy smile, her bloody, burned hand touching his as she nodded to the side. "They helped me."

He glanced there, and when he found a whole family crammed in the small kitchen and living room, he cursed his lack of situational awareness. Two large men, arms folded, considered him gravely. "Okay," he said, his mind on the struggle bus, "but . . . I saw you in there. When it was on fire before the RPG hit."

"I woke up in the smoke and fire," she said with a nod. "The other door had been ripped off—the side on the ground—and the SUV stopped almost perfectly over a wooden door." She indicated to the family. "Over their root cellar. They helped me get out."

"Unbelievable. I guess it was just the seat I'd seen. Or some gear? Either way, I'm just glad you're okay." Dante dragged his gaze back to the locals. "Thank you."

The younger man edged forward and spoke to McKenna.

Her expression tightened, and she touched Dante's forearm. "He says a vehicle is coming down the hill. Someone saw a man from the wreck limping down the road."

"Brick."

"That's my guess too." She bobbed her head toward the local. "We should go so we don't endanger these people. He says we can use his car." She replied to the man, wholly trusting and following him.

Dante didn't. "Hold up." He caught her hand. "You sure we can trust them? Standard ROE is to not engage locals or endanger them."

Her blue eyes seemed to probe his soul.

"What?"

"After all we've been through, you're still doubting God and His help?"

"No," he said tersely, though his chest thundered. "I'm doubting strangers who could be leading us to the enemy."

"Why would they haul me out of the burning truck just to go through all this to later betray us?"

"Reward," Dante said. "Alive, we buy their safety. Dead or gone, we can't."

She shook her head at him.

He hated the disapproval emanating from her, the way she made him feel . . . small. "AzerBs aren't going to play nice with them if they find us here."

Her gaze sparked with something fierce and hot. "Then let's stop stalling"—her eyebrow arched in an annoyance that felt as sharp as any blade—"so they don't get caught." Releasing his hand, she fell in step behind the man.

Dante had nothing except his sidearm, and he palmed it as they trailed the guy from their home, through a narrow alley, across a street, and down another alley. And another. Corkscrewing their way through the densely clustered village. They found a fenced yard in the north corner. There sat a gray car.

"Here."

The voice—clear English and loud—called from Dante's two. His gaze skidded into Brick. "Bro." Relief again chugged through him, but he spotted the quick field dressing on Brick's leg. "D'you stop to shower and shave too?"

"Anything to win the girl," Brick said, then indicated to Mick. "How's the shoulder, Olympian?"

She blinked. "It's tender, aching, but okay."

Dante cursed himself for not even considering that.

The local man pointed to a small rusted-out hatchback. No idea the make or model, but it was as nondescript as they came.

"Think this will make it all the way back." Brick tossed a ruck into the trunk. "Let's move, people."

McKenna said something in Armenian, the two conversing like they were old friends.

Made Dante itch. "Mick."

She turned to him with that severe expression again.

"Hostiles incoming, remember? No delay," he said, scanning the area for unfriendlies. Which was really about avoiding her expression. "Now. Go time."

A radio squawked and Dante glanced around, alarm buzzing

his veins. The guy who'd led them out here retrieved a radio and listened. Two things struck him—the way the guy's hands trembled, and the Cyrillic lettering on the walkie.

Ruger unholstered, Dante slammed into the man. Pinned him against the car and pressed the weapon to his face. "Where'd you get that?"

"What're you doing?" McKenna trilled.

"Whoa! Stop. Stand down," Brick said, peeling him off the guy.

"That's a Russian handheld. He's telling them where we are!"

"Check the radio." With one more tug, Brick gripped the man's hand with the device and angled it to Dante. "Talk button's damaged. He can't send. Only receive."

Dante released him. "Where'd you get it?"

McKenna scowled at Dante, then finally translated his question and waited for the reply. "He said"—her teeth were gritted—"he stole it off an Azerbaijani soldier. The town uses it to stay ahead of attacks by knowing when the enemy is coming." She cocked her eyebrow. "That's why he brought us out here and is giving us his car—he heard them sending a scout back to make sure we are all dead."

"Apologies," Dante said, still reluctant to let down his guard.

The guy motioned to them with urgency.

"He says to go, they're here." McKenna thanked the local and climbed into the car.

With a curse, Brick tossed Dante the keys. "You drive."

Dante folded himself behind the wheel. In a matter of minutes, they were wending through the village, headlamps off, heading for the main highway. He hoped the terrorists wouldn't bother the family—that much was owed to them for saving McKenna. He'd reckon it'd take the terrorists ten, fifteen minutes before they realized the targets they'd rammed off the road had found another vehicle.

Ramping up onto the highway stirred the dangerous embers of

hope that they'd make it back to Yerevan without more trouble. Dull, thick clouds moved into protective cover of the sun, dropping the temp and threatening to turn the rain into sleet or snow.

"Hope we beat the snow," Dante muttered.

"It ain't going to snow," Brick groused. "Ain't cold enough."

Road noise made it hard to hear, but Dante was pretty sure McKenna said something from the back seat. He eyed her in the rearview, her injuries all the more apparent. "Do what?"

"Nothing," she muttered, looking out the window.

"Don't go all passive-aggressive on me, Mick. Protecting you, being sure you get back home to your dad, is my job."

"Is rudeness too?"

"No, he hands that out free of charge," Brick cut in.

Dante glared at him.

"Hey," Brick said with a smirk, "if y'all want to keep flirting, get a room."

"Shut up, man."

Brick glanced back at McKenna and winked. "For the record, he has never beat the ground or shouted at God when he thought I was injured. In fact, he didn't even call out my name, wondering if I was okay after being thrown out the back. He was all 'McKenna'"—his voice pitched high, whining—"'McKenna!! Noooo.'"

Knowing the big guy knew the same close-quarters skills he did and would block any strike, Dante instead nailed the brakes. Which pitched the guy forward, his forehead thudding against the windshield of the small import and his mouth smacking the stock of his M4.

Brick cursed. "What the—"

"Uh-huh," Dante said, eyeing him. "How's that big mouth now?"

Dabbing his bloodied lip, Brick gave him a dark look. "You know what they say about payback, right?"

"That it's petty and beneath you?" In the rearview, Dante caught sight of something, and all his smack evaporated. He straightened and gripped the steering wheel. Checked again.

"What?" Brick asked, looking at his side mirror. "Holy—*how*?"

Dante ripped the wheel to the right, narrowly seizing the next exit. Barely avoiding being sideswiped by a car that had the right of way. He banked right, down the street. Gunned it to a tight cluster of structures and prayed the ground wouldn't leave a trail for the bad guys to follow. Zipping in and out of streets, he spotted a house with several cars parked out front. He yanked into a spot in the middle.

Dante cut the engine so the exhaust wouldn't give them away. "Crack the windows," he instructed, knowing the warmth of their bodies would fog the windows otherwise.

Thanks to the thick overhang of clouds and early evening, the dusk-like darkness should work in their favor.

Frigid January air stole into the car, chilling McKenna to her bones. Made every little cut and scrape ache like nobody's business.

Or was that Dante's cold shoulder?

What was with *him* calling *her* passive-aggressive? The accusation stung. Especially from him. But she wasn't above examining her actions and heart to see if there was truth behind his accusation. Maybe there was, but he should talk, with that icy reception he'd given her. And clearly that was the norm, from what his buddy said about Dante handing out rudeness free of charge. And yet, nothing could steal from her the image of Dante shouting and railing at God when he'd thought she'd been killed in the explosion. What did it mean that he'd been so upset?

She sniffed—probably just his fear over having to face her daddy. That realization did not help her bruised heart, mind, or body. She rubbed her aching shoulder.

"You okay?" he asked quietly from the front.

McKenna flicked her gaze to his in the rearview. She managed a small nod, gave up massaging her aching shoulder, then turned her attention to the early night.

"Stopped snowing," Brick muttered. "Works if we end up walking."

"Do not bring your bad juju up in here."

Brick snorted. "When'd you start believing in that?"

"Oh, I don't know," Dante grumbled. "Maybe after the helicopter taking a hit from an RPG. Maybe McKenna nearly going over the side of the cliff with the bird. Maybe us being rammed off the road. Taking a flying leap out a flipping SUV, and then the RPG that tried to end us." He eyed the guy. "Want me to go on?"

"Dude, you got a corncob stuck up your—"

"Okay!" McKenna hissed, then recoiled at her short temper. "I . . . um . . ." She thought of Daddy. Mom and her siblings. "I just want to make it back to Yerevan so I can take my vacation. Okay? So let's just . . ."

What, McKenna?

She had no idea. But the last forty-eight hours had felt like a month. Quiet settled around them as they waited out the vehicle trolling the neighborhood.

"Heard Ben went into the Army."

Glad Dante knew, that he'd paid attention, she took the obvious olive branch. "Yeah." She spoke to the window, her breath blooming over the glass. She hastily wiped it and shifted away. "He's at his first duty station—North Carolina."

"Bragg?"

She nodded.

"Airborne?"

"He wants to be like Uncle Canyon."

"A medic?" He sounded surprised.

A wry smile tugged her lips as she leaned her head back. "Yeah, never saw that one coming. Ben would run out of the room, gagging, every time there was some type of bodily fluid." She didn't miss the way Dante's buddy eyed him, then her. Time to intervene before he could rib Dante again. "You married, Brick?"

The big guy gave her a surprised look and snorted. "I'm too much for any one woman."

"Ah, afraid to commit," she teased before she could stop herself.

Dante covered his mouth. "Ohhhh, she did not just call you out."

"I'm sorry." McKenna felt chagrined. "I—"

"Down, incoming!" Brick hissed, hunching out of sight.

Lights swung onto the street perpendicular to them.

McKenna slid off the seat and onto the floorboard. It was cramped for her—she could only imagine how uncomfortable the guys were as darkness receded and the Humvee's headlamps glided closer . . . closer . . . From the floorboard, she heard rocks crunch and pop beneath the tires as it passed. Night became day as a beam traced the vehicle.

Brick muttered another curse and somehow folded himself deeper into the footwell.

Noticing Dante's hand on the key in the ignition, she prayed they did not have to attempt an escape. This old import had little chance against the big armored vehicle. While she had avoided a bullet wound or broken bone, she seemed to ache with every move and pothole. There was no doubt she'd have significant bruising by morning, if she didn't already.

Legs going numb and a throb pulsing through her side, McKenna tightened her jaw. Told herself she could endure anything and die tomorrow. Just not now. Not today.

"Nice and slow," Dante said, easing himself up in his seat. "But stay low."

Slumped, they remained there for a solid ten or fifteen minutes, silence their protector. Weariness clung to McKenna, and she let her eyes close.

"Okay," Dante said after a long void of light and convo. "Let's blow this place. Just stay down and hold tight till I give the all-clear." He started the car and made a beeline through the neighborhood with the lights off. He took the highway again. A few minutes of the vibrating car straining with the speed to which Dante pushed it helped ease the tension in her muscles.

"Clear," he finally said.

They sat in silence for a solid fifteen minutes before they accepted they might have actually gotten away.

Relief sagged through her, and she let herself relax. Rest. Thought of the whole day, all the miracles. Dante hovering over her, protecting her. Rehashing it wouldn't do any good. Nor would pining. He would leave with Omen once things were settled with Mr. Secretary. And while she would get a brief respite back home, she eventually would return to her job. Not that she would begrudge it—helping people was a good thing—but she really was getting pretty lonely.

She rolled her head in the other direction, sneaking a look at Dante as he drove. Handsome. Strong. He cared about her. She felt exhaustion tugging at her, anchoring her, pulling her back . . .

Thunder cracked and rattled the house. Glass shattered, bringing McKenna up out of her bed. "Daddy?"

Shadows scampered and slunk along the floor. Light exploded and another resounding crack made her jump.

"Daddy!" she screamed.

The door flung open, making McKenna jump again. She screamed but then saw Piper rushing toward her. Relief was hot and sweet as Daddy's girlfriend lifted her from the bed. They rushed out of the room and down the hall.

Clinging to Piper like a lifeline, McKenna knew monsters had come tonight. This time, they were not just in her dreams, but real.

They darted across the living room and into Poppa's bedroom, where Piper crushed her to herself. In the dresser mirror, McKenna saw shapes moving. Light flickered and exploded, making her flinch. Then she saw the shiny spots all over the floor. Walls. Daddy hunched over someone. Shouting. Nana was crying something fierce.

Then Uncle Canyon rushed into the room. "What happened?"

"Sniper shot," Daddy said. "Through the window."

Her gaze flicked to the window. Sure enough, there was a hole in the window. Glass on the floor. Someone shot . . . someone? But why? Only bad men got shot. That's what Daddy said.

". . . warning's a little late," Daddy said in his angry voice.

Uncle Canyon looked at Uncle Max. "We need a rig—he has to get to a trauma center. Call it in. Now!"

And then he tilted Poppa's chin up, kind of like Daddy did to her, when he was trying to see in her eyes all the way to her soul where the truth lay. But why would he be looking there?

"His breathing's agonal," Uncle Canyon said. "Get the shirt off! I need to see the wound."

Then Daddy ripped off Poppa's shirt.

Shaking his head, Uncle Canyon had that look, the one that said bad things were coming. "Pulse is thready." He probed the wound.

Shiny liquid slid from Poppa's chest.

Blood, she realized. That's Poppa's blood.

"C'mon, c'mon, c'mon!" Uncle Canyon grunted.

They were all so mad. McKenna lifted her head, but Piper cupped it and refused to let her turn. But she was breathing funny, like she was out of breath from running. And something wet kept hitting McKenna's cheek.

"Benjamin, please . . . please don't leave me." Nana cried as she bent over Poppa. "Ben, please . . . Oh God, please don't take him."

Where would God take him? God loved them, so he would let Poppa stay because they loved Poppa. Right?

Piper was moving again, this time shifting and angling to be sure McKenna could not see. But then there was a loud crack.

And that's when McKenna saw Poppa standing alone in the light. He was gray. Had a hole in his chest. "Be good for me, Mickey. Look out for your daddy, okay?" And suddenly, he was moving backward. Away . . . away . . .

"No!!" McKenna jolted, heart spasming as she snapped awake.

"Don't worry," Dante said, the momentum of the car rapidly slowing as he eyed her in the rearview. "You good, Mick?"

Sensing something amiss and realizing her shout had bled from her dream into the waking, she sat up, pushing her hair back, then seeing Brick alert, taking in their surroundings. "Y-yeah, I'm good. What's going on?"

"Car died." Dante eased the car to the side of the road. Rocks crunched and popped as it rolled down the incline, effectively hiding from passing vehicles.

Still entrenched in the dregs of the bad dream, McKenna struggled to clear the cobwebs from her mind. "What do we do?"

"Walk," Brick groused. He climbed out and went to the back, where he grabbed the ruck.

Backpack. Only then did McKenna realize she'd lost her backpack with protein bars and hydration packs. Not having her smartphone—security protocols demanded she not bring it—she couldn't look up their location, but she was pretty sure they were still at least two driving hours from Yerevan.

Dante ran a hand over his face and eyed her in the mirror. "At least it's not snowing."

She took in the darkness beyond the vehicle. "And good thing I wore my leathered personnel carriers," she muttered with a wry smile as she joined them.

"Now you're learning." Dante gave a wan smile.

Brick returned and ducked down to see into the car. "There's a drainage tunnel to the right." He pointed down the ravine a bit.

"Let's hide the car down there. Olympian, get behind the wheel and steer it. We'll push."

McKenna made the switch to the front seat. With her behind the wheel, they used brute strength to hide the car in the drainage tunnel.

"Alright," Dante said, tapping the hood.

"This works for me," McKenna teased, looking out the window. "Y'all push and I'll steer."

"All the way back to Yerevan?" Brick snorted. "You may be beautiful, but I'm not stupid."

Surprised at the open compliment, McKenna tucked hair behind her ear.

"You sure about that?" Dante challenged.

"What?" Brick shifted back and grinned. "Am I stepping in on your territory?"

"Whoa, hold up," McKenna climbed out, closed the door, and moved between them. "The only territory any of us are in is Vayots Dzor Province." She eyed the two operators. "Clear?"

"Lima Charlie." Brick brandished an unrepentant grin and winked at Dante. "I'll fight you for her."

"Only thing loud and clear is your vain self, thinking she'd be into you," Dante muttered.

Just then, the skies unleashed their venom again.

"You were saying?" Dante glowered at his buddy. "Not snowing?"

"This ain't snow. This is what we call rain." Brick swung the large ruck in a powerful arc onto his back. "Now. Single file and we're off to see the Wizard of Yerevan."

Dante held a hand for McKenna to go next, and she fell in behind the big guy, tugging her jacket tight and hunching to stop the rain from sliding down her neck and spine. Very soon, she was soaked through. The winter night turned brutal fast, and she shoved her hands in her pockets in a vain attempt to keep them warm. A dozen steps on and the rain turned needling.

"Yo, Brick. This is what we call sleet."

NINE

Vayots Dzor Province, Armenia

THE ICY TEMPS WERE MERCILESS, DIPPING and rising so they alternated between sleet and rain. Mick might've worn boots, but that jacket of hers wasn't waterproof, and now, drenched, the weight of it looked heavy.

"Hold up." Dante drew out a small rain slicker from his gear and skipped a step to tap McKenna's shoulder. When she glanced back, he held it out. "Here."

She took it, then frowned, walking sideways. "What about you?"

"Mine's waterproof," he said as they continued onward.

She gave him a concerned look but slid the poncho over her jacket and clothes. "Thank you."

Heads down, they beat a steady path off the main road, away from plain sight. Problem was, beneath the trees, they were also shielded from light. Between the dark and the rain, cold clobbered their bones.

When McKenna slipped, Dante reached out to steady her, hand too easily finding her waist. "You good?"

She nodded and kept moving.

The ground was turning to slush, their steps splashing. Swelling water up over ankles. This wasn't going to work. Between the cold, sleet, and slush, they'd end up with hypothermia if they didn't find shelter soon.

Brick stopped and angled back to them. "Need to hole up somewhere for the night or until the weather clears. Saw a building through my NODs about two klicks west. No lights or movement that I could detect. Let's check it out."

"Agreed." Trudging on, Dante knew Omen was doing what was necessary to get the SecState to a hospital. Another klick of nothing but trees and roads. Then another.

"Oof!" McKenna face-planted, then climbed onto all fours with a grunt.

Dante sidled up to her, aware of Brick still moving. "Hold!" he called over the elements, then crouched. "You okay?"

Hands wet and still red with burn welts from the SUV, she wiped her face. Black streaked over her forehead and cheeks. Only then did he realize she must've had ash on her face from the SUV fire. It looked like war paint now. She owned it, because McKenna Neeley was a warrior. He extended a hand to help her up.

"I'm not weak," she bit out and struggled to her feet.

When she tried to push past him, he held fast. Waited till those blue eyes came to his. "Never entered my mind, Mick."

Wiping off her palms, she faltered, gaze bouncing around his face, then down to her hands. Hold up. Were her lips blue? He edged in and angled for better light.

With a frown, she drew back. Swept around him. "We should go."

True. The sooner they got to that place Brick had seen, the sooner she'd be dry. Maybe warm up. Ten minutes more after they'd banked up and over a small hill, they came upon the structure.

Two defunct pumps sat in the middle of the dirt parking lot littered with scrub, weeds, and a layer of snow. The building had what looked like a small shop and two metal folding garage doors. The sign overhead wasn't much help, since he couldn't read the language, but it seemed pretty obvious this had been a convenience store and car repair shop, complete with work bays. Boarded-up windows hinted that the place was abandoned—but recently. The wood didn't look old, and the overgrowth was still young. Walking a wide arc around the station, Dante used a scrub branch to break up their footprints in the snow as they came up the backside.

Brick jiggled the door handle, then made quick work of picking the lock and urged it open.

"B-breaking in . . . ?" McKenna balked around a shiver, then followed his indication to enter and lowered the poncho's hood. "Is th-this legal?"

"Life or death changes a situation." Brick kept his weapon at the high ready as he walked the interior, ducking into a small room—an office?—then into another. Ambling back to them, he pulled a door shut and turned on his torch.

Dante flinched at the flare of light. "Bro—"

"Building's secure," Brick said. "No windows in here and nobody in sight." He jutted his jaw to a metal shelf. "Help me bar the door."

Hefting it, they carried it to the back wall. It scraped and groaned against the concrete as Brick nudged it flush with the door.

To ensure no light escaped, Dante stuffed a tarp against the threshold, then walked the building to get the lay of the land. The rectangular structure was divided in half across its length, forming front and back rooms, taking up two-thirds of the structure. The back corner had a framed-in office, its walls only spanning maybe ten of the fifteen feet to the ceiling. A desk and cot hugged opposite walls. He ducked into the darker space—confirmed car bays—and spotted a rack where coveralls hung on the crossbar and car parts sat on the shelf above. Two lifts anchored the bays and a wall with a window peeked into the front, filled with standard convenience fare. They'd skip that and stick to MREs and protein bars.

"Place seems recently abandoned." Dante returned, then noting the rickety table and chair in the corner. Break room?

"Probably boarded up when they got word of the incoming military convoy." Brick shrugged out of the ruck and dropped it to the floor.

"S-s-s-so d-do we j-just stay here?" McKenna's teeth clacked with each broken word. Her jacket had soaked up and held the rain.

Dante pivoted to her. "For now." He motioned to the ruck Brick had set down. "Thermal blanket. She's soaked through and looks hypothermic. Any clothes in there?"

"I'm f-f-f-fine."

"That you are, but your condition is not," Brick said, eyeing her. A scowl pushed into his broad face and beard as he studied a dark stain on the floor. "Uh, Goat . . ."

Dante saw it too and his pulse jacked. "Mick, you're bleeding!"

"What . . . ?" She swayed.

He lunged and caught her. "Whoa, easy!"

Her icy cold nose pressed against his neck. "S-s-sorry."

Arms around her shoulders, he hooked her legs and lifted her off her feet. Hurried to the small office and nudged open the door with his boot.

"You're so s-s-s-strong." Her breath along his throat should've been warm, but it too was cold.

He laid her on the cot, careful to ease her down gently. That's when he saw the sheen across her forehead.

"Back up," Brick said, coming in with his medkit.

Worried over the pallor to Mick's slack face, Dante did not want to yield ground, but the big guy pushed the thermal blanket into his chest, forcing him to surrender the space.

"She needs dry clothes."

Dante nodded. "I saw work coveralls in the garage."

"Get 'em and get her changed. Dry socks in the ruck. Then start a fire," the big guy instructed.

It grated to be ordered around. "And what are you going to do?"

"Rawlins isn't here, so I have to use my rusty medic skills." He nodded over his shoulder. "Get going."

Concerned about the ghostly tinge to her face, Dante forced himself out of the office. He hustled to the ruck and dropped to his knees—a move that immediately reminded him of being in the same position on the hillside. Seeing Mick hanging in that SUV when it'd blown. He'd come close to losing her then. And now.

Joke's on me, God. You made me care about her. Shouldn't be no take-backs. He dug through the ruck and found socks. Rushed to the garage and scanned the coveralls. They were all oil-stained and dirty.

"Nasty." Cringing at the thought of putting her in these, he wondered if there was anything else. Looked around, not sure—

There. Another rack in a walled-off area had two coveralls hanging over the slats, like they'd been washed. He snatched them and lifted them to his nose. Couldn't smell soap, but they didn't reek. "That'll do." He hurried back to the office where Brick hunched over McKenna, who was now propped on her side, arm dangling over the cot.

She seemed limp . . . like she was dead. But . . .

"D'you give her something?" Dante tried to steady his pulse.

"Morphine. Found an entry wound in her lower back. No exit. Have to find the bullet and wasn't into torturing her, so I helped her sleep."

"Bullet? But . . ." Dante struggled to think . . . "That would've been before we went down the hill."

"Yup. Which means chance of infection is high." Brick retrieved something from his kit, then knelt at her side.

The sight of Mick's back to him, a bloody mess evident just above her hip where her shirt had been drawn, stopped Dante cold.

"Bullet's visible," Brick muttered as he tipped his head closer. "I'll get it out and stitch her up." He cast Dante a look, then hesitated. "That going to be a problem, you getting her into dry clothes?"

The question wasn't one of ability but of character. "'Course not. Why would it?"

"Because you're into her."

He tightened his jaw as he went to work, removing her boots. "I'm a SEAL first."

"You're a man first," Brick countered, winging up an eyebrow. "But a smart one—if you don't strip off the icy clothes, you're expediting her death."

Surprise spiraled through Dante at the praise as he tugged off her wet socks. Slipped the black wool ones on her feet. Pants . . .

Brick focused on stitching. "She wasn't shivering when I ran the IV."

He realized what the big guy wasn't saying. "Hypothermia."

"And we all know you don't want to kill her with negligence but with your rugged good looks." Brick used his steri-tools and removed the bullet, then eyed Dante. "'Course, you're sorely lacking in that area, so I guess hottie here is safe, but you still need to get her dressed and warmed up."

— • —

Nagging pain pulled McKenna from the greedy embrace of sleep. She fought through the fog and forced her eyes open. Low light thrummed through the small office. She squinted at the strange ceiling, slowly working out that she was in a tent. A very warm one. On her side, she felt a pinch in her lower back and winced. Reached back and her fingers grazed a rough swath . . . A bandage? What . . . ?

Exhausted, she lay there, trying to clear her mind. Took in the room—tent? Tried to remember how she got in here. How long had she been asleep? Directly across from her was a metal desk.

Laid out atop it, arms folded over his chest and legs bent so his boots were on the edge, Brick was sawing some serious logs.

Was that what had awakened her?

Where was Dante? She grunted her way into a sitting position—and faltered at the thick black socks on her feet and the faded blue pants.

Which weren't pants. Her mind tripped and fell over what she was wearing. Coveralls? *Um . . . what?!* When had she changed? The foggy brain worried her, and she strained to recall the events that led to this moment.

What happened? Wait. If she had a bandage on her back . . .

She swallowed as her gaze drifted to the big lug laid out on the desk. Had he changed her? She vaguely remembered the shot he'd given her. Was he the one who'd . . . put the patch on? Did she have stitches?

Noises clanked beyond the tent, then came the repetitive grind of metal on metal. Was that Dante? Must be. What was he doing?

Bracing and wincing at the tug of pain, she stood, glancing down at the wool socks. Where were her boots? Shrugging the thermal blanket tighter around her shoulders, she slipped out of the tent, stepping gingerly so she didn't aggravate the pinch in her back. A door just outside the tent flap stood ajar.

Beyond it in the middle of the room, Dante was stretched out, toes and palms on the floor, doing push-ups. Then one-handed. And planks. He had a shirt on, so it was decent.

No, it wasn't. Those muscles of his were straining and glistening with sweat in one of those sweat-slicking shirts and basically sculpted to every dip and curve of his well-defined torso. It was a glorious sight.

Shame on you, McKenna Margaret.

Cheeks warming, she stepped out of the tent to break the silence and the distraction of her wayward mind. "What," she asked quietly as she crossed the room, "you don't think we got enough exercise hiking in the freezing cold and sleet?" She eyed the chair, but it looked ready to crumble beneath the weight of a mouse, so she was forced to tower over him.

"Our bodies are temples and all that." Dante hopped to his feet and dusted off his hands as he looked around. "How you feeling?"

"Weird," she admitted. "I'm . . . not really sure what happened."

"You passed out. Brick found a bullet in your side," he said, gaze searching the room.

"A bullet?" she gasped, recoiling, hand automatically going to the pinching spot. "I . . . never felt it."

"Shock can do that." He gave a cockeyed nod. Still hadn't looked her in the eye. "And being hypothermic—wet clothes were a hindrance."

Was he avoiding her gaze? She tugged at the collar of the coveralls. "Thus these . . . ?"

His eyes finally found her—more accurately, the coveralls—and he bobbed his head. "You were already at risk in your wet clothes. Weren't shivering."

Touching her temple, she was surprised at how dire her situation had gotten without her even realizing it. She'd just felt cold and exhausted. "I don't remember any of that."

"Morphine knocks you off your game for a while."

"At least I'm warm and stitched now." A thought struck her that made her want to squirm—had he been the one who changed her? Then again, did she really want to know? Did it matter?

Yes. Yes, it did. She could handle knowing a stranger—Brick— had changed her out of the wet clothes, seen her in her skivvies. But Dante? The guy she'd crushed on since . . . forever? Mortification soured her stomach.

When he shifted around and threaded his arms through his thick thermal, she cursed herself for being so distracted. For only being concerned with herself. "Any word on the others? Catalina, Mr. Derriscort, Omen?"

Tugging down the shirt, Dante walked to the table. Lifted a phone in display, then tossed it down. "Phones are destroyed. One when they rammed us off the road, and the other took a bullet. Tried to use the parts between the two to get one operational, but . . ." He shook his head.

Despair and alarm crouched at the edges of her mind, and she felt her heart skip a beat. "What do we do?"

"I'll give Brick another twenty to sleep"—his gaze skidded to the side, a shadow looming large by the tent—"then wake his lazy backside."

"I'll show you lazy, GOAT."

She smiled at the nickname, but noticed he didn't.

Brick smirked and stalked over. He pulled out a protein bar and stuffed it in his mouth, chewing as he grabbed some gear from the ruck. Then he donned his jacket. Did a press check on his weapon. "Going to scout the area. See what I can find. Hopefully a phone."

McKenna scoffed. "It's the middle of the night. No shops are open or nearby. Where do you plan to get . . ." But even as she said it, understanding washed over her. "But that's stealing."

"Not stealing it," Brick countered. "Just borrowing. Need to make a call."

Dante moved to the shelf blocking the door. He and Brick shifted it back, then the big guy left and Dante faced her. "Don't worry, Mick. We know what we're doing," Dante said, as he set the tarp back at the door following his buddy's departure.

"You think there's a risk the troops will find us here?"

"No," he said, pulling two bars out of the ruck, "but I also didn't think they'd be on us in that village." He handed her a protein bar.

"Same," she murmured as she straightened, then furrowed her brow and took the proffered food. "It all happened so fast, deciding to go out there. How could they possibly have found out?"

"Comparatively, it wasn't fast. They had all night to plan."

"Plan, yes," she said, feeling more than a little frustration and panic, then hoisted the bar up. "Thanks." She tore open the packaging. "Planning is one thing, but how did they learn we were even going out there?"

"Someone told them." Dante dumped a packet into a plastic bottle and added water from a Camelbak, then shook it and passed the bottle to her. "Drink up—it'll put some much-needed color back in your face."

Had he slapped her, McKenna was not sure she would feel more hurt or stung. "Wow, don't spare my feelings."

"I only meant after the blood loss—"

"I know what you meant." Chagrined at herself, she waved him off. Why was she being such a brat? Pacing away, she ate the bar and thought about the feeling she'd had, the questions that plagued her, that nagging sense . . . "It was so strange. They were always right there." Back aching, she glanced around, searching for somewhere to sit.

"Here," Dante said, pointing to the tent. "It's warmer and we won't have to sit on the floor."

Agreeing, she moved in there and eased up onto the desk, the bandage tugging at her skin and rubbing against the stiff coveralls. "It's so strange—why a tent inside?"

"It's a heat tent, designed to trap the heat."

"Then it has succeeded." Strangely relieved as Dante ducked in with a small bag of nuts and drew down the flap, she worried the details of the mission. Someone told the terrorists . . .

He hopped up beside her.

"Someone at the consulate is a traitor," McKenna decided, hating the words that escaped her lips. Hating the truth that someone she knew must have betrayed them. "Right?" She looked at the eldest Scion. "That's the only answer. Who else would have knowledge of all this?"

"Someone on the SecState's detail."

McKenna startled. "You really think someone on his detail would have access or connections to alert the Azerbaijani troops?"

"Anyone determined enough . . ."

She sipped the drink, which was almost sickly sweet, but then suddenly felt ravenous, so she gulped it down. "No," she went on, wiping her mouth, "it makes more sense that it was someone from the consular offices. An . . . officer. I might have suggested Vugar after all his vitriol but—"

"Could it still be him?"

McKenna shook her head. "If he'd still been at the consulate, maybe he could've, but he wasn't in the offices and remember"— she nodded to him—"you told me to revoke his access by the time we headed out, so no way he could've known." Massaging her temple, she tried to work through what she was missing. "And he was an LE, not an officer."

"What difference does that make?"

"Everything." Was he arguing with her? Considering his expression, she guessed not. "As a local employee, he wasn't allowed to remove any hardware from the consulate—no phone, tablet, or laptop. And I'm in charge of device inventories, so I know there weren't any missing."

"Could he have remotely accessed the system?"

Thinking, McKenna tucked her hair behind her ear and shrugged. "Even if he had, he wouldn't have access to the schedules—only officers had that clearance. And I suppose someone skilled could have hacked in, but . . . Vugar doesn't seem the type."

Squinting at her, Dante pressed. "But you had doubts about him at the dinner."

She sighed, feeling miserable. "I know . . ."

"Can you recall anyone who seemed interested in top clearance intel or VIP movement?"

Frustration coiled in the pit of her stomach—she did not want to think of her coworkers like that. "I refuse to believe any of them could be responsible for what happened today, for turning a beautiful, quiet village into a war zone. For trying to kill us . . . me." The mere thought hurt so much, she couldn't remain sitting. She had to move.

At her pacing, Dante lowered his boots to the floor and leaned against the desk, palming the edge. "I'm sorry. I know this is hard—"

"No, you don't," she snapped. "These are my friends, people I have worked with day in and day out, fighting for Americans in-country. We look out for them. We fight the bureaucratic red tape for them, going up against agencies and sometimes even local authorities, to ensure they can get back home. And now . . . now you want me to name one as a traitor, as the one who is trying to kill us!"

She heard her voice pitch and stilled, facing the side, staring at the doctored water bottle she'd emptied. Feeling foolish, emotional. She was tired and had been through so much. Obviously, she wasn't weathering it very well. Fearing he'd think her silly or stupid, she turned the bottle in her hand, then held it up. "Man," she breathed a hollow laugh, embarrassed for being so defensive. "What did you put in this?"

Tears stung. She closed her eyes and swallowed. When she opened them, Dante filled her periphery, sending giddy spasms into her belly. "I'm sorry," she murmured, turning away. "I'm just . . . really tired. Scared."

"Hey." He caught her arm. "You're doing great."

"No," she said, wilting. "I'm not. I'm falling apart, Dante." Being so close to him made it hard to think, so she used the excuse of setting the bottle on the desk to create distance. Hugged herself to remove his wildly distracting hand. "I want to be strong. A warrior—like you and Daddy. But this—seeing people hurt, killed. Seeing you in danger . . ." Shouts and screams from the past dodged her thoughts and willpower. Forced a tear from her eyes. "It's killing me. I can't . . . I can't do this again."

Dante stood next to her, facing her, and slid a hand around her shoulder. "Mick, chill. It's going to be okay."

"Chill?" she scoffed, avoiding his gaze because he was close again. Too close. "We have no way to get out of here. No way to call for help. What if they find us again? What if—"

He pressed a finger to her lips. "Mick."

Sweet mercies, her stomach flipped a flop, jellies swarming at his touch and proximity.

"I got you."

Finally, she met his gaze. Finally braved those beautiful eyes. Appreciated the way he was looking at her, the strength and warmth of his hand on her shoulder . . .

Wait, what was that look? The way his eyes were hooded . . . She drew in a breath. Was he going to kiss her? Oh, she wanted that. Had always wanted him to look at her the way he was now. But why . . . ? What changed?

Changed.

Mortification tore through her, and she jerked her gaze to the concrete. Dante had changed her into the coveralls. Now he wanted to kiss her . . . Was it because—

No. He wasn't like that.

"What just happened there, Mick?"

Heat soared up her neck and face. "I never . . . You . . ." She shifted away, humiliated that she'd think that. And yet, what else could explain the shift in his attitude? Then it made her angry. Real angry. She pivoted to face him. "You changed my clothes." She tugged the canvas overalls. "Put me in these."

He stared but said nothing. Most noticeably, no denial.

"For the love of all that's holy . . ." Touching her forehead, she moved in a circle to get away from the bald truth. "That—*that* is why you want to kiss me?" she balked. Whirled to him. "All this time I've liked you, wanted to get to know you, and you gave me nothing but that cocky, too-good-for-me cold shoulder. And now that you've seen me withou—"

"*Do. Not,*" he bit out, low and deep, eyes ablaze, "finish that sentence."

TEN

HIS WORDS REVERBERATED OFF THE WOUNDS, bouncing back to him after silencing her. Jerking her straight. Widening her eyes.

Regret clogged his ability to think. He hadn't meant to growl, but hearing Mick suggest that about him unleashed a violence he had trouble restraining. The vile accusation that his integrity was so lacking that the only reason he'd be interested was because he'd seen her . . .

"Not you, Mick." His pulse hammered in his veins, a war of denials drumming against his heart. "I can take that from the guys, questioning my character." Man, it hurt to breathe. "But not you."

Eyes puddling beneath unshed tears, she held his gaze as she stood frozen before him. Staring. But not taking those words back.

Dante feared doing anything—moving, saying the wrong thing—that might give that violence in him a voice. "You know me, Mick." That came out as a growl.

Wariness crouched at the edge of eyes that fought so valiantly to keep tears at bay. Chin bouncing beneath the restraint, she lifted her jaw and shuddered. "Do I?"

Her question crushed him. Crippled him. His defenses. "Mick … C'mon." He splayed his hand over his heart. "You *know* me." This time those words were pleading. "Always have."

"I thought I did," she whispered, tears slipping free. "But you have never looked at me twice, not in *this* way." She indicated to the side, where they'd stood when he had moved in to kiss her.

It hadn't been intentional on his part, but desire wore stealth tech and had him homing in for one.

"You've always brushed me aside, Dante. Treated me like someone patting a dog on the head." She hugged herself. "And just last night you called me your 'eternal friend.'"

Dante flinched. Couldn't deny that. His head had been in the wrong space at that dinner. Too aware of her. Of the beauty she had become. How natural she was in an environment that demanded professionalism and elegance. Which she'd owned. Her smile … her strength and confidence. So when he felt a fundamental shift in how he thought of her, he'd grabbed the nearest words and shoved them into the awkward heartbeats of the moment he realized he might feel something more for her than just being her Scion family.

Seeing the pain he'd caused with that careless phrase wrecked him. He hadn't thought about how pushing her away all these years might impact her. Yet, she'd always—*always*—been there for him. Believed in him.

"Now suddenly, after …" She tugged the coverall again. Her face tight beneath the hurt, rejection, and disappointment.

"Okay, stop. Just …" He pinched the bridge of his nose. "Please, listen. I'm an operator, Mick. You were frozen through, and if I didn't change you, you would've died. Getting you in dry gear was a means to an end. You're not the first person I've had to do that to."

"So … so changing me, seeing me … in a state of undress meant nothing to you."

He huffed. "You're twisting my words." Wouldn't lie. "What changed me, Mick, was seeing you at that dinner. How you navigated the politicians. You were so comfortable, casual—freakin' genius with the bureaucrats. And yeah—you're beautiful. Hot. Look, I'm not immune or blind, but my focus was on keeping you safe. Changing you was done out of concern, and respectfully."

She considered him, then looked away, uncertain. "What am I supposed to believe . . . ?"

Time slowed, giving Dante the space to process her question, the tone, the wrestling in her expression. This was years of saying she wanted his attention, and now that she had it, she wanted to know it was legit.

A single, spiked heartbeat delivered him to her. "This." He caught her in his arms and set his mouth to hers, kissing her and preventing doubts from lingering in her mind. In his own mind. He heard and savored her shocked, pleased gasp that escaped.

That moment, that epic moment, when she sank into his hold, he silenced fears and doubts that said he didn't deserve her. Slipping his hand to the base of her neck, the tangle of her hair snagging his fingers, he drew her closer. Deepened the kiss.

When he eased back, he had to appreciate the color flushing her cheeks. Her reddened lips. The blaze of eyes that were simultaneously soft as she gazed up at him. "Believe that," he said, his voice husky. "Don't doubt it."

"I . . ." She tucked her chin and set her hands on his chest. "I . . . never saw that coming."

He smirked, yet his conscience quailed. "That's on me. I'm sorry."

Her brow wrinkled.

"All my life, Pop played uncle real well. Never hinted that I was more to him than that. By the time he did come clean, the damage was done. I'd lived my whole life without my dad." He cupped her cheek, hating his inability to get things right. "Mick, I . . . hate that I hurt you. Never was my intention. I'd do anything to erase that, but I know I can't. But I don't want to make the mistake Pop made with me. Know this—what I feel for you is legit." He angled to take in her blue eyes. "I don't want to lose you. You're the only one who has always been there. But, Mick, I don't know how to"—*what, be more than a friend? Love her? Is that what this was?*—"do this."

"Oh, I think you did it very well," she said with a small laugh.

His heart popped a beat at her words. "For real?" He firmed his grip on her waist and drew her back across the two inches she'd put between them, glad for the distraction from tough talk and weighted truths. "You sure?" He angled in. "Maybe we need to test that. Y'know—just to be sure." When her eyes slid closed, he brushed her soft lips with his. Claimed them and her.

He had to figure it out—showing his feelings yet not drowning in the tsunami of them. As her hands locked around his neck, he felt himself falling hard and fast for McKenna Neeley.

"I'd say 'get a room,'" Brick's deep, mocking voice intruded, "but uh . . . guess you already did."

Dante veered off, acutely aware that this broke a dozen different protocols and good sense. Despite his instinct that told him to hold onto McKenna, he somehow found himself stepping back and guiding her aside. Even as he did it, the dagger of betrayal embedded in his own heart just as he'd lodged it in hers. "I—"

"And it's about time," Brick muttered, turning back toward the main room, "because something needed to loosen you up a little. It's been so long since I've seen you with a girl, I thought you'd forgotten how."

"Bro." Dante planted his hands on his tactical belt. "Not cool." The swarm of chaos, a battle raging in him—how was he supposed to figure it out with Mick while serving as protective detail, keeping her safe, earning the respect of the chief—that swept him far from that very thing. And now, he had no idea how to pull out of the awkwardness caused by Brick.

No—by your own foolishness.

Kissing her wasn't foolishness.

Then what was it?

Besides amazing? No clue.

McKenna hunched her shoulders, her hurt once more evident when she moved past him.

He caught her hand before she could exit the tent. "Hey. Wait."

Surprise spiraled through her tawny features as she stopped, one socked foot on the threshold between rooms. She hugged herself.

Dante felt miserable as he hedged closer. "I wasn't lying . . . I don't know how to do this."

She shook the hair from her face and fire roared in her eyes. "Do what, Dante?"

Though he skated a glance to where Brick was unwrapping a power bar, he focused on her. "Us, this."

"And what is this?" She folded her arms. "A distraction? Because it's very clear you have a lot happening in that head of yours, and you can't even seem to voice that you like me."

"It's not like that."

"I think it is," McKenna countered, her voice hoarse. "What Brick mentioned—about needing to loosen up—"

He groaned.

"It's true. Ever since I first saw you at the hotel, you've been . . . different. On edge. Defensive. Unrecognizable." Her words, though soft, were razor-sharp, shredding the shields from around his heart.

She repositioned herself in front of him. "The man I know," she said, her voice lower, "the one who left Virginia to forge his own way in the world, walked in confidence, intelligence, and"—she bobbed her head side to side—"some level of arrogance."

"Don't hold back, Mick."

"It's not a bad thing," she amended. "It's just . . . confidence taken too far, I think."

"Confidence?" His throat constricted as he inched closer, desperation screaming that she might ditch him. "Mick, I've never felt confident. All my life, I never measured up. Especially once I learned I'd spent my whole life with my dad right next to me— posing as my uncle. There had always been something missing. In here." He patted his chest. "When I found out who he really was, I wondered—what could I have done different that would've made him claim me as his own? What'd I do wrong? How'd I mess up so bad that my own dad didn't want me?"

The words shocked him. Pummeled him. He'd never spoken that to anyone.

"Oh, Dante," she said quietly. "You know that's not true. Our dads—what they did as special operators was dangerous—had to take strident measures to protect us. If anyone learned who they were, that the infamous Nightshade team had families, enemies would come after us. That was your dad shielding you, especially since your mother was gone." She touched his cheek. "I had no idea you felt that way. You were always so strong."

"I get it, Mick. I do. But he didn't own me. And what you saw back then was just a guy trying to hack his way through life and make sure he didn't make the same mistakes as his dad."

Brow furrowed, Mick stared at him, her gaze tracking over his face for a long second. She had this way of making him feel like a specimen under a microscope—a high-powered one that saw all the way to his heart. "Then don't."

He sniffed. "Glad you cleared that up."

She frowned. "Don't mock me. I know you've always thought of me as a little, silly girl, but I—"

"Never silly," he countered. "And you're not little anymore."

She stretched her neck and sighed. "Dante . . . Pike and the others think highly of you." Even when he started to object, she pushed on. "You can't argue that—they call you the Greatest of All Time."

He frowned at her. "Do what?"

"Brick said it earlier."

He tried to recall anything like that.

"He called you GOAT."

Groaning, Dante slid his eyes shut.

"It's sweet—"

"It's not—" He dragged a hand over his mouth with another groan. "It's literally a *goat*—I had a fight with one. Now that's what they call me."

She stilled. "Oh." Then she chuckled.

"No—no, it's not funny."

She wrinkled her nose. "It kind of is, really."

He sniffed again.

"Well," she said, "I know enough of paramilitary missions and their importance to know you would not be standing here if they didn't respect you. Especially with Pike Auberon. If he didn't think well of you, then you'd be a liability. We know from what our dads did that teams can't afford that and—"

"It's not that easy."

"—neither can I."

Snapping his gaze to hers, he faltered at her meaning. "Are you saying—"

"I'm saying," she said, then drew in a breath and did a quick look-see into the main room, before putting a growl into her voice, "get out of your own way before you lose everything you don't know you want."

He blinked. "Hold up." Did that make sense, what she'd said? "I know what I want." That hot viper coiled in the pit of his stomach slithered up his gut. Tightened his jaw and fists. "What does that mean?"

"Stop overthinking everything!"

———— • ————

Heart jarring in her chest, McKenna forced herself to walk away from Dante and head out of the heat tent. Silently berated herself for losing her temper and snapping at him. Kissing her senseless one second and pushing her away the next made her crazy.

"Boom!"

Brick gave a loud, resounding clap.

"That's what I'm talking about," he said around a laugh. He met McKenna, took her hand and led her to a folding chair he'd scrounged up. "Your throne, Your Majesty."

"The realm must be perilously short on coin," she muttered awkwardly around a laugh. "And why have I been crowned exactly?"

"Little Lady," Brick said, "we've been trying to pound that into his thick skull since he joined. Maybe that lip-lock and verbal head-smack will get through."

Feeling a little ashamed that her moment of weakness was being used to ridicule Dante, she eyed him. Her heart ached, recalling his very raw words about never feeling confident. About trying to measure up … About how Uncle Legend's well-intentioned desire to give Dante a stable life had produced insecurity in the very son he'd been trying to protect. She hated the void it'd left in Dante, making him feel unwanted and less-than. To her, he'd always been larger than life. A lot like Daddy and the other Nightshade "uncles" and operators.

Growing up, she'd always seen Dante as the Scion who knew where he was going and how he'd get there. The oldest of them all, he was the envy of the others, who watched him doing all the cool things. Everyone wanted to be like Dante, especially when he'd made it to BUD/S and earned his Trident. She hadn't been surprised—it was him simply living up to the legacy of their fathers and his Scion callsign of Atlas.

Jaw muscle flexing, Dante shot daggers at his buddy. Was it this kind of thing—Brick taunting him—that made Dante feel disrespected? "What'd you find out there?"

"Whole lot of nothin," Brick pronounced.

She glanced around their hideout. They couldn't stay here for long. What if the terrorists came looking and found them? Walking to Yerevan was out of the question, considering the weather and distance. "So . . . how do we get back?"

Brick lowered himself to the concrete floor and leaned back against the wall. "Welp," he said, chomping off half the bar. He continued around his food. "There's this thing called standard operating procedure."

"Don't talk down to her," Dante bit out, snagging a bar and sitting on the ruck.

Surprised that he defended her, she furrowed her brow. Hadn't he just pushed her away?

Brick swung wide gray eyes to her and flashed his palms. "Apologies. Never meant that."

"I know you didn't," she said, scowling at Dante, who was suddenly focused on the protein bar wrapper. Avoiding her gaze again? She looked back to Brick. "So, SOP . . . ?"

Brick smoothed a hand over his beard and nodded. "OTG had to get the VIP to a hospital, so the chief will stay with him, connect with our sponsors—"

"Sponsors?"

"Slow down," Dante said to his buddy, voice unnaturally calm. "She's not an operator."

"I may not be an operator," McKenna clarified, "but I understand more about SOP and ROE than most, since my dad has been an operator most of his life and I work at the consular office."

Now Brick seemed lost. "I . . ." He had a cursed-if-I-do-cursed-if-I-don't look as he dragged his hand over his beard again. "Goat, help a buddy out."

Dante bent forward, elbows on his knees. "It's simple—SOP will have Omen looking for us," he said quietly, gaze focused a hundred percent on the wrapper. "Pike will get the SecState to the hospital, check in with our sponsor—the one who funds and authorizes our presence in-country—and then send a couple teammates to track us down."

"But how will they find us? Armenia is big."

"We left a trail," Dante said quietly. "They know where the vehicle went over the ridge. They'll talk to locals, gather intel. Knowing we'd head back to Yerevan, they'll work their way north. Sticking to main roads helps."

"But we didn't," she countered, accepting more electrolyte water from the brawny man.

"Yes and no," Brick said with a shrug. "They can calculate time, note weather, and figure out we had to seek shelter. That limits where to look because they'd know we wouldn't check-in at the Ritz."

Ah, that made sense.

"They'll find us." This time, Dante met her gaze.

Was he just trying to placate her? "So, we stay . . . put?"

"Yep." Brick guzzled water, then wiped his beard.

"For how long?" McKenna did not appreciate the way they both looked at her, as if she were a child who needed reassurance, but her question was a valid, reasonable one, in her estimation. Even though she heard her own panic. "I mean, what if they don't come—"

"They'll come," Dante said.

"—and"—she glowered at his condescension—"the Azerbaijani troops find us?"

His jaw muscle bounced again.

Hoo-boy, she was getting miffed with him constantly countering her questions and statements. "It's logical to assume, isn't it?" McKenna hated the concoction of anger and fear rising through her. "I mean, if Omen can figure out where we are by tracking our progress and knowing where we were headed, it presumes the terrorists can too." When Dante opened his mouth, she held up a staying hand. "We were just talking about the belief that someone is tipping them off, that there may be a mole."

He gave Brick a look, and that just set her teeth on edge.

Since neither offered a rebuttal, she forged ahead. "Thus, my question—how long do we stay here?" She wanted to add "like sitting ducks" but refrained because that would be irritation talking.

"Till the weather clears," Dante said.

"And your boots dry," Brick added, then pulled on a ball cap, likely trying to keep warm. His gaze fixed on her. "So . . . theories on the mole?"

McKenna stifled a yawn and told herself not to take it personally that they wanted to point fingers at one of her friends or coworkers. "As I told Dante, I would've said Vugar, but he was too . . . softhearted." So, who else could be—

Her mind slammed into that morning at the office, when Dalita told them about the secret meeting. "Dalita Apkarian."

"Hold up," Dante said, frowning. "At the embassy, when I told you she'd hit my radar wrong and had Rawlins keeping tabs on her, you got upset. Said she was trustworthy, a good worker."

"She was—is," McKenna said, the needling defensiveness rising again. Determined to squash that feeling, she chose a painfully honest path. "When I saw Rawlins watching her, I . . . Well, it frightened me that someone I knew so well was considered a threat." She shuddered. "Even saying that, I feel like I'm betraying my friends, but Dalita always had this uncanny knack for hearing rumors—ones that proved to be accurate intel."

"Having intel doesn't translate as corrupt," Dante countered.

Ugh! So much for her attempt at a middle ground. Would he argue every point she made? "I did not say it did," McKenna ground out. "But when a person somehow has intel that even embassy and consular offices don't yet have, it raises suspicions."

"Fair." Brick nodded, adjusting his ball cap. "This Delina—"

"*Dalita*. Apkarian."

Brick's thick reddish-brown eyebrows lifted. "So . . . local?"

The way his tone and whole demeanor changed unsettled McKenna. Made her feel protective and defensive of her friend. "Dalita has been a good friend to me while I've been living here."

"Of course she has," Brick said casually. "What better way to win your trust and make you look the other way?"

The haunting truth of that pushed McKenna's gaze to the floor. "I don't want to believe this of her." She swallowed, thinking through it all. "But . . ."

"But you can see it works," Brick supplied. "I mean, you were suspicious of that intel she keeps producing."

"Yeah," she said, slowly accepting the facts. Her heart squeezed. "Why? Why would she do this? It's terrible. Dalita has seen what the people have gone through with this conflict. Selling them out doesn't make sense."

"To you," Dante pointed out. "Because you're loyal, sensitive."

Being accused of being "sensitive" had always felt like an insult. As if it made her weak or ruled by emotion. McKenna especially resented hearing it from Dante, but she focused on the real concern—Dalita. "She was loyal, I thought."

"She *is* loyal," Brick amended. "We just aren't sure to what, and that makes her dangerous."

"No." McKenna regretted the objection as soon as it escaped her lips. "I simply cannot imagine Dalita betraying me—us. She would know they were trying to kill us, and that's . . . It's not like her. She grieved one of our cases where a young American mom had watched powerlessly as Azerbaijani troops killed her son."

Brick and Dante silently considered her with matching expressions that said they could imagine it.

"You think I'm silly for defending her."

Brick gave her a solemn look. "Maybe naïve, in an innocent way. And we"—he thumbed between himself and Dante—"wouldn't want anyone we love or care about to get an education on the dark world in which we operate. Right, Goat?"

Dante gave him a terse look but nodded.

"Now, if y'all don't mind, I'm going to grab some shut-eye." With that, Brick tugged his ball cap down over his face and slouched until his chin rested on his broad chest. Knees up, arms folded, just like earlier when he'd slept on the desk, but this time his ruck offered the necessary support.

A cool silence settled over the room, walls creaking and popping beneath the storm's influence. An ache bloomed in McKenna's side from the wound. She touched it and winced, still unable to believe she'd been shot. Part of her couldn't wait to tell Daddy that she had a scar like him, but that wouldn't go over well. She'd always be his little girl, even when old and gray. It reminded her of Brick's comment that being naïve wasn't a negative because it meant she hadn't seen bad things.

Awareness pushed through her thoughts, reminding her of Dante sitting there. Still bent forward. Still messing with the wrapper of the bar long since eaten.

Too tired for more "figuring out," she struggled to her feet—the wound pinching and objecting—then headed for the cot in the tent. "I think I'll do the same."

"Mick," he said quietly as he rose.

Holding a dismissive hand out, she kept moving. "I just need rest." She did not have the energy to argue, not after all they'd been through. And each time she'd tried to make peace with him, it backfired. She heard his steps giving chase and quickened her pace to the cot. There, she lay down and gave him her back, tugging up the thermal blanket as she closed her eyes.

His boots squeaked to her side, then hesitated. Quiet rankled at the lack of conversation, but she was glad for it. He likely debated over pressing her. Uncertain of her own roiling thoughts and unable to figure him out, she kept her eyes closed. Told herself to go to sleep.

But her ears—traitorous little head wings—were attuned to him as he retreated. Only a few paces, probably to the threshold of the tent. Or maybe he'd gone back into the supply room and she hadn't heard him. If she looked and he was there, he'd want to talk. And while that was probably the right thing, sweet mercies, she was just so tired. Of it all. This wasn't the place to sort out "us," as he'd called it. Not with him still entrenched in his insecurity and demand for respect.

Even having this conversation with herself was strange. That all those years of hoping and dreaming he'd turn those rich, chocolate eyes on her in that way had finally come true. And now she was shutting the door?

Not shutting the door, she silently argued.

Well, maybe just the screen door.

ELEVEN

Vayots Dzor Province, Armenia

LAUGHTER DREW HIM DOWN A LONG, DARK *hall toward a lone source of light at the far end. Hardwood floors chilled his feet and sent icy shards up his spine. Ahead, out of sight, another laugh joined the first. Peals of delight echoed, then turned to shrieks of laughter. The merriment, the unadulterated joy of the sound, pulled him onward.*

He passed a door and peered in. Saw Pop sitting with Lyric and Kazi. Pop looked up, and his expression darkened.

"Pop, something up?"

Staying seated, giving him a long look, his dad bobbed his head forward, indicating the front of the house. "You know what you need to do."

"'Bout what?"

"You are not that dense." Pop again nodded toward the front. "Your wife and child."

"I don't have a wife. Or a kid."

Pop went back to the book he was reading to Lyric. Then just like that, he was all up in Dante's face. Gripping his shoulders. "They're in trouble. Hurry!"

"I know you're old, Pop, but not that old. Remember, I don't have a family."

In a blink, he found himself again in the narrow, light-deprived corridor. Alone, cold. It seemed longer than before. He started that way, then realized the hall was lengthening. Each step he took added another yard. And another. Until Dante found himself running, the source ever out of reach. The laughter pervaded the stretching night, then turned into a scream.

Dante flinched awake.

The scream reverberated into his mind, smacking sense into him—Mick and Brick were talking, smiling in his direction. Embarrassment washed over him with a heaping chunk of irritation. What were they mocking him about this time?

Brick touched the side of his mouth. "You were drooling, Atlas."

Before he could think better of it, Dante checked the spot. Dry. "Bro, you—"

Chuckling, Brick shook his head. "Too easy."

Thud.

Dante stilled, cocking his head to the side and training his ear on the wall behind him. On what lay beyond . . .

"Uh-oh, I think we ticked him off," Brick sniggered.

Snapping up a closed fist, head angled to the wall, Dante felt the tension in the room shift, the others understanding his signal for silence. He came up, swiveling toward the wall, and unholstered his Sig as he cut off the torch that lit the tent.

A soft buzzing came from the device strapped to Brick's arm. His expression went grim. "Perimeter alarm's been tripped."

Another soft-yet-loud-enough-to-carry sound had Dante backing up. Eyes on the wall, he caught Mick's hand and drew her around to his left as he exited the tent.

For a big guy, Brick was fluid and downright graceful in operator mode. M4 at the high ready, he rushed into the supply room, snuffed the lamp, and moved to the second side window. "Got company," he confirmed in a low voice.

"Mick, go," Dante said. "In the garage bay. Lie down in the well of the car jack."

Her eyes widened. "What? No!" she hissed. "I know how to shoot. Let me—"

"You don't have plates," he countered, passing her a Glock. "Use this if you have to, but go now before they start shooting through the walls."

Mick faltered, looking at him, expression wide and distraught.

His mind hiked back to the dream. To the warning of danger. *They're in trouble.* His wife and child. Man, he did not have the headspace to sort that right now.

He nodded and she reciprocated, then raced toward the bay. He couldn't see the jacks from here, but the sound of her settling between the two braces of the jacks reached him. At least she'd have protection if bullets penetrated the structure. And the top of the jack would protect her in the event of a cave-in. Not likely, but better safe than dead.

He pivoted and hustled to the other window and pressed his shoulder to the wall, angling to get a line of sight through the crack in the boards.

"Four, lightly armed," Brick subvocalized. "Haven't alerted yet, but if they notice the sensors . . ."

"Two coming up your six," Dante said, holstering his Sig and bringing his M4 around. "Handguns, no visual on rifles." He saw an unfriendly trip and stumble, then jerk around, gaze on the ground. "They found the sensors."

Crack! Crack!

"Taking fire," Brick said, his voice dull, bored, as he returned fire.

Rifle tucked into his shoulder, Dante aimed at the two he had sights on. Targeted the first guy. Sent a short burst to down him. The second scuttled up against the building. Backing up along the wall, farther from the direction the target had gone, Dante calculated where the target was and opened fire. Rounds chewed through the plaster wall without a hitch.

Crack!

Glass shattered above him.

Dante ducked.

A metal canister sailed in through the broken window.

Tink-tink-t—

"Flash-bang!" He'd no sooner pitched himself away—simultaneously opening his mouth, closing his eyes, and covering an ear—than the device detonated.

Bright white exploded through the supply room as the concussion punched him in the spine. Ears ringing, he rolled onto his back as a barrage of gunfire tore through the wall. Training and logic said to get up and bear down on the enemy. But instinct told him to wait . . . train his sights on the thin barrier that tried in vain to protect him from the elements and the enemy.

Darkness beyond the hole gaped.

C'mon . . . Where you hiding?

Muscles twitched to get up. Shoot. Anything other than lying on the floor waiting to eat lead. Locked on the wall, he waited for movement. For muzzle flash to betray the tango who tossed that grenade. The flight part of the fight or flight instinct railed at him. Hammered in his pulse.

"They're in trouble. Your wife and child."

A buzzing at the back of his brain told him it had simply been his mind aware that he'd heard something while being asleep. But . . . wife?

"C'mon," he growled quietly, shifting, his core tight as he aimed at the wall. A spark ignited as bullets pierced the plaster. Gotcha. Adjusting his sights to where that muzzle flashed, he released a short, controlled burst. Waited, breath ragged. Used the heel of his boots to scoot back, farther from the shooter, just in case he hadn't tagged the guy.

"They're going for the door," Brick bit out, firing, then announced, "Empty!"

Knowing his buddy would be out of commission for the few seconds it took for him to change out the magazine, Dante rose and provided suppressive cover.

Shots peppered the door, followed by a solid thud.

Dante sprayed and prayed to eliminate the terrorists before they breached the door.

Having smoothly and efficiently loaded another magazine, Brick was already back in action and did a look-see. "They're coming in!"

If McKenna had not been in the bay, she was pretty sure her ears might have bled. The detonation of the percussion grenade unleashed chaos. The terror of the situation sent her fears and tormenting past into overdrive. The night Poppa died had been like this. So many people hurt. So much blood.

Left hand over her head, right cradling the Glock, McKenna silently begged God for a different outcome this time. *I know You did not bring Dante all the way to Armenia, to me, so he could die in my sight. Right . . . ?*

A barrage of bullets and shouts demanded she check to make sure he was still alive. Safe in the jack well, she peered over the steel platform. Saw Dante moving into position next to Brick. With her ringing ears and drumming heart, she watched them get locked in a firefight. They needed help.

Where was Omen? Brick and Dante had said the team would come for them. But that hadn't happened, and now they were in this fight alone. A third gun would be helpful . . .

Would it? McKenna wasn't sure she could shoot a person—well, she certainly would to save her life. And was Dante's worth less? She groaned, remembering the time as a teen when Daddy had taken her up with one of his buddies for a hunting trip. She'd been thrilled to tagalong, feeling grown up and excited that he wanted her with him. But then Daddy handed her the Remington, which she had been begging him to let her have for years.

"This is yours," he'd said, *"if you can kill the elk."*

She'd recoiled, but bravado and her unwillingness to be seen as weak in his eyes made her take it. She lined up the shot. Even now recalled the loud thunder of her heart.

"Line up the shot just like at the range," Daddy said, oblivious to her panic.

Or so she'd thought. It'd taken her a hot minute, but she finally got her breathing under control as he'd taught her. Noted wind direction and speed. Staring through the sights, she aimed just behind the shoulder and halfway up the body so it'd be a quick, clean kill for the massive, powerful elk. She took the shot.

And threw up for the next hour, until she had dry heaves.

Daddy gave her the Remington. Told her she now understood what it was like to take a life. Said it'd taught her to respect life and respect the gun.

And now, the men attacking would kill them if they didn't defend themselves. But this line of work just wasn't for McKenna. Yet, if she stayed here, it was very likely she'd end up dead. She twitched toward the ridge to climb out.

No. No, Dante said stay put, she reminded herself, lowering back to the concrete. He was the operator, she the consular officer. She had to trust his experience.

Crack! Thud!

McKenna snapped her gaze up. In the supply room, dust plumed and a flurry of movement erupted as Dante and Brick, still firing, advanced toward the danger. Intent. Determined. One attacker barreled into Dante.

Breath in her throat, McKenna decided she was not going to watch him die.

Go. *Now.*

Jackknifing her body prevented her from seeing what was happening. Hoisting herself up, she negotiated over the steel jack. Scuttled to the far side, trying to keep moving. Shoulder to the wall, she felt the pinch of the bandaged wound.

A strangled shout went up in what was a surprisingly quiet moment.

Why was it so quiet?

"You good?" came Brick's gruff voice.

"You?" Dante must've nodded his answer.

"Got a couple of souvenirs, but I'll live."

Wait. Was it over? McKenna shifted around two large fifty-gallon drums and gingerly picked her way to the open door to the back room. Halfway there, something snagged in her periphery, stopping her cold. She ducked low behind the barrels, searching for whatever had caught her attention. Then she saw it. Through the dividing wall's window between the garage bays and the main shop . . .

Adjusting her position to protect herself, she peeked through the dingy window and down the aisle of the front shop. Unlit, it hung in dark, dank shadows. Ominous. Haunting.

What had she seen? Where she expected barren blackness, a long shaft of light from outside forced back the veil of night and darkness. The interior, powerless against the white blight, succumbed to an ominous glow.

Except . . . Her eyes struggled to decipher what she saw. Her gaze traveled down the shelving, the supplies, the counter, out the far, broken window to the two hulking black shapes prowling the side of the building.

Oh no! Her first instinct was to shout a warning to Dante. But if she did that, she'd draw attention to herself.

McKenna glanced at the weapon in her hand. Heavy yet strangely light, familiar. A lethal tool. She brought it up and aimed at the two, who were walking a wide perimeter and still in sight. Steadying her breathing, she slid into her sharpshooter mindset. She was the daughter of a MARSOC sniper. An Olympic sharpshooter.

Wait. What if that was Omen . . . ?

Well, if it wasn't and she didn't take the shot, warn Dante . . .

But killing someone? Her stomach quailed.

McKenna noticed a soft glare above the men. A power box hung on a pole. Likely used to light the station and pumps when the station had been operational.

Perfect. She firmed her grip, lined up the sights, and aimed above the transformer.

Firing would give away her position. Maybe. Likely. Probably. But at least the newcomers wouldn't take Dante and Brick by surprise. Or worse—take them out.

McKenna eased the trigger back. Heard the report, which punched her already hurting eardrums, and absorbed the weapon's recoil.

Glass raining down on them, the men shouted.

Adrenaline shoved her out of hiding. Ducking, she started for the door to Dante—but felt a jolt yank her backward. A thick, powerful arm hooked her neck. "Aug—"

The guy clamped a meaty, sweaty hand over her mouth, muffling her scream. She bucked back, nailing the guy's head as she writhed. A hard thud against her temple left her dazed, but cognizant enough to know if she did not fight, she would die.

TWELVE

Vayots Dzor Province, Armenia

NO SOONER HAD DANTE WHIPPED TOWARD the exploding transformer than his brain registered the shot that had come from behind. From the car bays.

Brick seared the air with more expletives as he fired at two more tangos coming around the west side of the building.

A sound erupted from the bay and froze him. He stared at the doorway. "That sounded like a scream." A cut-off scream.

"Check it," Brick barked as he continued engaging the terrorists.

Moving intentionally, weapon at high ready, Dante guessed that McKenna had fired at the light above the transformer to alert them to the additional tangoes. Smart. Yet it'd given away her position. That thought hurried him to the door.

He did a quick look-see, but found nothing. "Mick." Staring down the barrel of his M4 as he swept the garage, he advanced toward the large car jack, nerves firing hot. A quick glance told him she wasn't there. "Mick." He turned a slow circle, taking in the cold space.

Pulse pounding, he hustled through a perimeter walk. His gut cinched beneath the awful truth—she wasn't here. "Brick. She's gone!"

"Find her."

"Ya think?" he threw over his shoulder.

A fracture in the darkness yanked his gaze to the far corner. What . . . ? Was that light coming through a bullet hole? But it was so angular . . . His gaze traveled the beam to—

Huh. The garage door had a smaller, inset door, which sat ajar. Vehicle headlamps stabbed through the crack and pierced his gaze.

Why would she go out there? He moved to the right of the door. Pressed his shoulder to the metal barrier, a bad feeling swarming his gut. He nudged the door with his toe. Bobbed his head out. His split-second look-see proved a magnet for enemy fire. Headlamps blinded him. He jerked back as a barrage of bullets *tsing*'d and punctured the door.

Augh! "Contact!" Whipping to the concrete pillar between the doors, he took a sec to process what he'd seen. A dozen or so terrorists. Two more vehicles. And another wrangling someone— McKenna! Pulse jacked, he searched for options. "Brick! Need you. They've got her!"

"En route," Brick hollered.

Time took on a supernatural aura, slowing to an impossible rhythm that tightened Dante's chest and struggled against his need for air. He couldn't wait for Brick. No way he was going to let them take her. He slid to the door again, kicked it open, and laid down suppressive fire.

But the enemy was waiting for him and unleashed their own volley, driving him back. "Augh!" He gritted his teeth. Where on earth was Brick? He jerked to the side—and found himself facing a brawny chest. "What took you so long?"

Brick held up a flash-bang, his expression one of fierce determination. "Where's our girl?"

"Through the door, eleven o'clock."

"Ready?"

Adjusting for Brick to take point and send the flash-bang, Dante brought the weapon to ready. "Going left."

"On three," Brick said with a nod and pulled. "One . . . two"—he adjusted to the door—"three." With tactical precision, he reached out, pitched the flash-bang, and whipped back inside.

Dante huffed a breath, ready. The seconds between the flash-bang being thrown and the explosion of white light and noise felt like forever. When it finally hit, he barged out, quickly sighting the first target and firing. The second, fired. Again and again, always advancing in the direction of—

A scream diverted his attention to his nine.

Pale blue coveralls were a flaming beacon against the dark uniforms, thick night, and glare of the headlamps.

An impact drove him back, knocking his breath out. He stumbled, realizing he'd been shot. His vest had absorbed the impact. He huffed a breath, trying to stay on his feet. Gaze ever locked on Mick, who was fighting and giving her captor a run for their blood money.

Dante advanced, the fire in his lungs making it a struggle to breathe. But he didn't care. He swung out in a wide arc.

The SUV door opened, effectively shielding the terrorists.

"Let her go!" Dante neutralized the terrorist who'd been guarding the two forcing Mick into the vehicle. When they didn't yield, he advanced. "Last chance. Let her—"

The words died in his throat as the tall, lanky soldier hooked McKenna's throat and used her as a shield. Ticked at the cowardice, Dante shifted and double-tapped the second guy, dropping him. And in that moment, Lanky shoved himself backward, hauling her with him into the SUV.

Mick's scream assailed Dante's nerves and conscience. "No!" He lunged across the fifteen feet to the SUV.

Blue eyes wide, Mick surged forward, arms outstretched to him, desperation in her eyes and strangled cries, face contorted in terror.

His legs could not carry him fast enough. Caught her hand. Relief churned.

But the vehicle lurched forward, breaking their contact.

Grabbing the door, Dante pushed himself to stay up as the vehicle bounded over the bumpy parking lot, aiming for the street. If they made it there . . .

The realization threw him forward. He snagged her hand. Lanky rose and slammed a fist on their hands, tearing them apart. Dante aimed his weapon at Lanky. He was practiced at hitting a moving target. Might injure Mick, but she'd be alive. They could tend her.

The SUV banked hard right. Snatching her away. "No."

"Dante!" McKenna's face twisted in terror as distance grew between them. "Nooo!"

Her scream shredding his soul, he struggled against the icy conditions that slickened his grip on the fiberglass door, preventing him from finding traction on the ground. Feet bouncing and flipping, turning his waist this way and that, Dante gritted his teeth and held on.

A shot clapped through the night.

Fire licked his knuckles, making him flinch—just as the vehicle swerved. At the same time, hit a gulley. Crashed down, driving shards of pain into his knees and hips. For a half second, they went airborne as the SUV careened onto the road. When the tires hit, that was the final straw. The vehicle divested itself of the extra weight—Dante.

He flipped and bounced, rolling to a stop in the ditch. "No!" He thrust himself up and sprinted after the SUV as its engine roared. Tires lost traction and the tail swerved.

Dante caught the bumper—but the driver knew what he was doing. In a second, the vehicle straightened out and forward, yanking free.

Momentum suddenly lost as he scrambled to hang on, Dante face-planted. He struggled to get upright again. But the distance between them rapidly increased. "No." He sprinted, telling himself he'd die before letting it end like this.

Chest heaving, legs trembling, he was slowing . . . Staggered to a stop, watching the vehicle speed away. Bent, holding his knees, he panted heavily as the SUV got smaller and smaller. "Augh!!" He punched the air.

The other SUV.

Whipping around, he disregarded the pain in his ankle. Shoved himself back to the gas station.

Brick was there, going through the bodies of the soldiers and gathering gear and weapons. He held up a walkie crackling with convos in some language. "Russian, pretty sure."

"The other SUV," Dante huffed, hurrying to it and climbing in.

"Already tried." Brick straightened and made his way over. "Engine's blown."

Unwilling to believe it, Dante tried to crank the engine. Nothing happened. Banging the steering wheel, Dante gave a shout. Pitched himself out, his ankle wobbling beneath pain. "We can't let them get away."

"That ship has sailed," Brick muttered.

Dante threw himself at the big guy. Jerked him around by the tac vest. "What is wrong with you? You want her to die? You talk so big but you won't help me help her!"

Something dark and menacing morphed into the big guy's face, glinting with a latent threat. Full hands lifted in surrender. "Atlas, I hear you." His breathing seemed taut. "But . . . step off." Eyebrows lifted, lips thinned. "Now."

Dante swallowed, suddenly realizing what he was doing. Regaining possession of himself, he released his hold and looked down. Patted the guy's plates. "Sorry." Shaking his head, he dragged his hands over his face and head, hooking them there. Staring in the direction they'd taken her. All those words, those . . . promises to keep her safe. That he had her . . . and he'd let them take her.

"We need to clear the bodies off the road," Brick said. "Don't need locals wondering about dead soldiers."

"I have to do something."

"We will." Brick caught a body beneath the arms and hauled the terrorist around to the back of the shop.

Dante stalked inside, grabbed his jacket, ammo from the supply ruck, and threaded the Camelbak on, then headed out.

"What're you doing?" Brick demanded, dropping the body he'd been hauling to catch up.

"Going to find her."

"No." Brick stood in front of him. "Not like this."

"Get out the way," Dante said, his breath staggering around the words, the fury and the anger so powerful, he feared what he'd do.

"Dante."

"I'm not playing with you, bro."

Somber eyes held his. "Neither am I. Pull your head back into the game. I know she's your girl and important, but this isn't the way to find her. You start out there, get killed by the AzerBs or some wild animal . . . Dead isn't helpful. Dead is dead, and she needs you not dead."

Defeat stuck its claws in Dante's wounds. Glanced across his tongue, bitter and metallic. "I can't just sit in that shop with her missing. Not after . . . where she . . ." Where we talked. Laughed. Kissed. "I made her mad."

"Blinding flash of the obvious, Atlas—you do that to all of us."

Dante scowled and shoved him back. "Get off me, man. You don't understand—our last words—"

"No!" Brick said definitively. "Last words have not been spoken, so don't even go there. Omen is en route, and we'll find her." Another shoulder clap. "I promise."

"Man. You can't promise nothing. You know how it go—"

"That." Brick pointed over Dante's shoulder, turning him, where in the hazy sky whirred a sleek gray drone. "That's ours and how I can promise."

"About freakin' time." Relief warred with frustration, because that was a long-range drone. Which meant the team wasn't nearby. Still . . . he had an idea that might not only save time but save McKenna.

THIRTEEN

Gegharkunik Province, Armenia

HER NECK AND SHOULDER ACHED, PRYING McKenna from a heavy sleep and assaulting her with the memory of being ripped from Dante. *Where am I?* The utter darkness forbade her from seeing anything, but her mind warned that something was . . . off. Wrong. Pulling upright, she threw out her hands. Struck something solid. Bars—flat bars with gaps between them. She groped wildly, her mind quickly assembling her predicament—a . . . cage. Sweet mercy—they put her in a cage?

No . . . A whimper coiled through her, and she fought the rising shriek of claustrophobia.

I'm in a cage. It's dark.

Horror clung to her. "No, no, no," she whimpered, pushing herself straight—whacked her head again. Panic swelled. Churned. She slapped the hard, cold bars. Shifted, searching for a latch to free herself, but found she couldn't even turn her body. The cage was narrow and short. Trying to shift around got her leg stuck.

I can't breathe.

You're fine. "God has not given me a spirit of fear, but of power, love . . . and a calm, well-balanced mind."

But I can't breathe!

Muscles twitching, she smacked the metal bars again. As if that'd help. "It's okay . . . it's okay . . . You're fine." Cold. Confined. Captive.

This was absolutely not fine! Being in a cage was not a portent of good. It was bad. Very, very bad. She had to get out of here. Why had they even taken her? She was of no use to anyone!

Wrangling her leg out from under her, metal biting into her spine with icy teeth, she shifted. Now her legs were in her chest. "I can't do this. Get me out," she breathed, tears blurring her vision. "Help!" She pounded the bars repeatedly. "Help! I need help!"

Whoosh!

Light pierced metal bars that were several inches wide, disorienting her to what happened. How had the light suddenly gotten through? She tried to peer out. Only with the flapping of black material did she realize the cage had been covered with a tarp. In the whispers of moments when the tarp shifted, she was able to sort that the cage she sat in was in a large metal building. Through the thick bars, she could see across a dozen feet to a large opening. This was some kind of warehouse. Beyond that opening, the dirt road led to two structures that flanked an open gate. And a woman—

A woman was walking past the compound!

"Hey! Help!" McKenna shouted as loud as she could, desperate.

The woman faltered, her gaze finding the cage.

Yes! "Help me!! Heeeelpp! Get me out . . ." McKenna's voice died as the woman yanked down her gaze and all but ran out of sight. "No, no!!"

A man stepped in front of the caged, aimed his weapon at her, and fired. Bullets pinged and zipped. One tore through the finger-wide gap and found the fleshy part of her thigh.

"Augh!" McKenna screamed, the pain excruciating. Hand clamped over it, she felt the warm, sticky blood streaming out.

The man shouted at her.

McKenna tried to push herself into the back of the cage, as if she could get away from the man or more bullets. Crying, angry, she kicked at the walls—and immediately regretted it, the wound responding with a gush of hot warmth. She cried out, applying more pressure. Knowing enough of field medicine that she had to tie it off. Needed to elevate it. But she could only do that if she put her legs up and her body on the cage floor. To accomplish that, she'd have to be a contortionist. "I need something to bind the wound." When he made no move to get help, she growled. "I'm going to bleed to death!"

"Then die, American!" he snarled as he thrust the stock of his rifle at the cage several times. Steel rattled, sending vibrations through her limbs and body.

She stifled a yelp, trying to figure out how to stem the bleeding as he railed at her in Azerbaijani.

A second man stalked into view with a gun, moving with terrible calm and lethality. He aimed at the man and fired.

McKenna gasped, silenced by the cold, callous manner in which he'd killed him.

The tall man strode toward the cage. "Bring me that," he barked to someone in Russian. "No, th—*da*!"

What? Was he going to torture her? Shoot her again? Stab her? McKenna fought tears, along with waves of nausea and pain as she kept pressure on her leg.

The man stared off to the side, waiting, then extended his hand as a woman rushed a length of cloth into his hand. He turned and crouched before her cage.

McKenna diverted her attention to the other side, wincing at the sharp twinge in her thigh.

"Here."

Frozen in fear, she refused to look.

"American," he insisted, his English thick and awkward, "take it."

McKenna swallowed and glanced to the side. Saw the cloth . . . thick and wide. Perfect for binding her wound. Why would he help her? She braved his eyes.

Cold cruelty stared back. "You are no good to me if you die." He stuffed the cloth between the slats. "You were with American soldiers, so I assume you know how to tie it around your leg, *da*?"

Everything in her wanted to defy this Russian, but doing so would only hasten her likelihood of dying. She wasn't interested in bleeding to death, but she couldn't bring herself to take the cloth.

He worked the material through and let it go. "You have fire in you," he said, nodding. "I like that in my women."

McKenna recoiled, refusing to dignify those disgusting words with a reply.

"Good, you know your place. Most American women do not."

Fabric pressed to the wound, she ignored his putrid comment as she watched blood soak through the material. Not good. She would need—"Dirt."

He scowled.

"There's too much blood. You said you didn't want me to die, so I need dirt to pack the wound. It has to be packed, then bound."

Dark eyes weighed her heavily for what felt like minutes. His stonelike expression never changed as he scooped dirt and dropped two handfuls through the top of the crate. The dirt sprinkled her head and ran down her neck.

Scrambling as it cascaded, she shifted to catch what she could with her legs. She grunted her frustration, then glowered at him as he stood over the cage. Jerk.

"You thought I open it so you could escape?" With another whoosh, the black tarp settled back over her metal prison, plunging her once more into darkness.

"No!" she pleaded before she could think better of it.

Mocking laughter faded with the Russian's steps as he left her alone in the dark with dirt and a strip of fabric.

Assailed by panic once more, she banged her head against the cage and squeezed a few more tears around gritted teeth. Which were chattering.

God . . .

She moaned. Why was it so cold? Was there no heat in here?

Pain radiating through her leg made her refocus. Shaking out her shirt and hair, she felt and heard the trickle of dirt hitting the cage pan. Angling aside, this way and that, McKenna scraped up as much of the dirt as possible. Then she lifted the bloody fabric and packed the wound, a wave of nausea roiling through her. Swallowing, she coiled the material around her bloody right hand, which applied pressure to stem the bleeding, then wrapped the fabric under her thigh and up between her legs. Then slid her hand free and made one more circuit around the leg with the fabric. She crisscrossed, tucked—drew a breath for courage—and tightened the knot. Hard.

Pain exploded, spewing nausea into her throat. Her face went clammy and even in the dark, she saw spots sprinkling her vision. Head tilted back, she used breathing techniques to fight her body's sudden urge to pass out.

With the way that Russian had executed the soldier, she knew her minutes were numbered. What she would not do for more of that morphine Brick had given her. Shot twice in one day. Daddy would be proud.

No, he'd be ticked!

A yawn plied at her, as if in objection to exerting herself, but she had to stay awake. A shiver traced her spine. There was little chance of falling asleep with the frigid temps and the new throbbing leg wound.

Gaze tracking around the dark was futile, but she tried to recall what she'd seen when there'd been light. Had there been a latch or locking mechanism?

That was a dumb question—of course there was, how else would they have put her in here? But . . . where?

Pushing aside the alarm stirring in the pit of her stomach, she trailed her hands over the painfully cold, hard surface of the cage. Along each three-inch-wide bump and two-inch gap of the bars. No news there. It was highly unlikely they'd built the cage around her, so where . . .

Chattering teeth reminded her of the cold and pervasive aches, especially her wound, but she ignored it as she tried to figure out a solution. Trailed her hands over the top, searching for a mechanism. Still nothing.

This made no sense.

And mercy, her leg was hurting! She bent over, whimpering around tears she fought back. Tilted her head and exhaled. Spotted a hinge on the right side of the cage.

How can I see it?

That's when she noticed a hole in the tarp that allowed light to caress the hinge. Through that peephole, she spied three men standing near a couple of sleek sedans. The Russian and another man faced her, but the third had his back to her. The closer sedan blocked most of his physique, but their voices carried.

"Just make sure," the Russian snarled, "you take care of the Americans. They cannot intervene."

The third man didn't respond.

That dark cloud moved into the Russian's features again, and he got in the guy's face, stabbing a finger in his chest as he railed at him. He'd lowered his voice, making it impossible to hear, then he stepped back. "Kill them or I will kill you."

A gust of wind flapped the tarp, obstructing her view.

McKenna started, her mind racing through the conversation.

Were they talking about killing Dante and Omen? What other Americans could they be referring to?

Secretary Derriscort.

In the hospital.

Surely he would be under guard . . .

"God, please." There was so much happening, so much to pray about. She'd already been through a lot. When would it be enough? "I just want to go home."

No, she wanted to go back to Dante. The last words between them had been harsh, dividing. Even though she'd called him out on things, she could've been kinder about it. Then she'd retreated within herself, wanting to be alone. Feigned sleep to avoid getting into a deep conversation.

What if she didn't make it back? What if she was never found or able to get free? Then he'd go through life thinking she died angry at him. She should've just talked to him. But she'd been so sore and tired, felt like she had been at the end of her rope.

Now, kidnapped and shot—in far more pain than before—she had to own the painful truth: She'd been lazy. Selfish. Weak.

"Love is hard," Mama had once told her. *"You have to decide that, no matter what, the person you love is more important. Every choice about how to respond is in your hands. Whatever you decide is a choice of yourself or them."*

"But . . . what if they're really, truly wrong and you're right?"

Mama hugged her tighter. "What's more important—that they are wrong and you are right? Or that you love them?"

McKenna wilted, resting her head against the side of the cage. "Oh, Dante . . . I'm so sorry. I should've done better. I should have chosen you over being right, because . . . I love you." She always had.

— • —

Yerevan, Yerevan Municipality, Armenia

Banged up, both his body and his heart, Dante stared at the black-and-white screens relaying the aerial footage from the drones searching for the two vehicles that had fled with Mick. Pacing between the monitors did not make the footage come faster, but it went a long way in dealing with the buzzing in his veins as he trolled the concrete floor of the hangar on the outskirts of the capital that served US diplomats and VIPs.

Pike held a hand in front of Dante, stalling him. "Heard you did good out there."

Dante balked. "Seriously?" He stabbed a finger toward the monitors. "McKenna is out there. Because of me."

"No," Pike countered, his voice preternaturally calm. "She's out there because of the Azerbaijanis."

"Nah." Patting his chest, Dante shook his head. "I told her to hide in the garage bay."

"Smart move. The walls are plaster and bullets puncture it like paper."

"And now she's gone."

"She is."

Gut writhing from the viper coiled there, Dante tightened his jaw. Did not need or want one of the lectures the chief was notorious for, but maybe he deserved it.

Yeah, he definitely deserved it. Because no matter how this got sliced, the fault lay at his boots. "I failed . . ."

"Failure is success in progress."

"I do not . . ." Dante growled, "Please, no lectures. I don't . . . can't—"

"No lecture."

"Not yet, at least," Luther said from the table he'd hiked a leg up on as Dade Tycho, their comms specialist, controlled a drone scouting the area where McKenna had been taken.

"No," Dade said with a snicker, "Chief always hits when you're not expecting it."

"But you won't avoid it," Brick warned. "Not after that kiss I came in on."

Heat shot down Dante's spine, and he detected Pike's head swivel to him.

Whoops and whistles echoed as the team roasted Dante. It wasn't funny. In fact, it pretty much ticked him off as the chief's gaze bored. "Save your breath, Chief," he said, finally looking at him. "You won't say anything I haven't already said to myself or beat myself with."

The silence in the hangar felt piercing and ominous.

"Think so?" Pike's gaze blazed, then flicked to the hangar door, where an armored sedan pulled up and delivered Ambassador Robertson. Meeting Dante's gaze again, he pointed at him. "We'll talk." Then he strode over with Luther and met the ambassador.

Dante speared Brick with a glower but did not trust himself to speak. He should probably plant his backside in a chair before he went after the big guy.

"So," Dade said, still focused on flying the drone, "this kiss . . . on a scale of one—being henpeck—and ten, being—"

Brick smacked the guy's head.

"What? Too soon?" Dade sniggered.

Dante rotated and planted himself in a chair. Elbows on his knees, he rubbed his knuckles. They were here running their mouths, and Mick was out there . . . in the hands of violent terrorists.

Do not let her die. Not because of me.

Pike and Luther talked with the ambassador and another man off to the side. And that served Dante fine, saved him from facing the ambassador, Mick's boss. Last thing he needed was another disappointed expression or more condemnation.

Screams replayed in his mind like a tormenting B-movie—the

terror in her blue eyes; blonde hair whipping like a halo around her face; her soft touch as she strained for safety, seconds before being wrenched away.

"Dante!" The terror of her shriek tore at him even now.

Breath coming in jagged chunks, he punched to his feet and paced away from the others. *I failed her. I freakin' failed her.*

"Listen up," Pike called across the hangar as he walked the ambassador and the other guy—wasn't that dude at the dinner?—over to them.

Ambassador Robertson wore a sharp business suit. Classy, yet strong. That grim set of her jaw and eyes that looked like they could cut stone set the stage for this group chat. "Thank you," she said, lasering in on Dante, "for all you did to save Secretary of State Derriscort and his daughter. The United States came very close to losing a great man and patriot. The surgery was successful. While stable, he is still critical and remains in ICU. We will soon transport both him and Catalina back to the States."

Whoop-dee-freakin'-do. Rich politician was still alive because he was a priority. Whereas McKenna . . .

That was not a fair assessment, but it rankled him all the same that the SecState was safe and secure while Mick was out there. Maybe dead.

The thought pushed him away.

"I am told, Mr. Riddell," the ambassador called, "that you were integral in ensuring all passengers were saved. You found the SecState, who'd been thrown out of the chopper."

Turn around. Be nice. He angled to the side but just could not make the full circle. "Doing my job, ma'am. That's all."

The *clip-clip-clip* of her shoes echoed across the hangar, delivering the ambassador to his side. She touched his arm.

He glanced at the scrape down his forearm that he'd gotten trying to stop the kidnapping. Then her fingers.

"Thank you," she said quietly, "for what you did trying to save McKenna."

His heart jarred in his chest at the mention of her name.

"She means a lot to me," the ambassador said, her words thick with emotion.

Dante eyed her. Considered her, realized she really meant that. He bobbed his head. "Same, ma'am."

The ambassador sniffed, tears in her eyes as she held something out to him. "She had this at her desk. I thought . . ." She stuffed it at him and cleared her throat. "I wanted you to have it."

Dante glanced down and found a framed photo. Oh man. That tight band around his chest—the one cutting into his conscience and moral compass—tightened a fraction as he stared at the photo from ten years ago, after he'd graduated Airborne school. She'd been so jealous that he got to jump out of planes that he and Dillon had gone in on a birthday gift for her—a skydiving lesson. The photo had the three of them, geared up, and the biggest smile on Mick's face. Fearless. Dauntless. Beautiful.

For the first time, he noticed the way she leaned into him in the photo. How had he been blind to that all these years? He hadn't. He'd just pushed back, not wanting to ruin a perfectly good friendship. Not wanting her to realize he didn't measure up.

"She talked about you a lot."

Stupid eyes blurred. Dante looked up and away, swallowing hard. Breathing heavier. Harder to pull in O_2.

The ambassador touched his arm again. "I know you'll find her and bring her back."

He cut his gaze to her, jaw tight. "Or die trying, ma'am."

"There's an active threat against the SecState," Pike announced behind them, "so, Crow, Brick, go with the ambassador as tactical support to the security team."

"Good copy, Chief," Brick said with a nod.

Dante still stared at the photo, memorizing her irrepressible smile. Infectious laughter. Vibrant, she buoyed everyone around her. And now she could die . . .

Why had he made her go into the bay? Should've kept her close. "Atlas."

He flinched at his callsign, the way Pike snapped at him. Straightening, he came to parade rest without thinking and swung his gaze around. "Chief?"

"I said her dad needs to be notified."

Oh snap. A wall of dread slammed into him at the idea of calling Uncle Colton. *He'll kill me. Then Pops will resurrect me and kill me again.* "Right . . ."

"The ambassador will call Mr. Neeley. I thought—"

"No." Dante twitched toward the brown-haired ambassador, who seemed to like him. He hoped to tap on that reserve. "Respectfully, ma'am, I should be the one to talk to him." And then likely report to his next duty station six feet under. "This is on me. I need to do it. Our families are close."

Warily, the petite ambassador looked between them.

"You sure?" the chief asked, hands on his tactical belt.

"One hundred percent." Head cleared, Dante did not want someone who wasn't intimately connected to Mick delivering that news to the family. "She'd want me to do it, and I owe it to her. To him."

Pike gave a slow nod, one that carried more meaning in that simple gesture than could've been spoken in an hour-long lecture. There was approval, pride, confirmation. Affirmation.

Then it struck Dante—"I don't have the number."

"We do," Ambassador Robertson offered. "Back at the embassy."

"Perfect," Pike said. "Atlas will go with you to make the call. We'll follow and get those files you told me about outside." He gave another nod to Dante. "I'll see you there. Keep your phone close."

"Understood." Dante trailed the ambassador and the other dude to the car, then climbed in the back with her.

"Oh, you know Asher, don't you?" Ambassador Robertson indicated to the guy who took the front passenger seat.

Light-brown hair trimmed short, bro extended a hand over the back of the seat. "Asher Bøhn."

"Atlas."

"Wait." Bøhn shifted to face the rear seats. "You were at the dinner."

Dante wondered what his point was.

"McKenna introduced you as Mr. Homer." His brow rippled, the connection between Homer and Atlas lost on him.

Guess they didn't grow all of them smart for this job at the embassy.

But Mick had known. Right off the bat, though he'd had to correct her that he preferred Hesiod's Atlas. "In Homer's *Odyssey*, Atlas was a marine creature."

"Mm-hmm, and were you not a SEAL?"

Chest tightening at the memory of Mick's words, Dante fisted his hand. Furious with himself for losing her. For letting terrorists get hold of her.

He noticed the tension and exchanged glances in the car. Must've missed something. Did not care. Not with Mick missing. The car slid through the embassy's security gate without issue and rolled around to the front portico. When they exited the armored sedan, he followed suit and entered the building. They led him to a secure room and gave him the number.

"Do you need anything else?" Asher asked. "McKenna and I used to—"

"I'm good." Dante gave the dude a look.

Something slid through the sharp angles and prep-school pretty-boy face. "Okay . . ." Bøhn backed up, then stepped out and closed the door.

Dante drew out his secure SAT phone. This had to be handled delicately. Didn't want Uncle Colton alone when this news came.

He should call Pop first. He swallowed hard and lifted it. *He's going to kill me.* He punched in the number, nerves drumming as he waited for the call to connect.

Brrrt-brrrrt. The drill of the ringing with that international call sound felt like it was boring through his chest. He pinched the bridge of his nose.

"Go for Riddell."

Dante choked. Forced himself to chug air. *Speak, fool!*

"Hello?"

"Pop."

The unnaturally long pause felt as if all heaven and earth held its breath. "What's wrong?"

Dante couldn't catch a clean breath. His eyes slid shut. "I . . ." He swallowed hard. "I need you to go to Uncle Colton's and call me when you get there."

Another long pause, one filled with clear understanding. Pop had been an operator long enough. "Dante . . ." That was the sound of grief, pleading for this not to be what it sounded like.

"Please. Go to the ranch. Call me when you get there."

FOURTEEN

Leesburg, Virginia

CRUSHING THE PHONE IN HIS RIGHT HAND, Griffin leaned heavily on the counter. The drumming in his chest had nothing on what he'd do to Dante if McKenna Neeley was dead.

A hand slid along his back. "What is it?"

At his wife's leaden concern, Griffin turned and crushed Kazi into his arms, pressing his face into her shoulder. "Nothing good," he breathed. Lifting his head, he straightened, but the portent of death that hovered in his mind pushed him back against the island.

"Who was that?"

He held her gaze. "Dante."

Confusion rippled through her expression. "I don't understand."

"He . . . he's been on an op with Omen. In Armenia." Griffin knew BabyGirl was smart as a whip; she'd figure it out. "He asked me to go to the ranch."

Now her green eyes turned to saucers as she drew in a breath and shrank back. "Oh no . . ." She shook her head.

"First Max, now . . ." He roughed his hands over his face. "I can't do this, Kaz. I cannot go up there and tell Cowboy his girl is dead."

Kazi caught his arms. "That's not what Dante asked you to do." Steady and earnest, she held his gaze. "Right?"

Hand over his aching chest, Griffin struggled. "They're family, Kaz. She's like our daughter." A wave of grief threatened to drown him. "One of the kids . . ." He fisted a hand to his mouth. "God Almighty, please . . ."

"Hey." She straightened, lifting her chin. "What did Dante say?"

He fought the squall of emotions. Cleared his mind. Thought back to the call. "To go to the ranch. Call when I get there."

Determination carved a line through her expression, driving her emotion from her focus. "Then that's what we do."

"Right." Man, he was out of practice. He nodded and pushed off the counter, the weight on his chest like an anchor. "Oh." He glanced to the living room. "Lyric . . ." He still had his girl, but Cowboy . . . How was this happening? Why . . . ?

Kazi strode to him and framed his face with her hands. "G."

His gaze locked onto hers, hauling his brain out of warp speed.

"Don't go there. Obviously, this is not good, but I think Dante would've told you if she were gone."

His heart careened into her words. He wanted to believe that.

"And besides, if she were, it would not be Dante calling. It'd be someone official."

"Right. Sure." But he knew it wasn't true. If Dante had been there when it happened, he'd call, SOP be cursed. They were family. They looked out for each other.

"And Lyric is at cheer camp this week, remember?"

"Right." He was a broken record.

She jingled the keys and cocked her head toward the door. "Come on."

In the Escalade, he again roughed a hand over his face. "You better be right."

"One of the best privileges of being your wife is that I'm rarely wrong."

"True," he sniffed with a near-smile. "True, BabyGirl." He caught her hand and kissed the back of it. Then he put the truck in Reverse. But his heart was heavy, recalling the weight in Dante's voice. The tightness of his words. "I'm glad you're going with me. I can't do this without you."

"Like you said—we're family. And while Piper did not birth McKenna, she raised her. This is going to destroy both of them."

"All of us," Griffin corrected, wiping a lone tear as he thought of the pipsqueak and her bubbly laughter. "All of us."

━━━━━ • ━━━━━

Lucketts, Virginia

Thumb and tall finger in his mouth, Colton let out a shrieking whistle. "That's it!" he shouted, cheering on his Sophia.

"She has your way with them," Piper said, grinning big.

"Bring it on in, Soph," he called, waving his eighteen-year-old daughter over.

Trotting around the training yard in a victory lap, Sophia looked natural up there. She guided the stallion over to the side gates with a broad smile that made his heart soar. "That was the best yet! Cash didn't hit a single rail!"

About time—the stallion had an excellent jump pedigree and had cost him a small fortune, but seeing that smile on his youngest made it worth it.

"I'm ready—excited!"

Colton caught the reins to steady the stallion and patted Sophia's leg. "Told you a little more practice and you'd nail it. Now you're ready for trials next week."

"And your new boots came in," Piper said as she trudged up to them.

Arm around his wife, Colton led his daughter and Cash toward the barn. "A few more days running the rails and it'll be old hat.

You'll both be so familiar with it, that muscle memory will carry you through the competition."

Sophia grinned big. "It's taken so long to get to here."

"And next week, we pack up and head down to Lexington for—"

"Look! It's Uncle G!"

Colton glanced to the left, where a shiny black Escalade wound its way down the mile-long country road to the house. "Did I forget about a dinner?"

"Not unless we both forgot," Piper said, frowning at the incoming arrivals. "Maybe they just want to visit. Friends do that, you know."

He smirked and planted a kiss on her temple. "I'll have to take your word for it. Why leave the ranch when I have all the beauty I can handle here?"

Clap!

His gaze hit the screened-in porch as Spencer stalked across it, boots thudding hard.

That boy had a burr the size of Texas under his saddle. "Spence, where you going?"

His son stopped short, shooting them a look. Clearly hadn't expected them to be so close to the house.

"C'mon, Sophia," Piper said, taking the rein and giving Colton a meaningful look that said *take care of it.* "Let me help you get Cash into the stall so you can brush him down."

"Believe I asked you a question, son," Colton said, keeping his posture loose so he didn't set off the hotheaded kid.

"Out," Spencer barked, scowling. Hands fisted. Ready for a brawl.

A dozen long strides carried Colton to his son. "You're still grounded."

"Oh, c'mon! It's been three weeks!"

Colton planted a boot on a step, tilted his Cattle Baron back, and eyed Spencer around the sunlight streaking through the trees. "Which means you still have a week to go."

"That's insane! All I did—"

"Was defy the rules."

Dark hair framed green eyes that roiled with frustration. "Your rules are stupid!"

"Could be," Colton held his ground, undeterred. Determined to make sure his son finished his senior year and launched into life strong. "But they're my rules. You live here, so the rules are to be obeyed."

Spencer stomped down the steps, right in front of Colton, and stormed past him.

Or tried.

Colton caught the pup by the scruff of his neck. Hauled him back up the steps.

"Ow! Dad, let go!"

Even as he noticed the Escalade pulling up the drive, Colton opened the door and thrust Spencer inside. "To your room. If you come out, I'll add a week."

"You kidding me?" Face red, Spence whipped around. Pounded two steps away, then jerked back. "I hate you!"

"And I love you. Now"—Colton motioned to the stairs—"go."

"Ugh!"

Dawg. That boy had more fire in him than a bonfire. *God, help me.*

"Hi, you two!" Piper returned and came up alongside him.

Colton turned and saw Griffin's stiff expression. Must've seen the showdown with Spencer. "Sometimes that boy seems more like Max than me." He sniffed, but . . .

"What's going on?" Piper asked, her smile wavering.

Colton's gut clenched. *Something's wrong.* "Legend." Old habits died hard, and there was something about the big guy's expression that put Colton back in operator mode.

Griffin gave him an aggrieved look. "We should go inside. Sit down."

Obstinance wasn't in his particular skill set except when Colton was being handled. What . . . ? What could he . . . ? "Is Dante okay?"

Head angling to the side in a slow bob, Griffin exhaled heavily.

Colton watched in slow motion as Kazi rushed to Piper and hugged her.

A sniper round traveling at 940 feet per second would reach its target in roughly seven seconds. It took twice that for understanding to hit Colton. "McKenna," he breathed, his gaze arcing back to his buddy, who stood there, tears on his face. "No." Head shaking, he backed up a step. "*No!*" The porch stairs clipped his legs. He went down hard but didn't feel it. A howl of agony dislodged from his chest with a choked sob.

"Daddy?"

For a half second, he thought it was McKenna, but Sophia came rushing around the porch and clung to him.

"Let's go inside," Griffin said, pulling him upright. Bracing him.

Horror lanced that pride-puffed chest he'd had five minutes ago. "Tell me! Tell me she's not dead."

Griffin trailed him inside. "Don't know. Dante asked me to come here and call him."

Piper whirled around and dropped onto the leather couch, crying freely as Kazi rubbed her back.

"Do it." Colton wouldn't sit down. Couldn't. He wanted to hurt someone.

Griffin lifted his phone. Hit the call button, then the speaker icon.

"Hello." Was that Dante? Didn't sound like him.

"We're here," Griffin said, his voice hoarse.

Colton stared at the phone. "Dante, what's happened?"

"I'm so sorry, sir." Dante's voice cracked.

Colton pivoted to the mantel. Braced a hand on it, his heart galloping right off a cliff of despair. *Oh dear Lord, help me. She's gone. Someone killed my sweet girl.*

"Son, tell us everything," Griffin instructed, his words cold, sharp.

Dante cleared his throat. "I, um, I'm limited in what I can say over the phone, but I was with McKenna when she was taken."

"Taken?" Colton jerked toward the phone cradled in Legend's hand, hope kindling in that dark well that had stolen over his life. "What do you mean, 'taken'?" Dare he hope she was still alive?

"Unfriendly troops attacked our location and took her. I tried, Uncle Colton. I tried to stop them, but they . . ." Sniffling came through the speaker, then he cleared his throat again. "We're looking for her. We'll find her. I swear it."

"McKenna was alive when they took her?"

"Yessir."

"Something happened to Mickey?" They all turned toward the voice—Spencer stood in front of Sophia in the hall, their young faces pale and taut.

Piper rose and went to them both, wrapping them in a hug.

"Sirs," intruded another voice. "This is Pike Auberon with Omen Tactical. We've just been given the green light to bring in every resource we can to locate and bring her home."

Griffin's gaze slammed into Colton's. Hope kindled between them, like flint on a sparking stone. Two operators of the same mind. Same skill set. Their voices rang out in unison, "We're on our way."

FIFTEEN

Yerevan, Armenia

DANTE ENDED THE CALL, STARING AT THE phone. *Can't believe he didn't chew me out.*

"Were they serious?" Pike asked, gray eyes intense beneath his short crop. "About coming?"

"They lived and breathed combat for over two decades and were some of the best," Dante said with a slow nod. "It's what they do. So . . . yeah, pretty sure."

"I'm well aware of Nightshade's reputation. But they've been out of commission for . . . a while." The chief held his gaze, jaw clenching beneath his beard. "Any way to stop them?"

Dante sniffed. "Feel free to call them back and try."

Pike said nothing for several long seconds. "We need to talk."

"Figured you'd say that."

"Brick told me what you did."

What, the kiss again? Better to wait it out than offer himself as a sacrificial lamb before the fire was even lit.

"You went into a hostile firefight," he said, his tone razor-sharp and accusatory. "Exposed yourself to danger and recruited your teammate to do the same. Pitted yourselves against impossible odds." He came around the table, closing in on Dante. "Took extreme measures—"

"Which were effective."

"—and as if that wasn't enough, you threw yourself at a moving vehicle. Again putting yourself in danger and risking the life of not only your teammate but the objective and—"

"I knew if they took her," he said, the drum of panic and fear warring with the conviction in his chest that he'd done the right thing, "the chances of getting her back alive were slim to none." What was with the dressing down? A preamble to firing him?

"And yet you did not care. You threw yourself into a deadly situation to effect an outcome you could not guarantee."

Why's he all up in my face? "Yes, sir."

"And you're okay with that?"

"I am!" His pulse rapid-fired and he worked to calm himself. This was it—Pike would cut him from the team. But then he wouldn't be able to help find Mick. That could not happen. "In fact, I'd do it again—and more, if it meant I had even a chance of saving her life. Nobody, not you, not even my pop, can tell me what I did was wrong. Regardless, it wasn't enough. And that will never be acceptable." Nostrils flaring, he stared down the chief, mustering the last of his courage. "Look, I know I'm through—just please, let me finish this before you cut me loose. I have to find Mick. I can't live with myself if I don't."

Pike's gaze narrowed. "You think I should cut you loose?"

Dante faltered. "I . . ." Defeat clung to him like refuse. "I would."

"Guess that's why I'm the chief and you're not." A ghost of a smile hit the hardened operator's face. "Tell me something, Atlas."

"Yeah, Chief?" Why did he sound like he'd entered a second puberty?

"How's it feel to shed your anal-retentive obsession with rules?"

Surprise froze him. With the way things had gone—the chopper, the SUV, the shop, Mick still missing—he wouldn't let himself relax. Didn't trust himself, didn't know what that question meant. Except this had to do with him letting go of his death grip on policy and procedures to find his passion.

"Rules serve a purpose. We don't serve them." Pike nodded. "You did good." He gripped Dante's neck and shook him. "Real good. That"—he inclined his head to him—"is what I have been waiting to happen since you signed on. I'm just disappointed I wasn't there to see it."

"I wish *you* had been there. She might not have been taken."

"Probably." Pike smirked again. "But this way, you saw what you were capable of."

Disbelief spiraled through Dante. "You serious? She's missing! I failed!"

"Failure is success in progress," Pike said, repeating his favorite saying, then cocked his head toward the door and gripped the knob. "Let's go find your girl."

In motion, Dante recalled the conversation with Mick. "Chief?" he called, his gaze on the offices beyond the saferoom. "McKenna had a theory about who was responsible . . ."

Stalling his exfil, Pike focused on him. "Go ahead."

"She had a coworker here, someone named Dalita. Mick said the woman tended to be in possession of intel before the embassy had it. She thought it strange that a local employee would know key things that were classified, often before even the ambassador or McKenna knew."

"Okay," Pike said, cocking his head to the side. "Let's chat up the ambassador."

Stalking past a row of desks that formed a main aisle between offices and cubicles, Dante trailed the chief down the hall toward the ambassador's office tucked in the corner. A general din of conversation rose to a dull roar that was somehow still quiet and professional.

Lights off, door closed, the ambassador's office looked shut down.

"Everything okay?" asked the tall guy from the hangar, Asher Bøhn.

"We need to talk with the ambassador," Pike stated flatly. "Any idea when she'll be back?"

Dante skated a glance around, searching for Mick's workstation. He located her nameplate on a desk to the right of the ambassador's office. He scanned the open-floor cubicles and finally hit on a familiar face—Dalita.

"Ambassador Robertson had a lunch appointment," Bøhn said as he reached for the phone on his desk. "I could call her—"

"Unnecessary," Pike said. "I'll reach out to her."

"Hey," Dante asked, angling toward the guy. Even though he didn't particularly like the pretty boy, he could still pull intel from him. "What do you know about Dalita?"

Light-brown eyebrows rose in surprise as Bøhn started to look in her direction but stopped himself. "She . . . uh, she's worked here for five years. After McKenna, she's next in line of seniority. Good worker."

Interesting that the guy relegated all the intel to her work ethic. What about her ethnicity? Family? Social life?

"Ah, good," came a woman's stern voice, "I was hoping you were still here." Up the long aisle, the ambassador clipped her way toward them, a satchel slung over her shoulder. "Come in." She waved them to follow as she used a fingerprint pad and keys to access her office. Lights flared on of their own accord as she moved to the credenza behind her desk, secured her purse and satchel, then turned to them. "Come, come. Shut the door."

Dante entered behind the chief and felt the presence of the consular officer behind him.

"Thank you, Asher," she said, her tone polite but crisp as she shut the junior officer out of the conversation. "I'll be with you shortly."

Hands on her hips, she waited for Bøhn to shut the door. Once it clicked shut, she drove her gaze to them. "There is certainly a lot of Brass breathing down my neck over McKenna's kidnapping. I had to leave my meeting with the prime minister early because my phone was blowing up with messages."

Dante looked to Pike, then back to the ambassador.

Her eyes glinted as she met his gaze. "Apparently, you come from royal military stock, young man."

He felt chagrined.

Pike clasped a hand over the other fist, classic sign of annoyance at being ignored.

"Oh, don't get all ruffled, Chief Auberon. We all come after some greater name or hero," she said with a sigh. "I'm just relieved to have more assets to help find her."

"We've been green-lit to use whatever's necessary to ensure her safe return," Pike stated.

"And that means sixty-year-old gray-haired operators." She smiled.

"Fifty-something," Dante corrected, shifting when they both eyed him speculatively. "Pop's kind of uptight about that."

"Well." Her smile broadened, then slipped, a crease of concern forming between her brows. "Now, you both seemed rather intent when I came up the hall. Was there something . . . ?"

Pike adjusted his stance. "What do you know about the LE, Dalita?"

"Dalita?" Ambassador Robertson repeated, eyebrows vanishing beneath her bangs. "You can't . . ." Mouth agape, she then swallowed the objection, blinking several times as she collected herself. "Yes, well, we all know how people in our inner circles can surprise us, don't we?" She sat back and rested her elbows on the arms of her chair. "Dalita Apkarian is twenty-four"—her eyes narrowed in thought—"no, twenty-five. Half Armenian, half Azerbaijani.

She's lived in Yerevan most of her life, though she has family in the Nagorno-Karabakh region."

Dante understood that Apkarian's ethnicity and having family in the NK gave her plenty of reason to betray Armenia and want to stop the SecState from facilitating the peace treaty.

Robertson's frown deepened. "Why? What's this about?"

After Pike nodded, instructing him to share what he knew, Dante straightened in his chair. "McKenna voiced concerns over Dalita's 'all-too-accurate intel.' She said the LE often had intel on situations that even you did not yet have. Ma'am."

Concern tweaked Robertson's mouth, eyes darting over her desk, then out the window. Having one of her top assets come under suspicion couldn't be easy, and he gave her the space to work it out and process the potential betrayal.

Pike wasn't as patient or forbearing. He cocked his head at the ambassador. "That true?"

"I suppose it is," Robertson said reluctantly. "Dalita is very adept at her job. She has this uncanny knack for reading people and situations. As a local, she has connections that are likely filling gaps I can't due to security clearance limitations."

"Reading people and reading intel are very different," Pike said. "If she is getting information from outside this agency, then the possibility exists that she may be sharing sensitive intel from this agency with said contact."

The ambassador exhaled heavily. "I knew things were going too smoothly."

"Ma'am?"

She sniffed a laugh and flicked her fingers dismissively. "Just with the two countries exhibiting genuine interest in finally coming together to sign a treaty that benefits both parties, for my staff to be so strong and good, involved . . ." She shrugged, then considered the chief gravely. "You're right—there's cause for concern." She drew forward and pressed a button on her phone, activating the speaker.

"Security desk," squawked a voice.

"Jeff, I'm afraid I'm going to need a unit to take an employee into custody."

"Be right up, ma'am."

Unknown Location

Wakened in the dead of night—at least, it seemed dead—by beeping forklifts and creaking axles, McKenna lifted her head from the bar she'd fallen asleep on again. The bitter cold and the wound in her thigh fought her ability to find REM.

A whirring noise grew closer . . . closer . . .

What was going on?

The cage jarred violently, and McKenna swung out her hands to brace herself. Metal groaned against metal. Through the torn tarp, she saw the giant teeth of a forklift ramming up under her cage. It jerked the steel trap and hoisted it up . . . up . . . up. She steadied herself, noting the tarp rustling hard beneath a strong, icy wind. Shivering, she watched through the bottom slats, trying to make sense of what was happening.

They wheeled around and she yelped, half expecting the cage to slide off or careen to the ground. But it didn't. A second later, they were jouncing along at a steady clip across the dark night spliced by headlamps of several vehicles. The forklift slowed and finally, the cage lowered. A clang rang through her prison, jarring her, then the jaws retracted. She wasn't on the ground . . .

Clanks and voices carried through the night around her, dirt crunching and brakes squeaking.

THUNK!

The resounding noise pulled her attention toward the rear, the same direction where the forklift had been. Through the tiny slit, she struggled to make sense of what she saw. Brown and large, two pieces of wood swung in to block her view.

Doors! They'd put her cage in a box truck! A bolt secured the doors. She anticipated the truck leaving, but it remained in place long enough for her to drift off, only to be jolted awake when the truck finally lurched into motion. The violent movement thumped her head and made her stomach churn as they took a slow, lumbering pace, like they were picking their way over uneven terrain. The truck found a steady, smoother pace, awakening a keen awareness that she was getting farther and farther from Dante. From safety.

Scared, alone, she sat in the cage, jouncing and rocking. On the brink of tears and unable to take much more, she breathed a prayer of thanks that she was alive still and pleading that God would help someone find her. Dante . . .

How would he? There was no way for him to know where to look, which direction they'd taken her. She didn't even know! Though she wanted to cry, McKenna couldn't. She was too tired. Too cold. In too much pain. And her leg was radiating an unusual warmth—likely infection.

But at least one part of her body was warm.

It wasn't funny but she laughed. Too much. Until the laughter turned to tears. Dry tears. Because she could not remember the last time she'd had anything to eat or drink. They hadn't even let her out to use the bathroom, forcing her to soil herself.

I'm going to die here. I'll miss seeing Sophia and Spencer graduate. I will never know if Dillon is right and his dad is alive. I won't get to tell Dante I love him.

A jolt rang through the truck as it swung her aside.

Thud, crack! Groaaan.

A sudden drop slammed her into the bars. Her hand rang with pain. But the truck leveled out and quiet descended as the ride once again smoothed. Soon, they hit a pretty good speed—a highway?—that lulled her to sleep.

She did not know how long she'd been out when a swift slowing changed the rhythm, plucking her from slumber. A violent jounce pitched her about. Whacked her head against the bars. The top. Thudded against her backside—a painful reminder of the wound Brick had stitched—and warned her they'd again left the main road. The painful jostling went on for way too long, to the point she just gave up hope that it'd end. No use expending tears on this.

Once they stopped, the smell of petrol wafted through the truck. Getting gas. She shouted to no avail before they were in motion again. It was a lost cause.

Though she wanted to shout and rail at God, she would probably just scrape her throat raw. She fell asleep a few times, no idea how long each nap lasted. Losing all sense of time, she whimpered. Thought again about railing at God. At anyone. Another lost cause. At first, she'd let herself scream, but that just made her head throb. So the next time, when frustration and fear formed that volatile cocktail, she just told herself to sleep. What good would railing do? She remembered once telling Daddy she'd wanted to quit, and he'd asked her, "What's there to quit to?" This was the same. Giving up didn't change the situation.

"Oh, Daddy," she whimpered, trying to brace herself with blood-caked hands. "I came out here to help people . . ." And to run away from the heartbreak of Dante.

Except he'd come to her this time.

Kissed her.

Now she would die.

But hey, at least one bucket wish had been fulfilled.

Shaking off the ridiculousness, she pushed her thoughts to that moment in the abandoned shop. When she'd asked him what to think. How he'd rushed at her. Crushed her against himself and kissed the ever-loving daylights out of her.

Smiling at the memory, she sighed. It'd been divine. The way he'd held her so tight. Kissed her. Deeply. Passionately. It'd been everything she'd dreamed of—and more!

The truck slowed . . . slowed . . . then swung left. McKenna looked there, though she couldn't see anything because of the dark. Was that from a tarp or because it was night? She had no idea how long they'd traveled—so she trained her ears on the noises around her. Heard thumps against the box truck and guessed it to be someone hitting it. Then they were backing up . . . backing . . .

Another thud against the hull.

Clangs that sounded like doors being unlatched reverberated through the bed of the truck and her cage. She peered through the hole, silently begging for a glimpse of light.

The doors opened and the elevated prongs of a forklift drove at her cage. She yelped again as the giant teeth stabbed beneath the pan. Jerked her up and back violently. She canted to the side, somehow hitting her leg.

Pain sluiced through her. McKenna cried out, whimpering. But her desperate need for survival—to escape—ordered her to shut up and pay attention, check her surroundings. Catch as much intel as she could. Head on a swivel, as Daddy would say. She pressed her eye to the steel bars, trying to catch sight of anything around the flapping tarp. Dim lights peppered the area. She spotted a person. An old truck. A few small structures. In the distance . . . land. Lots and lots of it—rolling hills, deep valleys.

The forklift swung around completely, pitching her into the left wall, steel rattling pain up her arm and into her shoulder.

Fed up with feeling like a sardine in a can, she growled and steadied herself. A forward thrust of the forklift caused her to tense, her wound screaming in protest. But she gritted her teeth and focused. Through the small hole, she could see they were moving her toward a dark, gaping maw—a warehouse, if the steel crossbeams were any indication. She stiffened as they lowered her cage to the ground.

The steady tap of steps drawing closer made her still.

"Uh. *O qoxu nədir*?" a male voice said.

The *vrrp* of what seemed to be fingers dragging over the canvas made her draw back. Without warning, the cover ripped away.

Cold air swarmed into the crate as a man in black pants, tan shirt, and a thick dark jacket jumped aside, lifting his jacketed arm to shield his mouth and nose. "Ugh!" With his free arm, he waved over a woman. "Havva, *müdir gəlməmiş onu təmizləyin!*"

Humiliation acute, McKenna resented his accusation that she smelled, but relief rushed over her in two parts: one, he had ordered someone to clean up McKenna before some boss came, and two, the woman quickly crossed the warehouse to her. No idea who this boss was, but McKenna would be very glad not to smell like her own waste anymore. However, just washing her wasn't going to work because—

"*Ona təmiz paltar lazımdır*, Fazil," the woman—Havva, apparently—shouted at the man stalking away, saying new clothes were needed. "*Paltarları xarabdır!*"

When Fazil and Havva glanced at her, surprise and concern in their gazes, she ducked. Miiiight be better to pretend she only spoke English than to betray she knew their language. Could she get intel out of them if she did? Make this fiasco worth it? Working in the consular offices, she often found it benefited her to let people assume she was an ignorant American. Some were quite brazen in what they said directly beneath her nose, assuming she couldn't understand.

"*Sonra bunu et!*" Fazil barked, dismissing her with a flick of his hand. "*Tələsin!*"

And hurry Havva did. The short woman rushed out of the warehouse and headed to the left. Hadn't that been where the truck had come in from? So that would be the direction to the entrance of this . . . complex—compound? The structures outside were smaller, more like houses than shops. However, she didn't know many neighborhoods with a giant warehouse.

This must be some kind of work compound. Maybe the small structures were offices or specialty buildings? Complete guesswork. McKenna just knew one thing for certain—she had to escape. Before the boss showed up would be best.

So, it was time to get the lay of the land by studying her new holding place. Definitely a warehouse with black hard-side crates that were at least three or four feet tall each and sat like sentries along the back wall. They had deposited her cage along the northern side, near massive metal accordion-style doors that came together in the middle. A standard door bisected the long south facade—her left. Behind her, the top of what appeared to be a walled-in section peeked out from a dozen or so wood boxes that were roughly three feet high and four or five feet long. The size wouldn't have been an obstacle had they not been so close to her cage. But six of them stacked atop one another effectively blocked her view of whatever was beyond it.

Shouts pulled her gaze to the accordion doors, where two men hustled in, carrying two more long boxes between them. Both men were dark-haired, wearing jeans and jackets. One shot her a disgusted look.

Yeah, I know I'm aromatic. No need to rub it in.

They set the new crates behind her cage, making yet another grimace in her direction. But then the younger leaned closer to the older man and whispered conspiratorially about the crates. Older glanced to the accordion doors, as if to be sure they weren't heard.

Amid their whispers came a loud *crack* that startled her. Stifling her impulse to look in that direction, she listened harder. When she heard something about guns, she stole a peek. The boxes behind her were weapons! One had been opened—that must've been the loud crack she'd heard. Her heart pittered at the sight of a long-range rifle. She angled for a better view, wondering what kind it was.

Older pulled out another weapon, and together, the two stared down sights, checking the bolt action and internal magazines of—

Oh, be still my sharpshooting heart—a Mosin-Nagant sniper rifle! They drew out a few stripper clips and loaded a couple rounds. But Younger lost interest when he spotted something else. He nudged aside a lid and withdrew a Kalashnikov.

Pfft. Flashy but unreliable. Lacked sophistication.

Older abandoned the sniper rifle, then he and Younger gathered magazines for the assault rifle. They were too busy ogling the Kalashnikov to care what McKenna—or the Mosin-Nagant—was doing. The poor thing, all alone and neglected, must've known it wasn't loved because it began a slow slide along the crate it'd been propped against, silently slipping to the front, where it came to a quiet stop with a clink against her cage.

Breath caught, she stole a glance at the two men. Still preoccupied with weapons that had neither loyalty nor class.

Okay, Old Faithful—as Dante would say, I got you.

She worked to catch the edge of the tarp that had been thrown across the top of her cage. The slats were just wide enough for her fingers to catch the corner of the black canvas. Watching the two, she slowly drew the tarp down . . . down . . . down. It blocked more than half of her ability to see the back of the warehouse and—more importantly—the rifle.

Now. To figure out how—

A flurry of words flew at her from the front.

McKenna sucked in a breath and flinched in that direction.

The short, stout Havva strode in from outside, armed with a basket filled with clothes and a towel. If the woman was attentive, she'd spot the rifle leaning against the crate, and Havva had been the one who'd noticed she needed new clothes . . .

God, please blind her to the rifle. Blind them all.

McKenna had no idea how to retrieve the rifle once out of the crate. But it felt like a solid-gold lifeline. She adjusted the way she sat to hopefully block as much as she could.

Keys rattled as Havva bent and unlocked the bolt, riveting McKenna's attention. This was the first time she'd seen someone work the locking mechanism. Reminded her of Saucy's paddock bolt—up and over. Not complicated. Except for the key part.

Havva tossed in handcuffs, which hit McKenna's leg, and ordered her to put them on.

Slowly, McKenna worked them over her wrists, then locked them. "My leg," she said in English, pointing to the bloody wound. Surreptitiously, she glanced back and noticed the men were gone. Would it be possible . . . She eyed the woman and studied her size. Could McKenna overpower her?

Havva waved her out and shifted aside, revealing two armed guards behind her.

Okay, so no violent overthrow. At least, not on McKenna's part. She'd kind of figured she'd have to use stealth to escape anyway. Just . . . no idea how or when.

Havva again demanded she move faster.

Guarding her wound, McKenna gently unfolded her legs, which protested with spasms and aches that made her struggle. Even her arms protested, threatening to collapse as she levered her body out of confinement. She hoisted her backside over the lip of the crate.

Without warning, hands clamped her legs and yanked her forward, collapsing her arms and dropping her hard against the cage floor. A whack against the back of her skull made her yelp, but the momentum did not slow. Her skull struck the steel lip, then bounced on the concrete as she was hauled onward. Dots sprinkled across her vision.

Then he was bending over her—the Russian boss—with a mile-long sneer.

Oh no, what if he noticed the rifle? Flat on her back, head and neck throbbing, McKenna nearly choked on her own oxygen as she stared up into his cruel, dark eyes.

"Get up."

She swallowed, whispering a desperate prayer that he would not see the weapon, because she knew without a doubt he'd use it on her.

He knelt, annoyance in every clipped move—the stretch of his jaw, the cocking of his head, the stab of his hand when he grabbed a fistful of her hair. Jerked her face closer to his. "You stink, American."

Feeling's mutual. Scalp stinging from his grip, she refused to cower or whimper.

"My friend here, Havva," he said in his stilted English wrapped in that Russian accent, "will wash you. Give you clothes. You will not give her trouble, *da?*"

Nostrils flaring, McKenna wanted to tell him she had never given anyone trouble. But he probably wouldn't appr—

White-hot fire seared through her leg as he pressed his thumb into the wound.

"Augh!!" Head back, McKenna screamed, reaching to stop the agony.

"No trouble, *da?*"

Tears streaming down her face, feeling the bile rising in her throat from the excruciating pain, she yielded with a nod.

The boss must've seen her chest and throat heave, because he pitched her down, and McKenna turned to the side just in time to vomit. But nothing came up. Dry heaves.

"Get her cleaned up and fed," he said, then strode away, talking to someone on speakerphone. "It's a bad connection . . . but it's done, *da?*"

"Yeah," came a warbled voice, "just as you wanted."

"Good, because if the Americans live, you will have a very big problem."

"They won't make it out of the valley."

Shuddering from so many factors—exhaustion, pain, the cold, weakness—she lay on the ground, sniffling, her mind railing at the threat to the Americans. Which had to be Dante, right? Or . . . the ambassador? Secretary of state?

Likely any and all witnesses. Including her.

The two guards hoisted her up and hauled her to the back of the warehouse, out a small door she hadn't been able to see from the cage, and across a yard.

Self-preservation told her to look around. Check her surroundings. No concrete out here—just hard-packed earth covered in snow. Industrial bricks encircled the compound, interrupted only by two gatehouses and a small door that whipped in the winter wind.

Crack! Thwap!

The men jerked at the flapping door but then muttered curses and dragged her after the woman.

"Scared as field mice," Havva taunted them as she opened a door into the building, which turned out to be showers. Concrete walls three feet deep divided the six stalls. No curtains.

The guards dumped McKenna on the floor, and she barely had time to shove out her cuffed hands to break her fall and shield her leg. Gripping her thigh, she whipped around to object to the abuse. But the guards were gone, the door shut tight, and Havva was setting up instruments on a side table. A long metal table braced the wall.

"Strip and shower," Havva ordered without looking at her.

Skating a nervous glance at the door, McKenna feared the guards returning. Or worse, the Russian.

Havva clapped at her. "Go, go! Or I will hurt you," she said in Armenian. The terse brow and firm set of her jaw warned she was not posturing.

Pulling herself up, cuffed hands impeding her, McKenna used

a half wall that blocked off three sinks for support. Upright, she hissed when her thigh throbbed violently. Nausea swirled. Even as she reached for the zipper of the suit, she realized the impossibility of complying with the orders with the cuffs on.

"I—"

Havva walked over with a ring of keys—the same ones that held the distinctive latch key for her cage. She chose a small one to free McKenna's hands. "Now—go! Hurry." She tossed the keyring on a medical tray, along with an array of instruments and bandages. She patted a stack of clothes that still had tags and plastic wrap, fresh from a store. "Once you are clean, get dressed." She shook a finger at her. "No pants yet. Fix wound first."

There was nothing for it. McKenna fumbled with the knobs on the shower, expecting the water to be cold, so she wanted to give it time to warm up. She also wanted to test whether the guards would return once they heard the water running. When nothing happened, she unbound the wound, wincing at the way it stuck to the injury, then stripped, cursing these people for the humiliation. When she stripped off the overalls, she saw the swollen, angry flesh with pus already sitting in the well of the wound. *That is not good.* She groaned but forced herself into the water.

Which was ice cold.

She gasped but made quick work of using the bar of soap that smelled like a men's fragrance and scrubbed herself clean. Didn't care about her hair—she didn't want drenched hair in the freezing cold anyway. Trembling violently, McKenna took the fastest shower of her life.

When she hobbled out, Havva pitched a towel at her.

Humiliated, McKenna dried off and donned the undergarments, then threaded her arms into the thick wool sweater. Glorious warmth! Desperate for more body heat, she reached for the pants and bent to thread at least one leg in when she spied the keys on the tray. Glanced at the woman, busy laying out strips of gauze.

Would she notice?

McKenna stumbled, planting her hand right over the keys as she pretended to be catching herself.

Havva scowled over her shoulder. "No pants." She looked to the other side and patted the table. "On here."

Sliding the keys off the table, McKenna knew she had to get the distinctive cage key off. An entire key ring would be missed, but one key? Hopefully not. The cage had been left open, so they wouldn't need it to lock the deadbolt. That should buy time. But she had to work the key off . . .

Havva again slapped the table, her words terser this time, then a distinctive tearing sound rent the quiet of the showers as Havva tore a section of the coveralls. What . . . ?

Focus—keys! McKenna's gaze hit the toilets. Fake throwing up. She started fake-heaving and hobbled to the toilet, already working the key off the ring. The brown, broken toilet was beyond gross, but it was a means to an end. She made hurling noises that she hoped sounded real. Felt the last catch of the key and tugged it free, stuffed it into the sports bra, and clutched the keys tight. Spit into the toilet, then straightened, wiping her mouth.

Havva gave her a disgusted look and handed her a bottled water. "Wash your mouth. I won't have you smelling bad while I stitch your leg."

Accepting it, McKenna took a swig, swished, then spit it out in the sink. She hobbled back over and used the noise of dragging herself onto the table to hide the moment she returned the keys to the spot.

With more than a few strident words, Havva went to work. It wasn't a hospital, so there was no numbing medication, but there was a shot of morphine. And honestly, McKenna wasn't mad, even as she felt the pain, the exhaustion, and the world falling away into the dreamy, weightless abyss.

SIXTEEN

Yerevan, Armenia

TWO DAYS AND TWO DRONES DOWN.

"Augh!" Dante banged his fists on the table and turned from the Command center. Hands hooked over his head, he paced the special-use hangar. They had spent the last twenty-four hours sending drones, reaching out to forces in the field to see if they'd spotted anything. Scoured aerial footage from satellites. "How do we not have anything? They were AzerB military—they don't just vanish!"

"I'm with you—doesn't track." Pike smoothed a hand over his beard, the sign he was in deep thought, then he relocated to the wall map. Tapped a region in the south. "Best bet for them to meet with success would be to get over the border."

"Maybe they're already there," Brick suggested and lifted his hands in surrender. "I'm just saying . . ."

"Negative." Luther leaned back in his chair and dragged a hand across his bald head. "That many vehicles—we'd have sighted them. It's too far and too long for them to have made it there without being spotted."

"Agreed," Pike said.

"Hate not doing something," Dante muttered. Without somewhere to search, they could easily head in the wrong direction . . . but at least they'd be going somewhere—not sitting here while Mick was out there fighting for her life.

But I *should be fighting for her!*

"Don't we have anything?" Dante balked.

Tariq sniffed a laugh. "Only strange activity mentioned in Sector 12 was an old lady complaining about a box truck taking out the stone wall around her front yard."

Dante fought the urge to curse and instead chose to pray. He prowled over to the map they'd hung on the wall to make notes and track reports. *Last thing I need is her pop coming up in here to take me out.*

"Atlas."

He glanced at Pike, who nodded to the open hangar doors. Beyond it on the airstrip, a sleek white jet screeched onto the tarmac.

Brick eyed him. "You write your last will and testament?"

Failure and defeat gnawed at Dante as he pushed himself out to meet the plane taxiing up to the hangar. The door lowered, and a large shape filled the hatch.

Something rattled in Dante's chest at the sight of Pop and that "I been there, son" look.

Straightening his spine, Pop waited—gaze locked on him—as the stairs were lowered, then hustled down them amid the whining of the engines powering down.

"Pop—"

His father's shoulder swallowed the rest of the greeting as he pulled Dante into a hug. And just like that, Dante was seven years old all over again, Pop holding the shattered pieces of his dreams after he'd taken a baseball to the knee, ending his chance to play in the city league for the rest of the season.

"It's gonna be alright." Pop eased off, gripped the back of his head, and stared at Dante, whose screaming-red eyes no doubt betrayed all the sleep he'd missed and the tears that were once again threatening.

When Pop angled aside, Dante flinched to find Uncle Colton looming behind him, ruck in hand and grief in eyes that were trained on Dante, who told himself not to look away. Breaking eye contact would show weakness, the same weakness that caused him to fail Mick so egregiously. "I . . ." There just weren't words. Only one thing to say . . . "I'm sorry."

Uncle Colton stared at him for a long second. Then stepped nearer, glanced to the side, then down at Dante—at least, it felt like down, but he was pretty sure he had an inch or two on Mick's dad. As much a legend in the spec-ops community as Pop. Probably the quietest member of the infamous Nightshade, Colton Neeley held more wisdom, strength, and honor in his little finger than most men carried in their entire bloodline.

Expecting to be coldcocked or railed at, Dante stood silent and cowering beneath that penetrating blue gaze so like Mick's. He searched for anger but found only that steady, penetrating strength.

He should be pummeling him about now. Where was the anger? The sharp reprimand for being so negligent?

Uncle Colton's hand landed on Dante's shoulder, making him twitch visibly and his gut seize. His uncle gave a clap on his bicep and turned away. "Let's talk." Adjusting his Cattle Baron, he strode to the hangar, giving requisite introductory handshakes to the Omen team.

Pop glanced back and waited for Dante to fall in line, so he did. But another back slap startled him. He looked askance at—"Uncle Canyon. What—"

"Don't worry," Canyon "Midas" Metcalfe said. "Whatever damage Cowboy inflicts, this team medic can fix." He winked. "We got you covered."

Aw man . . .

Another man had exited the plane—John Dighton. He wasn't quite an uncle, but pretty close, since he was part of Nightshade. They exchanged nods and headed inside.

The drop in temperature when he stepped out of the sun into the shady shelter of the hangar sent a preternatural chill down his spine.

He followed the Nightshade team across the hangar to the tables on the far side. Brick came up behind Dante and unleashed a low whistle. "I do not envy you."

"Is this where we say we're praying for you?" Dade taunted.

Ignoring the sarcasm, Dante kept moving, a metallic taste glancing off his tongue. He swallowed and rubbed the back of his neck.

"Nice knowing you, Atlas," Luther taunted.

Bro, this was so messed up. He felt like he was going to the principal's office.

He forced himself not to slow or look around, but he sensed someone next to him. Dante felt his pulse skip a beat at the steadfastness in the chief's expression. He gave him a nod of appreciation but didn't slow.

Uncle Colton dropped his ruck against the wall.

With each additional step Dante took, someone fell away, until he alone reached the conference table where her pop stood, arms folded, stance squared.

Dude was not small.

"Walk me through it," Uncle Colton said as the Nightshade team arced around them, expressions serious, attention laser-focused, and grim determination carved into their weathered features.

Dante eyed and waited for the chief's clearance, since this mission had been classified. Once given the go-ahead, he plunged on. "Omen came to Yerevan as additional operational security for the SecState, whose daughter was working with a humanitarian aid organization in one of the villages an hour or so south. We came under attack—"

"Hold up." Uncle Colton drew something out of his thick jean jacket lined with wool and laid the item on the table between them. "I think you've skipped some details."

Dante furrowed his brow, wondering what he meant, then edged closer. A photo lay on the table—of Dante next to McKenna, who was all decked out and beautiful at the VIP dinner. Both of them laughing. "Where'd you get this?" he asked, picking it up. "Who sent it to you?"

"Is that relevant?" Uncle Colton asked, his entire posture like a coiled spring.

"No—yes. Maybe." Dante worked to recover from the shock of the photo, his heart constricting at seeing Mick so carefree. "We were at the dinner—"

"What. Dinner?"

Dante faltered at the tight words, again stealing a glance at the image of Mick. "Ambassador Robertson hosted a dinner for the Azerbaijani and Armenian Ministers of Foreign Affairs in the hopes of fostering the will to sign the treaty. Mick"—his heart tripped over using his nickname for her—"McKenna was in charge of planning and execution."

"And you're next to her, seated, not working perimeter or patrol because . . . ?"

"My call," Pike stated flatly from behind Dante. "SecState's detail picked up chatter about a possible attack. We tried to convince the ambassador to reschedule or cancel the dinner, but she refused—said it was too important that the two countries meet on generally neutral terms. They didn't want an unfriendly shooting up the gala, so they asked for someone plain-clothes in the middle of it. Because of his CQ and BJJ skills, I recommended Dante. Made sense since he already knew Miss Neeley."

"How was that made clear?" Uncle Colton asked.

Please do not tell him she hugged me. I want to live.

"Miss Neeley said their fathers worked together," Pike answered.

"And then there was the hug she gave Atlas when she first saw him," Brick said around a snicker.

I am going to kill him. Dante skewered the guy with a furious look, then refocused on Uncle Colton. "It—"

"A hug." Uncle Colton lasered Dante. "That right?"

"It was innocent," he said, maybe a little too fast. "She was handling the hotel for OTG when we showed up. She saw me and was surprised."

"What I'm not understanding," Uncle Colton said in a tone that felt like a dad reprimanding a punk youth, "is how a junior consular officer ends up on a tactical mission to a remote part of a country that has been experiencing heavy and constant conflict with not one but two countries."

"Robertson had a meeting with parliament," Pike said calmly, "so when the call from the SecState's daughter came in, insisting he visit the village she was working in, the ambassador demanded Miss Neeley go because of her familiarity with the region and her skill with multiple languages."

Pop nodded, pursing his lips, apparently accepting the logic. "So you go out there . . ."

Pike glanced at Dante, handing him the reins again.

"Yessir," Dante said. "We were out there a few hours with locals when we spotted a military convoy en route from the southeast. It's Azerbaijani military SOP to push into a town, destroy it, desecrate graves, effectively forcing people to flee and yield their city or town. We called for an aerial extraction of the VIPs, to include McKenna. But the troops shot down the chopper, critically injuring the SecState. We loaded back up in the vehicles and fought our way out of the village, our priority being the safety of the locals and the SecState, his daughter, and McKenna."

"How many vehicles?" Pop asked.

"Three."

"Which was my daughter in?" Uncle Colton asked.

"Mine," Dante said with a hard swallow. "Third. The terrorists were on us fast. Drove us off the road. Our SUV rolled down a hill."

"At that point," Pike put in, "we got separated. No way to get down to them without endangering the SecState and taking hours to circle back around to the valley town. Two vehicles were needed to get the SecState to a hospital—one transporting the Secretary, another to provide protection. We decided to separate. Atlas, Brick"—a nod to the burly guy—"and Miss Neeley would make their way to Yerevan, and once the SecState was secure, the rest of Omen would circle back and pick up the three."

"But that clearly did not happen, since my daughter was taken," Uncle Colton said, his expression darkening.

"Ice storm slowed us in getting the SecState to the nearest trauma hospital," Pike said. "Local hospital wasn't equipped with the necessary trauma doctors, and with the storm, no rescue flight could happen. So we were forced to push on to Yerevan."

"Brick, Mick, and I borrowed a car and managed to avoid the Azerbaijanis for a while until the car died, and we had to go to foot," Dante said, remembering every step. "Mick was . . . amazing. She never whined or complained. She warriored through. With the ice storm and dropping temps because of night, we had to take shelter," he said, nodding to Brick. "That's when he noticed McKenna had been hit."

Uncle Colton jerked visibly. "Hit? As in shot?"

"Yes, sir—apparently while we were fleeing the convoy. She hadn't felt it, and with her thick jacket, I never saw blood."

"We got her stitched up," Brick said in his gravelly voice. "After some rest, she was good to go so much that . . ." The big guy flinched and shot Dante a look.

The kiss. Holy Mother, would the guy never shut up? Silently,

Dante threatened violence and torture if the guy said one more word.

"What is that?" Uncle Colton pointed between Dante and Brick. "What aren't you saying?"

It took him a minute to gather his courage, but Dante knew it had to be said. And he might as well get it in the open before anyone else spoke up and got it wrong. "It's my fault," he said, owning the blame. "We were tired. Irritable. We argued—"

"*Who?*"

"Me and Mick. I don't even remember what it was about, but . . ." Dante couldn't bring himself to say it, that he kissed her, and then ticked her off . . . because his regret was overripe and rank.

"Give us the room," Uncle Colton said, moving around the table to stand in front of Dante as the others relocated to the side, Canyon and Dighton intensely studying the maps and intel. "Read me in."

Dante met the blue eyes so like Mick's. "I kissed her . . . then pushed her away when Brick came in on us." He swallowed that bucket of regret. "I hurt her, and she wouldn't talk to me after that." Finally, he braved his uncle's eyes. "When we got hit, I told her to hide in the bay." He swallowed—hard. "That's how the AzerBs got her. I screwed up and she paid for it."

Uncle Colton lasered in on him. "Mickey called home shortly after you got here. Know what she told me?"

Dante eyed him warily.

"'Dante didn't want anything to do with me.' So wanna fill me in on how you went from cold shoulder to hot and heavy with my daughter?"

Mind and heart racing, Dante scrambled for an answer. Anything that would justify how he'd treated her. "I . . . can't."

"So that kiss meant nothing?"

"No!"

"Just a thing to do while shacked up during a storm?"

"No, sir!" The answer crackled through the hangar.

"Then. What. Happened?"

"I . . . I've had . . . issues," Dante said, feeling like this was so wildly disconnected to what happened at the shop that he wasn't sure why he'd mentioned it. "I wanted to prove myself—to Pike, my dad—that I'm worth it."

"Worth what?"

"Believing in me, trusting me." He exhaled heavily. "Getting caught kissing Mick . . . I panicked. Brick is relentless. He would've told Pike, and I—"

"You were afraid you'd lose your contract."

Holy crud. It sounded so lame when put like that. "Yeah . . ." Dante lowered and shook his head. Covered his face. "I was stupid."

"Say it again," Uncle Colton said.

He faltered, looking at those familiar blue eyes. "I was stupid," he repeated, miserable. "She's the best thing that has ever hit my life. She has always seen me, the real me—not the one everyone else sees. I mean, she drives all of us crazy, acting like she's our mom, but she's . . . good. Pure. Amazing."

"You love her?"

Dante twitched, eyes snapping to Uncle Colton. "I . . . I don't know."

Uncle Colton tucked his chin and gave him a stern look. "It wasn't a question."

Frowning, Dante didn't understand. "I . . . I've only been with her a week—haven't seen her in years."

"You've been her friend for nearly two decades," Uncle Colton said. "Love doesn't need a time stamp for X number of days to be valid. And I'll tell you from firsthand experience, love often uses stealth tech to slip past our barriers and embed itself in our hearts. I know—much to my dismay—that it's always been in her heart for you."

That word—*dismay*—struck him center mass. Stirred up all

Dante's old demons and fears. "You don't think I'm good enough for her."

"Do you?"

Dante struggled to breathe as his mind fought for purchase on a solid answer. Instead, he weakly pushed out, "No . . ." He did not compare or measure up to the firestorm that was McKenna Neeley. "She's like white fire—deceptively hot."

"Wanna try that again before I make you regret it?"

"Oh—*oh*!" Panic thrashed his ability to think. "No, I didn't mean that. I meant that we know a red flame is hot, but not many people understand the strength of white fire. Her fire is in her beauty, her sweetness, intelligence, her humor. She's amazing and confident and—"

"My little girl," Uncle Colton warned, then wiped a hand over his mouth. "Not sure anyone will be good enough for her."

The words conjured old wounds that had erupted when Dante had learned Uncle G was actually his pop.

"But you're pretty close," Uncle Colton added.

Shock froze Dante, then that strange pressure that had suffocated him all his life eased, lifted. Then he released the captive breath.

"Hey, listen—as you talked about what happened, I heard your words, but more than that, I heard your heart. And it's desperate to fix this and get her back."

"I am—"

"What you have to figure out is why. Is it to prove to me or your dad, or even Omen, that you have what it takes to get this done? Or is it because within you there's a McKenna-sized hole that will never be complete without her in your arms?"

Thunder had nothing on the pounding of his heart at the thought of not getting her back. Of never hearing her chastise him again. Or hearing her laugh. Or seeing where this thing was leading them. Life without Mick . . . It'd be meaningless. Empty. His eyes stung.

"Yeah," Uncle Colton said quietly. "*That*." He nodded, cocking his head to the side. "Let me tell you something, son. You don't lose situational awareness and focus over something that doesn't have meaning to you."

Dante felt the ghost of a smile flicker through him. "She was . . . very distracting."

"Keep the details on that kiss to yourself, okay? I don't want to hurt you when I've done such a good job obeying my wife's order to be nice to you."

Eyes wide, Dante started.

"It's a joke, relax," Uncle Colton said. "At least, I think it is." He grinned at him. "Oh, and don't let the devil get up in your business—you're a born operator. Everyone knows it, and Pike told me he's never seen someone like you. So get those doubts out of your head, get focused, and let's go find her."

The wound care may have been too late.

Flat on her back, McKenna had worked to get her thigh above her heart because of the inflammation. About an hour ago, she'd noticed fever around the site. She could only pray that rescue would come or an opportunity to escape arise.

Either one, God. I'm not picky.

But maybe desperate. She'd been in this cage two—three?—days now, and she was done with it. Although, she was grateful she had not been violated or otherwise assaulted. At least they'd stored the cage in the warehouse, where an old heater struggled to provide warmth, which was a welcome change from the biting cold that had threatened frostbite at the other location. But in here, while not necessarily warm but also not freezing, she was shut out of being able to discern what was happening in the compound. There was little indication as to the time of day. She guessed it must be getting close to dawn, because after she'd showered and been stitched up, she had been given a plastic bag filled with cooked rice. No utensils, but you bet your buttered biscuit she'd eaten every last grain.

Daunted, desperate, she had nothing but her thoughts to keep her company through the night. So she'd allowed herself to think of Dante. A lot of time to weigh the *un*likelihood that he'd consider her for any type of future. He was an operator, like Daddy had been. That meant missions . . . gone for weeks, if not months, at a time. While she wasn't sure she'd give up her career as a consular officer to become a wife and mother—

Ha. Bull. She'd give it up in a heartbeat because it's what she'd always dreamed of—a family.

But one safe. At home.

Oh, the twisted irony. Safe—she wanted safe because of how Poppa had died. She didn't want to date—let alone love—an operator who lived and breathed danger and violence. Every time Daddy had been spun up, she'd had nightmares. So much that she hadn't wanted to sleep and end up dreaming that Daddy died too. In high school, she'd resorted to taking sleep aids to avoid the nightmares.

To willingly walk into a relationship with a man who'd chosen the same profession . . . It wasn't that she was reconsidering that love—it was there, real and powerful—but maybe it wasn't a bad thing that he didn't see her the same way.

Oh, who was she kidding? It destroyed her every time she got her hopes up, had a chance to catch up with him, only to once again realize that to him, she was as invisible as Wonder Woman's jet.

Groaaaaan. Scraping preceded the retracting of the folding doors. Light shoved its way inside, impatient to scatter the darkness.

McKenna shielded her eyes against the brightness, but stayed on her back to keep her leg elevated.

Men rushed and shouted in stiff, tight voices that made her

shift to see what was the excitement. They completely bypassed her, hurrying to the rifle crates, which they hustled out of the warehouse. What was going on? Were they loading up, getting ready to leave?

No, no, that would be bad. Please, no—each mile from Dante seemed to strain the possibility that he'd find her. The thought pulled her up, and she struggled into a sitting position, wincing at the dull throb in her thigh.

Shouts erupted again, along with the blare of a horn.

McKenna whipped her attention to the accordion doors of the warehouse that were still open, letting in the bitter winter air and giving her a full view of the vehicles. A lot of them.

No no no . . . please. Definitely looked like they were clearing out.

Men hollered to one another, and one word in particular snagged McKenna's attention—American. Did they mean her, or . . .

Oh, please . . . please, please let it be Dante coming.

"Hurry—Americans!" someone shouted in Azerbaijani.

Okay, there was no doubt about that one, even though the rest were talking fast and loud, words and meanings blurring in a frenzy. The chaos of it all made it hard to think and translate their words. But as panic spurted through her veins, she heard this one, quiet phrase rush into the core of her being: *It's time.*

And while doubts assailed her thoughts, she couldn't let them take root. She would not. There was no place for panic and confusion at a time like this. She must be calm, focused. Just like when lining up the shot.

Heart steadying out, she surreptitiously reached for the latch key tucked in the sports bra. The one Havva had never noticed was missing. Casually, slowly, she turned her attention to the rifle. Eyed how it was positioned. The tarp would catch it if she yanked the wrong way. Then she checked the doors, searching for her exit.

Front wasn't an option with all the men and vehicles. So she'd have to go out the back, the way they'd taken her to the showers. Then up into the hills beyond the compound. Maybe she could snag a radio or phone on her way out. A jacket—she'd definitely need one. Only problem was, she hadn't seen one since the Russian had been yelling on the phone at the man who vowed to kill the Americans.

As if thoughts had conjured him, the Russian stalked out of one of the smaller buildings, phone tucked to his ear. Face red and strained, he yelled into the phone. "Take care of them! They are close. Too close!"

McKenna's heart ticked up a beat. *They're close?*

"Make them go south," he barked, his voice carrying easily through the tangle of other noises as he stomped to a black sedan. "We are not ready, and if they do not go south, if they find us, I will make sure you and everyone you love dies a very painful death." The Russian's black eyes flicked to McKenna. "And I will kill the girl if you fail."

Yep. All doubt gone. Definitely time. If they were close . . . and the Russian wanted them to go the wrong direction, then it could mean it was Omen. Dante.

Heart crashing into her ribs, she struggled for a clean breath. She had to leave. Now. While there was chaos and confusion. Fazil and another man hurried into the warehouse, hoisted three black-side crates, and hurried out, around the corner.

Key between her first two fingers, McKenna slipped them through the slats. Negotiated the key toward the hole. It flicked from her fingers. "No!" she gasped, eyeing it.

Fazil and the second returned for more crates.

Breath trapped in her throat, she stilled, not wanting to draw their attention. Which she got regardless—Younger slanted her a look and asked what would happen to her. Fazil sniffed and said the Russian would take care of her.

Watching them retrieve more crates, she secretly worked her

fingers toward the key. Felt it and picked it up. Waited as the men left the warehouse. As soon as she had their backs, she tried again. Closed her eyes, slowed her breathing. Focused . . . Felt the key slip in. Exhaled in relief as she turned it. Heard the clank of the lock just as Fazil and the man came back for more.

McKenna tilted her head back and tried to steady her racing nerves and pulse, all while holding the door closed. Praying they didn't notice the key in the lock or the rifle propped beneath the cage tarp.

Mercifully, they were too intent on loading up and were gone in a minute. Returned and got the last of the crates. This time, when they left, the doors blessedly closed.

Now!

McKenna shot a glance around to be sure she was alone, then eased open the cage. Angling her body out, she prayed for some mercy. That nobody would come in. She hauled herself free of the cage and swung her legs around. Closed the gate and locked it.

Holding onto the steel crate, she pulled herself up. Her legs trembled, protesting the weight she forced them to support. She pocketed the key and limped—holy cow her leg throbbed!—as fast as she could on unsteady legs to the back side of the cage, where she retrieved the rifle. Slung it over her shoulder. It wasn't a close-quarters weapon, and she would need her hands to help her hobble free. She tossed the tarp over the cage in the hopes it'd convince people she was in there, being isolated as punishment maybe. Hopefully nobody would check on her until much later.

It hurt each time she walked. Prickling pain, like her legs had fallen asleep and were waking up, pulsed through her muscles. Holding her thigh, she hissed and rushed to the rear of the warehouse. Pressed herself to the back door, listening over the roar of her own heart to hear if anyone on the other side was close. That's when she spied the jacket tossed over a crate.

Seriously? Finder's keepers.

She snatched it, remembering the open stretch beyond the door. Threading her arms through the sleeves, she knew if she got across the road, she could hide among the buildings and make her way out of the compound. Hoped the irritation of the guard when he'd hauled her out for a shower had meant this door didn't lock. She tested it and was relieved to find her theory correct. Carefully, she peered to the right. Cars were nearby, but the people rushing about seemed only concerned about getting going.

Which I should do too.

After checking to the left, McKenna slipped out of the warehouse. Braced herself, gave one last check, then hobbled into the open. Fire and agony tore through her leg. She nearly cried out at the crushing pain that threatened to send her to the ground. She stumbled but kept moving, aiming for the shadows of the alley between two white plaster buildings.

Her leg felt thick, heavy, and refused to bend. She stumbled again, this time losing her balance. She crashed into the wall even as she heard people talking nearby. Whipping around the corner, she flattened herself against the wall, prayed the dark clothes Havva had put her in would cooperate in keeping her hidden.

Chest heaving, leg screaming, she took a second to steady herself. To be sure the two hadn't seen her. As her heart beat out the seconds with thunderous thuds, she told herself to calm.

Two men, heads down as they chatted, strode past the alley.

McKenna drew up and held her breath. Felt the sling of the rifle sliding down her shoulder. With slow, intentional movement, she curled her hand back and caught the rifle just before it dropped. However, the stock hit the wall with a firm thump.

"Oy, what's that?" one of the men asked.

Pushing herself, she scampered down the length of the alley and banked around the corner. Prayed she'd been fast enough to not be seen. She stayed there for a second, lifting her leg, toe providing balance, but desperate to alleviate the riotous pain, and listened to the alley. Heard steps, but they blessedly retreated.

Taking a breather, she thought through her next steps. Now in a narrow lane, she'd have to cross over to reach the wall. There, she'd have to figure out whether to go right or left to find a way out of the walled city. Hobbling across the skinny road, she bit down to avoid crying out from the pain and let the tears flow freely. A slight incline made the journey more brutal. She hissed with each step. Made it to the stretch between a small shack and a larger structure. Limped onward.

A side door flung open.

Adrenaline exploding, McKenna's body buzzed with a dozen warnings—the loudest being she could not afford to freeze. This man had to be rendered unconscious before he saw her—and he would. There was no avoiding it. Rifle in hand, she grabbed the muzzle and with all her might, swung at his head before he had time to register her.

The impact whipped his head back. It struck the plaster wall. He dropped hard.

She gasped at the thud he made on the ground and hoped she hadn't killed him. Knowing she couldn't leave him to be found, she struggled to drag him around back, step by agonizing step. Gritting her teeth, she growled and tugged him the last few feet. "I'm so sorry," she whispered.

When she straightened, the world tilted. She slumped against the wall and whimpered. Felt herself collapsing. "No," she ground out. "You do not have time to fall apart."

Tears of pain and tears of mortification at injuring the man roiled together. Using her elbow, she wiped her eyes free of the tears so she could see. To the right, nothing but a long wall. To the left . . .

Thank You, God! She hurried toward the wood door, teeth clenched against the pain. Pushed through the gate, the hinges and old wood groaning. She dropped back against it with her own groan. Took a moment to assess her location. The right would lead her to a main road, but also to the front gate. Not good. She shuffled to the left and took in the overgrown path.

"You have to be kidding me," she moaned and slumped against the wall. The path was overgrown—a good thing that meant it wasn't often used—but also aimed into a steady, steep rise.

This was going to hurt. She hung her head and let the tears fall. At least for a second. She was sure Daddy would have some perfect inspirational phrase to match this steep incline and the pain it'd cause her to reach the top, but right now, she just really wanted a break. Some mercy.

Go! Get moving, you dolt! Knowing whining wouldn't get her anywhere, she palmed the wall and used it to help avoid putting her weight completely on the left leg. As she hiked the hill, she marveled that nobody had noticed her missing yet. A good thing. While she might have a mountain before her and a terrible, infected injury, she had experienced mercy—the key, the rifle, the escape . . .

Picking her way up the hillside, she chose the thicker vegetation and kept as low as she could, praying—begging—that Dante would come. That he'd find her. That she wouldn't die in the hills of Armenia.

SEVENTEEN

Gegharkunik Province, Armenia

NOTHING LIKE THREE SCION DADS BREATHING down his neck.

Dante resisted the urge to cower as they stood watching the drone footage. They'd reviewed the maps and come to a consensus that the border was the most likely destination. However, Pop and the uncles weren't convinced.

Too easy, they'd said. Too obvious.

But then, terrorists weren't known for being clever. They were known for being violent and desperate to bring about their means.

"What I don't get," Uncle Colton said, "is why they took Mickey. It doesn't track—she's a junior consular officer. No access to high-level intel or classified data. Immigration visas, yes, but ..." He shook his head.

"It did seem deliberate," Dante admitted. "She was there, hiding out, next thing we know, they're not even trying to kill us anymore and are exfiling."

"Yeah, there's more here," John Dighton said.

"Well," said Asher Bøhn, "she is the ambassador's right hand. I have no idea how many times I heard Ambassador Robertson call

McKenna that. Maybe they think they can force the ambassador to do something. Or force a trade."

"Of what?" Dante frowned at the guy the ambassador insisted attend in her stead, since she had been called away. They needed a language and cultural expert with them on this mission, especially with the peace treaty wagging in their faces. Over the guy's shoulder, Dante eyed the drone footage the uncles were watching. Saw something glaringly white in the black-and-white landscape. He squinted. What was . . .

"Hold up—wait," he said, hurrying around the suit. "Dade, back that up." Even as the footage rewound, he glanced at Omen. "Wasn't there a report about a box truck . . . ?"

"Affirmative." Tariq swiveled his chair to face his monitors, searching the intel. "An old lady in Sector 12 said a box truck wrecked her garden wall when it took a corner too sharp."

Dante wagged a finger at the screen. "What drone is this?"

"Uh . . ." Tariq craned his neck toward the screen. "Eight."

"Wait, didn't Eight go down?" Crow asked.

"It did. This was what it relayed right before."

"Look—a box truck and six other vehicles trailing it," Dante said. "That's . . . interesting." He rubbed his jaw, thinking. Hoping this was what they were looking for. "So, Eight went down . . . This footage is what, thirty hours old?"

"Thirty-two," Tariq confirmed.

"Has the drone been retrieved?" Pike asked, edging closer to the screen as the vehicles continued on.

"Not yet," Crow said. "No troops in the area for retrieval."

The team watched the black-and-white footage of seven vehicles, led by a box truck, barreling down a highway.

"Tight formation," Pop muttered. "So not just six vehicles stuck behind a slow truck."

"And Eight was reconning an area remote enough that, if these are our guys, they could avoid interference, yet could reach AzerB or head into Ukraine or Russia." Pike grabbed a tablet and accessed a map. He put it on the wall. "This is the area."

"Aren't we chasing a wild hare?" Bøhn asked. "Shouldn't we—"

"We explore all possible options," Pike said. "Dade, Brick, get on sat relays and see if we can backtrace that truck."

"What's this?" Uncle Colton moved to the screen and pointed to two black dots. "These."

Tariq zoomed in on those. "SUVs." He cocked his head. "Moving at a pretty good clip."

"Those cars look armored . . ." Uncle Colton said, then glanced at him. "In a remote location . . ."

"Yeah-yeah-yeah. I got you." Dante positioned himself in the middle of the screen. "Tariq, can we overlay the map on the footage?"

"On it," the comms officer said.

The chief's gray gaze rose to the screens. "There, you can see the region."

They watched the drone following the two coming at each other from opposite directions. Then the camera jarred and fuzz filled the screen.

"Wait!" Dante grinned, looking at the chief. "D'you see that?"

"I just saw the drone go down," Bøhn said, the other embassy guy confused.

"Run those last few seconds—slow," Pike ordered.

And in slow-mo, the camera flicked, then went gray.

"Someone shot it down," Dante said, grinning. "I think we found them."

Uncle Colton studied the overlaid map. "The caravan and the two cars—whatever is between the two, that's where we need to search."

"Agreed. I'll make some calls to get this underway." Pike strode toward the Command center and retrieved a SAT phone. "Suits are with us for language skills and PR in case we need it."

Three hours later, they boarded two cargo planes packed with Dante, Omen, the Nightshade team, the embassy reps, and two Bastion armored personnel carriers packed with weapons and equipment. Another hour and they were queued up at the rear of the cargo plane, holding the line in prep for the jump. Wind roared outside, offering them a thirty-three-thousand-foot freefall. Braced at the back, the jumpmaster had his teams deploy the APCs.

Dante couldn't help noticing his uncles seemed more than a little excited to make the jump. How long had it been since they'd thrown themselves out of a perfectly good airplane? And his pop, who had more jump hours than anyone aboard, had Bøhn strapped to him for a tandem jump. The other suit was harnessed to Brick Archer, who was tormenting the guy with fake jumps.

The jumpmaster green-lighted Nightshade, then Dante. He had no problem doing HALO or HAHO jumps, but it wasn't something he loved. Give him the ocean or terra firma any day.

He executed a textbook landing and hauled in his chute, watching as Pop and Brick landed with their tandem rides, the embassy suits. Bøhn looked white as milk, stumbling his landing, then face-planting when the big guy released the tether. Bøhn's mask went askew. Heaved himself onto all fours, ripped off the mask, then heaved another way—sacrificing his regurgitated food to the desert.

The other suit, meanwhile, landed like a pro. Once he was cut loose, he threw a fist in the air. "Whoop! Yeah!"

The team had all landed within a quarter-mile of each other, and within a ten-mile radius of the last-known location of Drone Eight. Pike had already secured his chute and was making fast work of removing the rigging from one of the armored personnel carriers.

Luther trotted over to the second, where he secured his chute in the APC and went to work clearing the carrier's chute rigging.

Dade joined them, stowing his chute in the APC, then drew out a tablet. "Eight went down about three-quarters of a klick from our present location," he said. "But it's not giving off any readings."

"Atlas, Nightshade, Brick—with me in APC-1." Pike considered the two suits. "Bøhn with me. Everyone else in APC-2 with Landry."

They piled into the indicated vehicles.

"Mr. Neeley—"

"Call me Cowboy."

Pike nodded, his expression clearly speaking his appreciation of that. "Take the jumpseat?"

The four Nightshade team members glanced at each other and nodded, then Uncle Colton headed to the front while the rest of them climbed in the back with Brick, Dante, and the suit. They stowed the chutes in the rack between the front driver seats and the eight bucket seats with harnesses, four on each side and facing one another.

Dante sat next to Pop with Uncle Canyon directly across from him. Dighton and Brick fell into easy conversation, chatting and chuckling, both watching Bøhn across from them struggling with the five-point harness. And this dude was supposed to help with cultural and language expertise? He finally gave up and eyed the bulletproof window up over his shoulder.

Pike cranked the engine, and they pulled away from the LZ, taking the lead.

"You good?" Pop asked, his deep voice defying the din of the APC and road noise.

Dante gave his pop a sidelong glance. "Yeah." He smoothed a hand over his mouth and jaw. "I'll be better once she's found."

Nodding, Pop fell quiet. For two seconds. "She's special."

It was weird, awkward, talking to Pop like this. About Mick. "Very."

A smile ghosted Pop's mouth. "Good." He looked at his longtime buddy and smirked. "Took him long enough to figure it out."

"A'right, I see how it's going to be," Dante said.

"Boy, you haven't seen nothing yet," Pop said, hooking a hand around the back of Dante's neck and squeezing. "Going after a Scion . . . you inherit five dads."

Four. Pop had clearly forgotten Uncle Max was gone. Or . . . "Hey—Mick told me Dillon was here."

Pop leaned forward suddenly. "Here?" Hands pressed together, he stabbed them to the steel deck. "In Armenia?"

"She said he'd found proof Uncle Max was alive."

Uncle Canyon sat back with a grunt, glanced at Pop. Both gave a slow nod.

"You think he's right?" Dante asked. "Could Uncle Max still be alive?"

"If anyone could, it'd be him," Pop said, running a hand over his bald head, which was more about hiding his gray hair than looking tough. "The real question is, why here? Why would Dillon go to McKenna?"

"They've always had some weird connection," Dante admitted. Pop considered him.

"That sounds a lot like jealousy," Uncle Canyon said with his trademark smirk.

"This ain't about that," Dante countered. "Besides, Mick said he's like a brother to her."

"But she said that about you too," John Dighton added.

"Not after that kiss," Brick tossed in with a chuckle. "He was practically eating her face."

"Bro. No." Dante gave him a dark look. "Inappropriate." He indicated to the Nightshade team. "And it could get you killed."

"You mean, get *you* killed."

Pop glanced at the burly guy. "You talk about one of ours like that, we help you remember what pain feels like."

Brick adjusted his ball cap. "I'd be mighty appreciative if you'd direct that collective weight to finding her instead."

Yeah, now he knew how it felt to have people breathing down his neck.

"Tycho's spotted the drone," Pike called from the front as they veered to the right over the undulating terrain and slowed.

A minute later, they deployed from the vehicles and hiked out to help retrieve the pieces of the downed drone. Back at the APCs, the teams huddled around Dade as he tugged out his ballistic laptop, synced it with the drone, and downloaded the data. He took a few minutes to run back the footage until the box truck wasn't in sight, then he brought it back to where it came into range, marked the time in the video, then extracted the longitude and latitude. Cross-referenced it with the map. "Okay . . . yeah, this truck came into play on the feed just south of that village."

"So, since an old man in the other village we'd sighted on the peak said he saw a blonde woman being manhandled by troops," Pike said, "and this is the one with the old woman who said the box truck took out her wall, there's a very good likelihood this truck is our lead on finding Olympian."

"And we're far enough south," Dante said, "that if we do not locate and interdict now, we could lose her for good if they cross the border."

"Not that enemy-controlled territory has ever stopped us," Uncle Canyon said.

"Wait," Bøhn said. "I . . . I want to find McKenna like the rest of you, but going into Azerbaijani territory—as a consular officer, I can't disregard protocols."

Why was he griping now? "Then we'll leave you water and protein bars and catch you on the flip side," Dante said without hesitation.

"You can't just leave us out here!" Bøhn balked, then wagged a hand in Dante's direction. "International relations cannot be compromised because someone thinks he's in love. No girl is worth losing a historical and vital peace treat—"

A loud *crack* sounded, and Dante didn't realize it'd been his fist against the suit's jaw until pain ruptured the nerve communication in his hands seconds before Pop and Uncle Colton pulled him off the guy. "You been countering everything we've tried to do since she went missing. You're not a help—you're a burden," he said, his breathing ragged. "She's worth ten of you!"

"Easy, easy," Pop said, patting Dante's heaving chest.

"Stand down!" Pike ordered, coming around the vehicle. He studied Dante, then turned his rage on the suit. "I appreciate you have things to protect, but if you aren't comfortable taking every measure possible to retrieve Olympian, you will be left here with provisions. I'll radio in your position to Command, but rest assured, we will not be slowing in our mission to find her."

"I'm in," the other suit said. "He always complains too much. Probably better without him."

"Hey!" Bøhn barked. "You can't leave me!"

Luther got in Bøhn's path, all but daring him to try something. "What's it going to be, Pretty Boy—hoofing it or riding?"

The suit's eyes blazed, fists clenched at his sides. His hand shifted to the bulging jacket pocket. "Riding," he bit out.

Pike considered him for a long moment, then focused on Dade. "Launch the new drone. Eight was shot down, so that means someone was nearby. Let's hope they're still here and we can find them, along with the box truck."

"Find Mick, you mean," Dante countered.

"Chief," Dade said, turning with the laptop. "Found two small villages within a ten-kilometer radius and about three klicks apart. There's also a third about fifteen klicks in the opposite direction."

"Box trucks?"

"Unknown." Dade shook his head as he controlled the drone while monitoring the footage. "Can't see one, and it'd stand out— that glaring white against the grays of the buildings."

"Unless they're camouflaged," Luther countered.

"We'll hit the nearest first," Pike instructed. "Get the drone over it so we aren't surprised by anything."

"Good copy," Dade said.

Dante stared the suit down as he turned toward the APC-2, appreciating too much the blood smeared over the guy's upper lip.

"Bøhn, with me," Pike ordered, motioning the suit toward APC-1. "Let's load up and head out."

EIGHTEEN

Gegharkunik Province, Armenia

MIRACLES WERE HAPPENING TODAY.

Shouts erupted from the compound, along with barked orders. McKenna stretched prone in the scrub and tall weeds of the hill, unmoving . . . watching a spider crawling down her hand. *That* was the miracle—not screaming or freaking out. She hated spiders. Frogs, toads, lizards any day of the year. But a giant Shelob-birthed one?

When the black arachnid neared her fingertip, she flicked it away with a shudder. Released the breath she'd held since first sighting it and started low-crawling again, even amid the violent protest of her leg, each muscle contraction feeling like a massive charley horse. Pausing in her stealthy movement, she plucked another dark-colored weed and threaded it through her hair, which she'd earlier rubbed dirt into to hide the blonde and added several pieces of sticks and shrubs. A few broken branches. She'd also threaded a branch and more foliage into the loops of her pants to dangle down her backside and up her borrowed jacket as a makeshift ghillie suit. All in the hopes of concealing her clothes and position.

Silently, she'd thanked God for all those times she and Daddy had contests to see if they could cross a field and reach the other without being seen.

Over the last hour of negotiating for a better vantage at a snail's pace—vital in not betraying herself—she'd worked her way toward the south-facing edge. It should give her a long line of sight on the valley that spread out below.

"Find her!" came the shout from below.

Her disappearance from the cage had been noted. The clock was officially ticking down. But it'd taken them long enough to discover she was missing, and spoke to their complacency. Not all were like them, but the men in the compound believed they were far enough from any conflict or threat and had let down their guard.

Farther from the camp and closer to a better vantage. Even from here, she could hear the troops shouting, "Americans are close!"

At that shout, her heart skipped a beat. The Americans had to be close enough to cause concern yet far enough away that the Azerbaijanis weren't yet firing on them. Or perhaps this contingent here did not have the long-range firepower to defend against an American spec-response.

Finally in position, she drew up the rifle ever so slowly, not wanting any glint or scrape to give her away, and shifted into position next to a log. Adjusted so the Mosin-Nagant was tucked against her shoulder and peered through the attached scope and scanned the outlying area.

Where are you . . . ?

A voice erupted behind her, then another.

Using slow, deliberate movement, McKenna lowered her head and drew the rifle beneath her. Scope poking into her chest, she prayed she'd done a good enough job with her own ghillie suit. She was about to find out.

Boots crunched closer, the two men calling out to each other that there was nothing up here. That Fazil was crazy.

Yes, very crazy. Go back down to the compound, she willed them. Regulating her breathing was a crucial part of not giving away her position. She closed her eyes. Silently prayed for God to blind the enemy's eyes . . . Drew in a slooooow breath. Exhaaaaled slowly. Innnnnn . . . ooouuutt.

Crunch.

On her immediate left.

Instinct told her to tense, but training ordered her to keep doing the rhythmic breathing.

With a grunt, the guard pivoted. "There's nothing here," he shouted down to his buddy in Azerbaijani.

"Same."

The nearest one shifted his feet. Then came a creaking. A sound that . . . was that a lighter? A moment later, the acrid odor of cigarette smoke spiraled over her head.

Are you kidding me! The soldier was sitting on the log right next to her, smoking!

Well, she had asked God to blind the guy to her . . . and apparently He had.

Cigarette smoke burned her eyes, making them water. Throat thickening as she fought the smell, McKenna knew that more than ever, she had to rely on focused breathing.

Steps approached from behind, the two soldiers chatted quietly. The smoke doubled. Were they both smoking now? They chatted about leaving, about going back home, about their families.

Hey, guys, wasn't there an emergency?

A shout came from somewhere distant. The soldier on the log stood, the wood cracking.

McKenna flinched and cursed herself.

"Nothing here," one bellowed to the compound, then said in a quieter tone, "We better get back."

A cigarette butt flicked against McKenna's cheek. Caught in the branches of her camouflage as the men stomped away. Kindled by the dryness of the weeds, a spark flared. Slow, deliberate—the men could look back at any second—McKenna reached with two fingers to the waxy leaf just beyond her fingertips. Curled her wrist slowly toward the smoldering butt. Pressed it down, feeling the heat through her fingers. Ignored that as she pushed the butt into the dirt.

With extreme care and slowness, she lifted her head. Rotated it in the direction the soldiers went. Relieved to find it clear, she refocused on her task. Kept her movements stealthy in case someone was watching via binos from the compound. She brought out the rifle and set her cheek to the barrel. Peered through the stock, ready—desperate—to get out of here.

Where are you? She scanned left . . . then right. She angled farther out. Frustration mounting, she wondered if maybe they'd moved on. It'd been a while since the first reports of Americans in the area. What if she'd been too late? What if they were gone? What then? *Please . . . please don't be gone.* She took her time searching, doing it in a standard search grid. But still she could not find them.

Defeated, she lowered her head. What would she do if they were gone? Her perusal of the vast expanse of land warned her she could walk for hours and not find anything.

Her heart—and leg—couldn't take that.

Well, she was not a quitter. Could not quit.

But . . . what? What was she to do? She fought the tears—they'd blurred her vision and made it harder to see through the reticle. Something tickled her cheek and she flinched, seeing something black out of the corner of her eye. With a gasp, she swatted it away and bumped her weapon. Cursing herself for being so careless, she readjusted and looked in the scope, automatically moving to adjust it farther—but a dust plume rose to the left.

Breath snatched, she diverted her scope there. Two armored vehicles. Were they Azerbaijanis? Had to be or the compound would be alive with chaos and gunfire . . .

The vehicles veered off suddenly and came to a stop. Doors opened, as well as the rear hatch, and men spilled out—not wearing the AzerB uniforms, but not everyone in the compound had. So maybe a group of the enemy troops was out looking for her. That'd make sense and explain why nobody was shooting at them. She'd evaded capture, so perhaps they'd sent out teams in all directions. Yet . . . she wasn't *that* important . . .

And there was no way she could've gotten that far with a leg injury.

A lone man rushed away from the vehicles, around a path of scrub. Potty break?

Two others strode after him, a handful of others hanging back. She traced her scope over the contingent. Scanned to see if more were coming. No? Just these two . . .

When she returned the crosshairs to the three, the loner returned, now waving something in the air. His back shifted to her as she tightened up on him. She stilled, her heart powering down to a dreadful rate—that . . . that man . . . he looked just like the third man from the encounter at the first village! The one who'd had the argument with the Russian. The one who'd said he would make sure the Americans died.

So, he was back. And he'd brought trouble . . . ?

He pivoted, waving a piece of fabric as he motioned to the south. Away from the compound.

Were there more . . . ? She checked but saw nothing. What was he doing? Peering through the scope, she zeroed in on him. Froze as his face came into focus. No . . . that could not be . . .

Holy moly—it's Asher!

Wait wait wait.

Asher was the third man? So that meant . . .

Asher was working with the Azerbaijanis? The facts crashed in on McKenna—recalling when Havva made her change, then cut her overalls . . .

It was . . . planned? That thought almost made her miss another shock—

Dante! A strangled noise climbed her throat as she recognized his very familiar, beautiful form and stride. *Oh, thank You, God!* Why hadn't she noticed them before?

Dante was here! Looking for her!

Heart racing, she watched the encounter with Asher waving something around. Dante arguing with him. Asher repeatedly motioning south. Another man strode toward them, his shape, build . . .

It couldn't be! Her pulse rapid-fired. "Daddy," she breathed, tears pricking her eyes as she realized her dad had come looking for her too. *They're here, they're here! I can't believe it!*

Her heart beat so hard and erratically that she was sure it would come out of her chest or alert the others by its thunderous sound. She blinked away the tears and forced herself to shed emotion and maintain line of sight.

Daddy took the piece of cloth from Asher and studied it. Walked it over to another man—no way! That was Uncle G!—who took the cloth, glanced at Daddy, then Dante. All three turned the backs of their heads to her. Looked out toward the mountains. South.

What was out there? Why was that cloth so important to get all their attention?

Well, she knew what *wasn't* out there—her.

Dante shouldered into Daddy, pointing at the cloth, talking. He looked ticked. Something dark seemed to pass through Daddy's expression. What was going on?

The other men had gathered at the rear of one of the armored vehicles as the conversation continued with Daddy, Dante, Uncle G, and—

Oh my word! It was all her Nightshade uncles!

When Asher tried to butt into the conversation, Dante pivoted and made a move like he was going to punch him, but Daddy drew him away. Pointed at Asher, who backed off. Wait . . .

Asher . . .

If Asher was with the Russian, that meant he was the one promising the Americans' deaths. And by *American* that meant Dante. Daddy. Uncle G.

Tension and fury coiled through McKenna. If Asher indicated for them to go south, did that mean there was an ambush? What other reason could there be?

Me. He's leading them away *from me.*

No way she could let that happen.

"I'm telling you, something is wrong," Dante insisted.

Rubbing the bloody strip of dingy blue fabric, Uncle Colton eyed Pop, then Bøhn over by the other vehicle. "You sure this was hers?"

Dante shouldered in, tucking his chin and lowering his voice, calling bull that the suit had found this strip of Mick's fabric stuck to the bush he'd just so happened decided to do business behind. "It looks like the coverall she put on, but it wasn't bloody when she left my sight."

Visage a stone, Uncle Colton considered him, then the torn, bloodied fabric.

Dante leaned in and lowered his voice. "And how did he see that through the small APC ballistic window and behind a hill?" He shook his head, gut coiled tight. That viper hissing in anger and frustration. "Dude's pocket was bulging before, and now it's not. I'm telling you, he had that the whole time."

Pop winged up an eyebrow. "You realize what you're saying . . ."

It was a stiff, terrible accusation. "Yes. But I'm not wrong." He held his ground, unwilling to be deterred. "I'd kill him myself if we didn't need him to tell us where she is."

"You'd have to beat me to it," Uncle Colton bit out.

"So, we agree," Pop said, slowly unfolding his arms and letting them hang at his sides. Near his sidearm. "We—"

"Augh!" someone screamed.

Crack! Tsing!

"Gun!"

"Sniper!"

"Down, down!"

In a swarm of instinct, every operator dove for cover even as Dante noticed Uncle Canyon pitch himself toward Bøhn. Tariq collided with the guy first, knocking a gun from the suit's hands. Where had that come from?

Shoulder pressed to the APC, Dante considered the situation as curses peppered the team.

Uncle Canyon and Tariq hauled Bøhn to cover, a field of blood trailing the suit's mangled left leg. A big chunk of his calf missing. The guy's screams raked the air as Canyon and Crow worked a tourniquet onto the leg to stop him from bleeding out, while Tariq held the guy down.

But Uncle Colton was positioned with his shoulder to the APC, M4 out, peering up the hill in the distance. "Sniper shot came from the north."

"Good copy," Pike answered, searching for the shooter.

"Suit aimed this Glock at Dante seconds before the sniper tagged him," Brick muttered, dispelling a magazine, popping out the round in the chamber, then handing a gun over to Pike.

What? Dante glanced to where the suit had gone down. Hold up . . . if Bøhn had been about to shoot Dante and a sniper took him out . . .

He snapped his gaze around. Looked at the hill. That . . . it couldn't . . . Could it?

A reflection glinted in the afternoon sun.

"There's a compound over there," Uncle Colton said.

"Box truck," Pop confirmed as he peered through binos. "Two o'clock, behind—"

"Sniper, two o'clock," Pike called.

"What if it's her?" Dante asked, looking at her dad. "WAIT!" he shouted in unison with Uncle Colton, their gazes locking. "It's her."

Smiling and nodding, Uncle Colton straightened slowly . . . "Hold! Hold your fire! Pretty sure that's my baby girl—it's McKenna."

Heart hammering, Dante stared at the spot where the reflection had glinted, thought about Bøhn getting shot . . . about the same time Brick said the suit had aimed that Glock at Dante. Whoa, that could only mean—"She saved my life."

"If that's her, it would necessitate she's escaped somehow. I'd think that means she's hiding," Pike said gravely. "That means saving you, firing that rifle, just gave away her position."

<hr>

Gegharkunik Province, Armenia

Shouts echoed in the afternoon. Even as she watched Dante and Daddy stopping the teams from firing on her position, McKenna heard the compound come alive with shouts. While she had a clear line of sight out across the open valley, she didn't have the same vantage on the compound, not from here. But she could hear the pounding feet.

They were coming.

The soldiers. And Dante, who would be too late. If the Azerbaijanis—or, God forbid, the Russian—discovered her, they'd kill her on sight. She was now a massive liability and threat, because by giving away her position, she'd also betrayed the location of the troops. How many were coming didn't matter—she was one woman, injured, and had nowhere to flee. Firing a sniper rifle was inefficient and cumbersome in close quarters.

It was foolish to think she could outsmart them again, especially with so many coming this time. After threading her arm through the rifle's sling, McKenna scrambled forward, toward the steep descent. Perched on the cleft, watching in the direction of the camp. Prepared to pitch herself over the side if necessary. She hoped not. But she knew the odds were slim that they wouldn't find her this time.

Before, they weren't sure where she was. Now they knew.

But Omen and Nightshade were coming. They'd raid the compound.

What if she warned them? Would the troops flee? "Americans!" she shouted, hands cupping her face in an attempt to throw her voice toward the compound. "Americans coming," she said in Azerbaijani.

Even as her shout echoed, she saw two men storming up the hill with Kalashnikovs in hand. Both paused, glanced back.

When they did, she angled her rifle in their direction. She could take one down, but she wouldn't likely get the other before he started firing. That was just tactically. She wasn't sure she could just shoot to kill . . .

Please, please . . .

The two spotted the armored vehicles tearing up the ground to reach the compound. "Go back, tell them," one warned. "I will find her."

Defeat pushed McKenna down. She flattened her body, cursing herself for not finding a better spot. Just one man . . . But she knew better than to let down her defenses, thinking herself evenly matched. It'd cost her a competition once. She wouldn't let it cost her life this time.

Not with Daddy and Dante so close.

Why couldn't this be simple? Easy. She knew some women felt being rescued reduced their strength, robbed a girl of saving her own life. But why would it be so bad that someone loved a woman so much he fought life and limb to save her?

It's terribly romantic. I wouldn't be mad.

Especially if said man was Dante.

Forget romance—she'd even be glad for Daddy. Anyone, as long as she walked—hobbled—out of here alive. Though . . . seeing Dante barrel in to save her . . .

Yeah, stuff of her dreams. Literally.

Heart ricocheting in her chest, she watched the soldier prowl closer. *No, go the other way.*

But he plodded onward. Nearer. Closed the distance.

The man turned and he tilted his head, eyes squinting. A slow smile slid across his face. "Got you."

NINETEEN

Gegharkunik Province, Armenia

DANTE SPRINTED UP THE HILLSIDE, HAVING bailed out of the APC before the team hit the compound. Calves burning, he pushed up the steep incline. Heard a shout—a man hollering something from ahead.

The sound threw him the last three yards. As he crested the top of the hill, Dante snapped up his weapon. Stalk-ran forward, tracing the area. Finally spotted a guy in a field camo jacket fifty feet to his three, aiming a weapon at the ground. What did he see? Mick?

She was a sharpshooter—a sniper. Improvised ghillie suit.

Only then did his mind let him sort the vegetation. See the variegation. He advanced, fighting the instinct to just barrel in. That'd lead to mistakes, and he'd already made enough of those. When the man said something, Dante knew the time was now. Focused as he stalked forward, he fired a controlled burst at the soldier.

The AzerB soldier twisted, mouth agape in surprise, saw Dante as he fell away. Thudded hard to the ground.

Rushing him, Dante fired two more rounds into the chest to

make sure he didn't come back to life and attack. He searched to the grass for the ghillie suit. Turning a half circle in the direction the guy had targeted, he probed the knee-high grass. What in all the crazy?

"Mick," he rasped, trying to stay quiet and not draw more attention up here. But he was legit freaked—and impressed—that he couldn't see her. Yet he knew . . . *knew* she was here. "McKenna."

Rustling came from his left. Like a caterpillar rolling, the grass shifted and splayed. Widening greenery morphed into the most beautiful woman he'd ever known—inside and out. "You brought my dad," she grunted as she gripped her thigh.

"'Course I did." Dante took a knee, eyeing her bloodied pants. The stain looked both fresh and old—but there was no hole in the fabric. "You're hurt."

Lifting her other hand to her forehead, she cried and shook her head. Chin dimpled as she fought tears.

"Hey." He touched her shoulder. "Hey, it's okay."

She cupped her hands over her face, and sobs wracked her body.

After a quick scan to ensure there weren't any fresh wounds, he drew her up to himself, the branches and grass of her ghillie jacket crunching softly as he held her close. "I'm here, Mick. You're safe now."

She grabbed onto him as if she were falling and pressed her face into his chest.

Though his heart twinged that the one thing she mentioned was her dad, he tucked it aside and held her tight. "I got you, I got you."

She sniffled and shuddered a breath. "I was so scared I'd never see you again, that the last thing you'd remember was that I wouldn't talk to you."

"Hey, hey, easy now." He checked their surroundings, heard the shots and shouts coming from the compound. Nobody new was coming up the hill.

Mick adjusted in his arms and settled there, breath staggering.

"When I saw Asher aim that gun at you," she murmured into his tac vest, "I was terrified to kill someone, but even more terrified he'd kill you. I know what a sniper round does. He'll lose his leg. But he was going to kill you."

Dante swiveled in front of her. "Hey. Listen—what you did had to be done. And you did it. You saved my life. Mick, you did good. *Real* good. That shot let us know where you were. That was smart." He would've kissed the top of her head, but she had all kinds of brush and grass threaded through her hair. "That was some legit-impressive strategy, you and that sniper stuff."

She shuddered a sigh and eased out of his arms, a loss he immediately hated. "You almost passed me," she murmured and started pulling her homemade camouflage from her hair. "I was invisible to you."

Dante nudged her chin up so she'd look into his eyes. "Not anymore, Mick. Not anymore."

She smiled up at him, then faltered, something like disappointment in her expression.

He frowned—first at the sudden distance she put between them, and second at the possibility she was hurt and they were up here chatting like they had all day. Again, he assessed her bloodied leg. "There's no visible wound. What happened?"

She gave him an aggrieved look. "A rogue bullet caught my thigh. It's feverish—infected."

"Tariq can fix you up. Can you walk?"

"No, but I can hobble."

He sniffed. "Let's get you vertical." He braced her shoulders and helped her upright. "You good?"

She gave a clipped nod even as more chaos and shots spiraled from the compound. With a gasp, McKenna pivoted and looked toward the compound. "Guess Daddy and Omen have arrived."

"*Arrived*? I think you mean interdicted. Don't worry, they're handling it." Almost as soon as the words left his mouth, the afternoon fell quiet. "See?" He smirked.

"I'm amazed you brought my dad," she muttered and started hobbling.

"I want to play hero and let you think I did, but"—he shook his head—"when I called and told them what happened, they said they were coming. Nobody could stop them. So, sorry to disappoint you again."

She caught his hand. "I am very glad my dad is here . . . but . . ." She gave another shy smile. "You were the one I kept praying God would send to swoop in and rescue me."

"Seriously?" That dangerous root of hope dug into his heart as he angled closer. "You've always seen me, Mick. Known me. Better than anyone—even myself. I couldn't see past my own issues to realize how much I cared about you." *Tell her you love her, fool.* But somehow, he couldn't. No idea why.

She nodded, a fake smile replacing the genuine one that had him hostage to those blue eyes. That's when he noticed the smudges weren't dirt—they were bruises. And cuts.

He cupped her face, something primal rising through him. "I could kill whoever did this to you."

McKenna nodded to the dead body. "You already did." And with that, she indicated to her injury. "My leg hurts too much to make it down the steep slope."

Dante knelt. "On my back."

"Seriously?"

"Do it."

Awkwardly, she climbed onto his back, careful not to jar her leg.

As he picked their way down the sharp incline, he argued with himself about fessing up. It wasn't every day he told a woman he'd known most of his life that he loved her. And love meant things. Like a future together. And how would that work . . . him on missions, her here in Armenia?

"After this," he said, carefully negotiating sideways down a particularly stiff patch, "embassy work will be boring."

She huffed a laugh next to his ear. "I'm not sure there will be embassy work in my future."

Dante startled. Eyed her, face so close to his. Blue eyes bright, even rimmed in red from her earlier crying. "Seriously?" His heart felt like it was doing hip-hop.

"I came out here to help the locals—well, that's what I said, but I realized . . . I really wanted to prove that I wasn't weak. That my softer nature, the one that wants to help people, wasn't a weakness. I wanted to be strong, like you."

He sniffed, catching her uninjured leg and hiking her into a better position. "I'm not strong, Mick."

"Have you seen your biceps?" she teased. "You're the strongest person I know, outside our dads."

"That's seriously whack. I screw up all the time."

"But you always try. You don't let it stop you." She strained to see his face. "You're the one who said I saw you, that I knew you—so trust me on this: You're strong. You keep looking for people to respect you, but I don't get it . . ."

"What? Why they'd respect me?" He sniffed, her words painfully close to the trigger of the weapon aimed at his heart.

"Don't twist my words," Mick said. "You can't see it, but they already respect you. That whole fear of yours, that they don't? It's a massive lie, Dante. The Dark One keeps you guessing and desperate, making you believe nothing you do is good enough. It's a lie that traps you in bondage to some search that is already finished."

"You get a theology degree while I wasn't looking?"

"Yeah, from the Bible. You should read it sometime."

"Don't hold back, baby girl." Dante reached the base of the hill and threaded through the small foot gate.

She laughed, then straightened her spine and pressed a kiss to his cheek. "I respect you, and really, that's all that should matter."

"Because you love me?"

"See? I knew you were smart." She wrapped her arms around his head.

"Are you really hugging my head right now?" He laughed. The hole in his heart that had always done exactly what she'd said—told him he wasn't good enough—filled with a heady warmth. No idea what it filled it, but he wasn't mad. "I—"

"McKenna!" Uncle Colton surged across the open yard of the compound.

She gasped. "Daddy!"

"Why are you carrying her?" he demanded as he reached them.

"She was shot." When he realized Uncle Colton intended to take her from him, Dante diverted around him, rushing her to the ACP where Tariq waited. "Days-old bullet wound, left thigh. Infected."

"How old?" Tariq asked as Dante set her in the ACP.

"Two days," she said, wincing as she hoisted herself onto the seat. "It's feverish and swollen. A woman stitched it yesterday, but the infection was already setting in."

And with a pair of tactical scissors, Tariq cut the pant leg up the middle until he found the bandage. "Breakthrough bleeding."

McKenna nodded. "Happened when I was running up the hill to escape."

Tariq reached for his medkit as he eyed her. "That had to hurt."

She shrugged. "If I didn't, they'd kill me or y'all. Maybe both."

Uncle Canyon joined them, watching as Tariq removed the bandage. He let out a low whistle. "Mickey, you're a regular petri dish of bacteria."

After dousing the wound with antibacterial and rebandaging it, Tariq ran an IV. "I'm giving you fluids and broad general antibiotics. That wound will need to be debrided back at Yerevan."

"Helo's inbound. It'll land two klicks out," Pike said, patting Dante's shoulder, then looked around the compound. "We'll leave this to the Armenians. Let's get your girl back to Yerevan."

Yeah—his girl. He liked that. A lot.

EPILOGUE

Washington, DC

TWELVE MONTHS AGO, SHE NEVER WOULD'VE believed where she'd be today—at the awards ceremony honoring individuals involved in the intervention that protected peace and prevented disgruntled individuals from getting their way. Terrorists from succeeding.

For McKenna, the bigger victory that deserved honor was convincing Dante they were meant for each other. After returning Stateside, he'd spent as much time with her as he could between missions with Omen. It wasn't the ideal life—and each time he left, her heart climbed into her throat and remained there till he returned. But she loved him, and if he could make the sacrifices for their country, she would support him in that. Besides, it made their dates all the sweeter. And she meant that literally because Dante apparently had a sweet tooth the size of Texas and a passion for adventure-seeking. Her favorite memory she'd made with him had been their day on the Potomac in a sailboat. Just the two of them.

She lifted her phone from the table, eyeing the image of them together that she'd set as the lock screen. Wishing he could be here. It wasn't about the award—really, she found it silly they were giving her a medal for getting shot.

Dalita should have been the one receiving a medal here, because it turned out the intel she'd been gathering? It'd been sourced by a terrorist who'd befriended her uncle. Mick's small mention of that to Dante, his relaying of that to the ambassador, led them to taking down a Top Ten Most Wanted terrorist working to disrupt negotiations between Azerbaijan and Armenia. Peace still hadn't been cemented, but she prayed it would one day.

"In recognition of sacrifice of health, in the performance of official duties while serving at the United States Embassy - Yerevan, the Secretary's Medal is awarded to McKenna Neeley by the Department of State for her strategic thinking and actions, which led to the capture of a known terrorist cell and thwarted further harm from being perpetrated against the people of Armenia."

Her phone lit up, and she gasped when she saw the face that flashed onto the screen. Dante! She swiped without thinking, her mind racing even as she noticed Daddy eyeball her. "Dante," she whispered, hunching to avoid disrupting the ceremony. And yet her heart sang as his visage with the—as usual—blacked-out background filled her screen. "The ceremony is going."

"Am I too late?"

She hunched even more. "No, I'm about to walk up."

"I'll be right there with you."

"Aww," she said, eyes tearing. "I sure love you."

"And had I not taken six months to recover from the injury I sustained in the same endeavor, Miss Neeley"—the mention of her name yanked her gaze to the speaker, Secretary Derriscort—"would not have been forced to wait so long for this recognition. Miss Neeley, if you'll please join me."

"Have to go—hang on." McKenna turned to her daddy, handing him the phone. "Here, help him watch." She rose from the table, smoothed her navy-blue ballgown, and moved to the stage, feeling self-conscious. A Marine offered his gloved hand for assistance on the stairs, and she ached for it to have been a certain former Navy SEAL.

Heart thumping at the attention, she strode across the stage and met Secretary of State Derriscort, who affixed the blue-and-gold medal to her gown, handed her the certificate in a black padded folio, then a black velvet box that held more variations of the medal. They turned and posed for a photo, then the Secretary hugged her. "Thank you for saving our lives—Cat never stops talking about it."

"God saved us all," McKenna countered solemnly.

"Now," Secretary Derriscort pronounced as he held her elbow, keeping her in place.

McKenna inwardly frowned—she would not do it publicly since they stood before two hundred Department of State employees— wondering what she'd forgotten that he kept her in place. The ceremony was supposed to consist of the award explanation, the presentation, and a photo op. Mercifully, that was it. No speech on her part.

"The same incident that wounded Miss Neeley," Secretary Derriscort said into the mic as he held her in place, "involved a contract team, as well as our own security details from the State Department. One particular operator, Dante Riddell, went above and beyond his duty as well. His efforts, combined with Miss Neeley's, provided critical intel that made the difference in slowing the aggression against Armenia. At least for the time. Miss Neeley." He nodded to her and pointed behind her. "On behalf of Mr. Riddell, would you accept this?"

"Of course," she said, touched that he would honor Dante, and smiled toward her daddy, who wasn't holding up the phone. Oh no, Dante would miss this. She turned to receive the medal and certificate.

It wasn't a Marine assisting this time. Instead, a man in Navy dress blues. A six-foot-two Navy SEAL with three yellow stripes marking his deployments, gorgeous mahogany skin noting his heritage, and chocolate eyes smiling just for her.

"Dante!" With a strangled shout, she threw herself across the foot that separated them and into his arms. Hugged him tight. Felt tears prick her eyes.

"Just like old times," he murmured into her shoulder, clearly referencing the hotel incident a year ago when she'd done this same thing.

A swarm of *awws* filled the air and pushed them apart.

Tearing up, she couldn't stop smiling. "What're you—"

Dante held her at arm's length, a very serious intent in his gaze as he then lowered to one knee.

McKenna gaped—then yelped, covering her mouth with both hands.

He opened a small black box, revealing an antique ring that had belonged to Madyar, his great-grandmother. "Mick, you have always been the only person who saw me, respected me, even when I did not deserve it. And I don't deserve you, but please—save my life again and agree to be my wife."

"Of course!"

Amid a roar of approval and applause ringing through the ballroom, he slid the ring on her finger, then rose, pulled her into his arms and kissed her.

"You're not married yet," Daddy objected as he tugged Dante back and pulled him into a hug. "Welcome to the family—again."

"'At's what I'm talkin' about, Goat!" Brick Archer bellowed from the back of the room.

Thank You!

Thank you so much for reading *Atlas*. We hope you enjoyed the story. If you did, would you be willing to do us a favor and leave a review? It doesn't have to be long—just a few words to help other readers know what they're getting. (But no spoilers! We don't want to wreck the fun!) Thank you again for reading!

We'd love to hear from you—not only about this story, but about any characters or stories you'd like to read in the future. Contact us at www.sunrisepublishing.com/contact.

READ ON FOR MORE FROM THE

DISCARDED HEROES:
SCIONS

SERIES

APOLLO
DISCARDED HEROES: SCIONS
RONIE KENDIG
AWARD-WINNING, BESTSELLING AUTHOR

HE WAS TRAINED TO SAVE LIVES.
SHE WAS BORN TO LIVE A LIE.

Owen Metcalfe thought his military career was over— two failed attempts at becoming an elite operator leave him questioning everything he believes about himself. When a desperate mercenary seeks help to rescue his daughter—a kidnapped princess—from the most dangerous royal family in the world, Owen discovers his true calling isn't about earning a beret or proving his worth to the Army.

It's about saving her.

Leighton Kingslake has spent her entire life guarding a deadly secret far from the Saudi princess who gave birth to her and the brutal king they fled. She's lived in the shadows, knowing one wrong move could end not just her life, but her mother's as well. When she's violently torn from her safe world and imprisoned halfway around the globe, survival becomes her only goal.Until a blue-eyed warrior crashes into her world and threatens everything.

This isn't just a rescue mission—it's a collision of two hearts that will either save them both or destroy them completely.

When Owen infiltrates the palace as Leighton's bodyguard sparks fly! She doesn't want him ruining her plan, and he holds fast to his promise to bring her safely home. But with a vengeful king, murderous princes, and a deadly enemy closing in, they're forced to set differences aside. Soon, begrudging respect breeds something far more powerful that becomes both their greatest strength and their most dangerous weakness.

ONE

Two Years Ago
Sterling, Virginia

DEPOSITING HIS SEVENTY-POUND RUCK JUST inside the foyer, Owen Metcalfe kicked the door shut behind him. "Mom?" He shed his backpack, never slowing as he aimed for the kitchen. "Mom, you here?"

Lights out, fridge humming noisily like always, the kitchen offered little welcome as he slid his truck keys onto the island. He checked the living room and hall for signs of life but came up empty. Huh. Where was she?

The rumble of his gut had him tug open the fridge and eye the contents. He grabbed a piece of leftover pizza. It wasn't the on-the-fly fast-food kind that he'd had too many times on his last rotation, but the mom-and-pop, legit Italian place that was a Metcalfe staple. Folding the slice in half, he grabbed a paper towel and headed to the stairs. "Mom?" He stuffed half the pizza into his mouth and chewed, waiting for her response before ambling to the sliding glass doors that led to the North Forty backyard. The place his aunts and uncles had played many a game growing up. Nothing.

"So much for a 'welcome home,'" he muttered and took another bite. Back in the kitchen, crust sticking out of his mouth, he snagged the last slice. "Serves you right for not being here—"

The heavy thrum of the garage door rising reverberated through the house. He tossed the last piece back in the box and headed into the garage bay. Over the roof of her silver SUV, he saw Mom step out and move to the rear hatch. "Need help?"

His mom's brown head and eyes swiveled his direction. She gave him a broad smile. "Hello, handsome." Retrieving a satchel, she walked over and waved him into her arms for a hug as the hatch shut. "I thought you weren't getting released on leave till tomorrow."

He bent down to accept the embrace and kissed her cheek. "Got things tied up quicker than expected." *Please don't ask if I'm okay. Or about the future.*

"I'm glad." She eyed him with an assessing look, then started into the house. "I take it you already raided the pizza."

"One slice."

"Dad left it for you, so have at it."

His phone buzzed, indicating a text, and he eyed the screen.

Sophia
____

Glad you're back. Bonfire at the ranch. 8pm.
You're my date.

With a sniff, he shook his head, hit the garage door button, and stepped inside. "Soph's having a bonfire again."

Mom nodded. "The twins' graduation party."

Dude, already? "Oh, right."

His mom turned as she drew a glass down from the cabinet and arched an eyebrow. "You going?"

"Apparently I'm her date, so I guess so." He opted to snag the last slice after all.

"Will you two ever make it real?" Mom asked as she filled her glass with filtered water from the fridge.

"Negative," he chortled, biting back the laugh at the way his mom gave him a concerned look. "She's my sister."

"*Tala* is your sister," Mom corrected. "Who's doing great, by the way, not that you asked."

"Tala is always okay," he said. His half sister had gone off to New York to pursue a career in art and never looked back other than to provide occasional updates so Dad didn't track her down and get in her face about communication and familial bonds.

"But Sophia Neeley is *not* your sister." Hair down past her shoulders, Mom looked smart in a blouse and slacks. Had she been to an appointment? "There is no biological connection there, and—"

"Like I need you to tell me that." Owen sagged beneath her blinding flash of the obvious. "That dog will never hunt. She's *always* been the kid sister I never had. And Scions have a strict no-dating rule. Too weird." He grimaced and shuddered. "For Soph, I run interference for her at parties. Dudes are always in her face, asking for a date."

"It wouldn't hurt you two to—"

"Nope." He waved a hand in the air and nuked the pizza. "Not doing this. I've got another year on my contract, and nothing happens till then." Though he had hoped to make Selection and go career with the Rangers, that hadn't happened. And now failure hung over his head like an anvil.

In two large bites, he finished off the pizza and went for a protein bar from the pantry. The Spidey sense said Mom was about to unlock "mom mode" and start drilling him with questions and lectures, so he needed to beat her to the gate. "You look nice. Last-minute meeting?"

"Nice diversion," she said with a wry smile. "I was visiting Uncle Stone."

"Cool, how's he doing?"

"He and Brighton are expecting again," she said, shaking her head, clearly aware he was still diverting.

"Isn't he, like, too old for that?"

She arched an eyebrow. "He's only a few years older than your dad."

"Exactly." Owen knew Dad was sensitive about his age. "Uncle Stone'll need a walker to get to his kid's graduation."

Mom yanked a towel from where it hung on the oven handle and snapped it at him. "You menace."

Laughing, he held up his hands. "Seriously," he said around a laugh. "I'm glad he's happy." He remembered the brooding Uncle Stone too well, and the tension radiating through the family after the scandal broke. "So, was it just a casual chat or was this about the trafficking shelter?"

She nodded, peeling an orange. "He asked if I could work my connections on the Hill to make some more headway on improving anti-trafficking laws."

"Yeah?" He wolfed down the bar and pitched the wrapper. "You going to do it?"

She drew her hair into a ponytail, a sure sign she was getting down to business. He'd need to bug out before it got tense in here. "Not sure. I know it needs to be done, but I'm not sure I have the time in my schedule to do it justice. Agreed I'd look into it." And then, just like that, she folded her arms and launched her heat-seeking missile. "So, you're home. Since Rangers didn't work out . . . what're you planning?"

What little air was left in his chest deflated. "Mom, c'mon. I'm home ten minutes and—"

"I know you, Owen Navas, and the longer you think about something, the worse it gets. You're like you're father—a man of action. Sitting around doesn't help."

That was the thing of it—he *wasn't* like Dad. God knows he'd tried to be. Believed that same tough mettle was in him, but Uncle

Sam disagreed. Selection board disagreed. "Just let a guy breathe, 'kay?"

Quiet settled between them, but that blaze in her eyes said she wasn't going to leave it alone. "You're not a failure."

Bam—right for the heart. "I, uh . . ." He aimed for the living room. "Gotta get the rest of my gear from the truck and grab a shower before heading to the ranch." He kept moving, not looking back. Avoiding the Mom look. Mom guilt. She was an expert at it.

———— • ————

Later that night, he made his way out to the Neeley ranch. Long before turning off the county road, he spotted the raging bonfire. That and the fifty or so cars lining the gravel driveway. "What in blue blazes . . . ?" he muttered as he lumbered past the many vehicles. Finally found a place to park his Raptor, cut the engine, and stared out beyond the hood that even now caught the firelight in the reflection.

The old barn had been converted into a wedding and party venue, staying pretty busy. Soph had helped her mom with the business and had a good head and eye for it. Light and music filtered out from the buzzing barn, spreading its revelry toward the riding corral. A lot of people—way too many, in his opinion— loitered there.

For a half second, he wondered if sitting at home and getting an earful from Mom might be less painful than this. Probably.

A lone figure striding toward him squelched the idea, especially when she waved at him. Soph. Wearing jeans, boots, and a plaid shirt, she let her hair loose in waves down past her shoulders. She looked pretty.

Abandoning the thought of bugging out, he exited the truck and met her halfway.

She leapt at him, wrapping thin arms around his neck and

laughed. "You made it!" Her blonde hair smelled of smoke from the bonfire. "About doggone time."

"You didn't give me much warning," he said, releasing her.

She swung around behind him, caught his shoulders, and hiked up on his back for a piggyback. Arms looped around his neck, she rested her face near his. "Someone didn't tell me he'd be coming home. Or I would've had it all planned, the million ways you can save me at the party."

"Huh. Wonder why he didn't tell you . . ."

She lightly popped the other side of his head. "How long you here for?"

"Couple weeks." Arms hooked behind her legs, he hoisted her into better position. "Ben or Dill here?"

"Ben, yes, but as usual, he's ticked at Dad and pouting in some corner, no doubt. But Dillon . . ."

At her tone, he angled to look into her eyes. "What?"

"Your parents haven't told you?"

He frowned and let her down, considering her seriously. Had a bad feeling about this. Dillon had been in communication on and off, but that wasn't unusual. "What's happened?"

"He vanished two months ago after an argument with Auntie Syd."

Slowing, Owen huffed and looked at the night sky, guilt haranguing him.

Soph gaped at him, those green eyes piercing. "You knew and didn't say a thing? Even to the Scions?"

"I didn't think he was serious," he balked.

She slapped his shoulder. "Usually, thinking is your strong suit." She clucked her tongue, looped their arms, and resumed walking. "Apparently, he told Auntie Syd he was going to find his dad."

"Holy . . ." He swiped a hand over his mouth, still unable to believe Dillon really thought he could resurrect the dead.

"Nobody's heard from him since," Sophia said as they neared the barn and pulsing music. "Because he's an adult, local authorities can't do a single thing."

"Maybe I need to try to reach out."

"You know he won't tell you anything. Of the Scions, he's always been the most stubborn."

"Says the girl who held her breath till she passed out when she didn't get her way."

Her blue eyes widened. "I was four!"

"Uh-huh." He jutted his jaw to her feet. "How long you hold out for the boots?"

She frowned, but it was fake and surrendered to a smile that she topped with her nose up in mischief. "Not long at all. Daddy's so proud I got into Carnegie Mellon, I could've asked for the moon and he'd have roped it for me."

"Think Jimmy Stewart already did that." Scanning as they entered the barn, replete with the smells of the country—hay, animals, and BBQ—he followed her to the refreshment table and grabbed a bottled water.

"Owen!"

He pivoted and spotted Sophia's parents arcing out from behind the food table. "Ma'am, sir."

Uncle Colton pulled him into a hug. Patted his back like he was providing life-saving measures. "Good to see you, son."

"Thank you. Same, sir."

"Has your dad talked you into Special Forces yet?"

Heat-seeking missiles apparently ran in the Scion family. Did everyone know? "Not yet." He took a swig of the water. "But I'm sure it's coming."

The barrel-chested guy laughed. "You're bred from good stock, so I'm sure you'll find the right MOS."

Stretching his jaw, Owen searched out his charge. Found Sophia in a huddle of girls and spotted some guys homing in on her. "If you'll excuse me, Uncle Colton . . ."

"Appreciate the way you watch out for her."

"Family," he said with a cockeyed nod. "We protect our own." With that, he strode toward her but slowed his roll, suddenly realizing he was legit out of place here.

Most of those partying were from the twins' graduating class, so only a couple years younger than him, but with three years of Army under his belt, he felt a decade older. These people were just getting started. Hadn't felt the sting of failure like he had.

"Sorry, Corporal. We just didn't see what we need for the Regiment."

As he reminisced that day, he slowly grew aware that he was staring at someone. Not intentionally, but his gaze had inadvertently locked with brown eyes. Olive complexion. A breeze swept through the barn, swaying the string lights crisscrossing overhead, and rustled her long, dark hair. Light hit her eyes and turned them caramel. She held his gaze for a second, then focused on her friends and lifted a red cup, which she sipped from. Smiled at something a friend said. Those caramel eyes found his again. And like that tiny zap of a hot socket, he felt the connection.

"Owen!"

He twitched at Soph's shout and pivoted her way.

"C'mere!" she said, lacing her arm through his and drawing him into the huddle. "Look who it is."

Owen grinned at the dark-haired guy she pointed to. "No way!" He pulled him into a one-shouldered hug and shook his hand. "Khalon Russell." He patted the guy's shoulder. "How's it going?"

Two years younger, Khalon Russell had always been a like-minded individual. They'd met when the guy had joined the private academy the Scions attended, then Principal Hamrick chose Owen to mentor Khalon through his first few weeks. They'd struck a solid friendship.

"Good." Khalon gave a slow smile and nod. "Glad to finally be done with school."

"What about college?" Owen asked with a laugh, and something in his periphery lured his focus away.

Her. Red-Cup Girl was drifting closer, trailing a bunch of rich kids who didn't really seem Soph's speed. Or RCG's speed. In fact, she seemed to hold back. Was that because of him, or the company she was keeping?

"I'm going to spend a year in Nigeria with my godfather," Khalon said. "Then . . ." He shrugged. "We'll see."

Huh. That sounded a lot like Khalon had things to work out. Once again, they were on parallel paths. "You'll figure it out."

Khalon gave him a speculative look. "I thought of joining the Army. Any tips?"

"Yeah, *don't*." Owen snickered, telling himself not to look at the girl now hovering to Soph's ten o'clock. "Nah, seriously—if it's what you want, do it. What's your dad say? And your uncle?"

It'd been a hot minute since Khalon's uncle was president, but former presidents wielded a lot of influence. Could get his nephew into any school he wanted.

Even as the guy answered, Owen noticed RCG shift into view over Khalon's shoulder. As her friend leaned into her, she again lifted that cup to her mouth—used the thing like a shield as her friend nodded to Owen and whispered something, turning RCG's gaze his way.

Yeah, not needing that complication, he refocused on Khalon, whose mouth was still moving. Shoot. What had he missed? No idea because his ears were still straining to pick up whatever RCG's friend said that caused them to laugh hard over the din.

RCG stood about five-six, had an athletic build, and by that outfit had a good sense of style. Yet, while she hung out with the rich crowd, there was something . . . different about her. She didn't look relaxed or comfortable here. Was it the barn? The country atmosphere?

It seemed more . . .

Her friends were laughing and likely had something else in their red cups other than the punch the Neeleys were serving. Her, though? Straight-laced. Alert. Those pretty brown eyes searched the crowds more than once. And they weren't just looking for him or a good time. It was . . . *awareness*. But something else too. Maybe vulnerability? Cloaked in . . . wariness.

"Hey!" Soph punched his bicep.

"What?" he balked, flinching as he touched his arm. "What was that for?"

"I was talking to you!" Soph's furrowed brow lifted, then smoothed when she saw what had distracted him. "Oh." She let out a huff and faced him full-on. "You *don't* want to get involved with that."

He arched an eyebrow at the way she said "*that.*"

"No, trust me, Owen. She's Holland's older sister."

"Holland?"

"The girl who threw herself at you when we went to prom last year—she was *lit*, and I don't mean in the good way. I know how you feel about stuff like that."

Fair. He'd seen too many friends wreck their lives with substance abuse. "Oh."

"Yeah. Don't waste your time—with any of that crowd." She sniffed. "You're way above all of them."

Was Soph sure about that? Because the beauty seemed light-years beyond him.

RCG looked away, pretending she wasn't trying to avoid him, but she was close enough to have heard Soph's comments. He'd already told himself once he didn't need the complication.

Yet like a riptide that yanked him from shore, her presence demanded his attention. Sucked every bit of common sense out of him. And somehow he found himself heading in her direction.

A weight plowed into his back. "Metcalfe! What's up, dude?"

Owen turned to find Ben Neeley in a big black Stetson. They

clapped hands and drew each other in for a chest-bump. "Congrats on not failing too many classes to get flunked."

Ben's green eyes sparked at the taunt. "Dude, that is so wrong." He thrust his pointer finger up. "What matters is I got the stupid diploma. Now, I think I'll trail Khalon to Nigeria."

"Don't think so," Khalon said with a smirk.

Even as the group started chatting again, Owen felt a seismic shift that sent his gaze to the girl shrouded in mystery. Wondered at the strange thing plucking at his conscience that said to protect her.

"You must be really into the older sis to stare at her like that."

He glanced at Soph. "Jealous much?" he teased as he combed the crowd for RCG, but she had vanished, leaving him with the haunting sense that she was in danger. A lot of it.

Ronie Kendig is a bestselling, award-winning author of over forty books. She grew up an Army brat, and now she and her Army-veteran husband have returned to their beloved Texas after a ten-year stint in the Northeast. They survive on Sonic runs, barbecue, and peach cobbler that they share—sometimes—with Benning the Stealth Golden and AAndromeda the MWD Washout. Ronie's degree in psychology has helped her pen novels of intense, raw characters.

To learn more about Ronie, visit www.roniekendig.com and follow her on social media.

BESTSELLING AUTHOR
RONIE KENDIG

WITH **STEFFANI WEBB,**
JJ SAMIE MYLES, & **VONI HARRIS**

We solve the problem of what to read next.

WE THINK YOU'LL ALSO LOVE...

Fire Department liaison Allen Frees may have put his life back together, but getting the truck crew and engine squad to succeed might be his toughest job yet. When a child is nearly kidnapped, Allen steps in to help Pepper Miller keep her niece safe. The one thing he couldn't fix was the love he lost, but he isn't going to let Pepper walk away this time.

***Expired Return* by Lisa Phillips**

Infiltrating a dangerous militia to save her troubled brother, Jamie Winters finds herself kidnapped. Only Logan Crawford, the man she once broke, can rescue her—but he demands a promise in return. As they navigate peril in the Alaskan wilderness, their unresolved feelings spark a chance for love and redemption.

***Burning Hearts* by Lisa Phillips**

When an attempt is made on Grey Parker's life and dead bodies begin piling up, suddenly bodyguard Christina Sherman is tasked with keeping both a soldier and his dog safe... and with them, the secrets that could stop a terrorist attack.

***Driving Force* by Lynette Eason
and Kate Angelo**

We solve the problem of what to read next.

WHERE EVERY STORY IS A FRIEND,
AND EVERY CHAPTER IS A NEW JOURNEY...

Subscribe to our newsletter for a free book, the latest news, weekly giveaways, exclusive author interviews, and more!

follow us on social media!

Shop paperbacks, ebooks, audiobooks, and more at
SUNRISEPUBLISHING.MYSHOPIFY.COM